Bo'Glin: The Prophecy
Written by Richard Leblanc
Covert art by Craig Ferguson
copyright Richard Leblanc

This book is rated PG14

ISBN 978-0-9783237-0-7
www.jack-and-pookie.com

Bo'Glin
The Prophecy

DREAMSCAPES AND NIGHTMARES

It is the same always the same but each time different. It was an early hour of the day. That much she could tell through the flowing mists and clouds of smoke that wafted up from hundreds of still burning fires. There she stood. Her name was Qu'Tee Pie the last survivor of the war cleric to the fallen Order of the Butterfly. Her armour was badly damaged. Her arms, legs, and face sported wounds that despite her best efforts would not heal.

Around her thousands of bodies littered the blood stained battlefield. She could hear the sounds of war. She could see flashes of fighting as though permanently etched in her brain. She closed her eyes and dropped to her knees. She covered her ears in a vain attempt to block out the screams, voices, sounds, and the explosions. Yet no matter what she did the echoes remained; reminding her of the failure and its horrific cost. It took great effort to block out the pain but she forced herself back up to her feet.

She staggered but managed to steady herself. A gentle breeze wafted carrying some of the mist and smoke away. Qu'Tee looked to the east and saw the ravaged remnants of a small village. She knew the name but for some reason she couldn't remember it. Everything was too chaotic. Reality hit her in the form of a jolt of pain. She fell to her knees, the bandaged wound on her leg was bleeding again.

Visions flashed in her mind. Visions of brutal fighting . Visions of Orcs, Undead, Humans, Elves, Dwarves, Wizards, Mages, Merfolk, and Ken. It was a brutal war; a war to end all wars in the lands know as the Veil. It was a war of good against evil, it was a war of destiny; a war that would free the Veil of the shadow of evil. It was a war that good lost. Her body felt limp and yet like chiselled stone.

Footsteps. Through the sounds of wind and fire; she definitely heard them. Her head spun around. Through the mist she could see others! She wasn't alone. Through the fog and smoke she could see the silhouettes of ten figures. Each stood strong and defiant. Each one wielding a banner that fluttered in the wind. She tried to speak but her throat was sore. It seemed as though the ten were discussing something, but from where she was she could hear nothing.

Then to her horror one by one the silhouettes vanished, their war ravaged banners falling to the bloodstained ground. She gasped. It was as though icy fingers had reached into her chest and were squeezing her heart. She was alone; so alone. It was then that she heard it. Laughter; amidst the carnage and destruction she heard laughter! Laughter that was not human.

"Look around whelp," the voice demanded. As if controlled by some ethereal power her head turned around taking in the carnage, the bloodshed, and destruction. "Tell me oh chosen one; what do you see?" the voice mocked. She wanted to challenge the voice, deny its words, but she couldn't make a sound. "Tell me!" the voice ordered. She shuddered at the tone.

"Death. Death everywhere." she said her voice weak. The laughter taunted her.

"Did you really think that on some level that you could make a difference? Did you really think that you could stop me?" the inhuman voice demanded as though amused by her defiance or in the very least her attempt at defiance.

"Why?" a raspy voice groaned shocking her. She looked over and saw the body of a long dead dwarf beginning to stir.

"You... you said we could win if we stood as one," a gutted pirate gasped as it crawled towards her. Qu'Tee backed away.

"You did this to us." an impaled mermaid strained from the pike she was trapped upon. She flailed trying to free herself unable to move from the pike which had her pinned . Qu'Tee looked to the river that was turning red with the blood of the hundreds – no thousands that had perished. She tried to run, but tripped over a dead horse. She crawled over to a toppled cart and watched as all of the dead began to rise.

"Not real," the cleric stammered. She closed her eyes as though trying to will all of it away. But even with her eyes closed she could smell the decay of death, she could hear the staggering shambling footsteps coming closer. A blood soaked hand grabbed her shoulder! It was real! It had to be! They were all around her. "No!!" she screamed out. A power all but exploded from her shattering everything as though it were forged of fragile glass. For a few moments she shuddered in the darkness. Again she heard the laughter, only this time it was quiet as though amused. She opened her eyes. She was in a circle of light, around her there was only darkness – total darkness.

Hesitantly she reached towards the darkness, but as soon as her hand touched it, she was burned. She jerked her hand away. Again there was laughter.

"You are crafty beyond your years," an inhuman voice hissed.

"Who are you?" she demanded, cradling her blistering hand.

"You know what I am . I am darkness. I am power. I am pain." the voice remarked. She swore the sound came from behind her. She spun around and something in the darkness moved.

"Why are you doing this to me?" she asked. Trying to find what was stalking her in the shadows. But again; all she could hear was laughter. All she could see beyond the circle of light was darkness.

"Why? You defy me and ask why?" the voice asked. It sounded like it was right behind her. She spun around, but there was nothing there.

"Defy you? I don't even know you!" she challenged. A pain caused her to double over. Voices screamed in her head.

"Oh but you do. You think that pleading ignorance will save

you?" the voice taunted. around her in the background she could hear inhuman chattering. Before she could react an giant wart covered amphibian hand grabbed her. She couldn't move. She could feel the hand crushing her, squeezing the life from her.

"Those you serve oppose me. As such you oppose me," the voice hissed. She could hear her ribs cracking under the pressure. "All that seek to oppose me will perish. All that seek to oppose me will suffer." the voice echoed. A shuddered window appeared beyond the edge of the circle of light. The hand thrusted her towards it. Just before she was about to slam into it the shudders opened and she found herself back in the battlefield. The stench of gore and death almost made her gag.

"Look!" the voice ordered. Hesitantly she opened her eyes and saw the thousands of dead bodies.
"This. All of this is the reality. All of this is the truth of those that seek to oppose me! Can you see them? Friends, family, loved ones? Look closely!" the voice hissed. Her eyes watered as she saw the thousands of lifeless bodies.

"But..." she began. "But so many are suffering. So many people are in pain." she closed her eyes as memories of the poverty and the sickness of the people she had seen flooded her mind. She remembered the hatred that was brewing between the nations. It was then that she blinked, and her eyes spaced out. "All of this it isn't because of me. This is your plan. This is your desire." her voice was distant. The hand released her as though she was white hot. Slowly she floated to the ground. "You desire the death of every living being in the Veil." she looked over her shoulder and saw the dead beginning to rise again.

"You are a crafty little bitch, but your tricks will not save you," the demon taunted. "Slay her!" The demon commanded as the undead masses closed in on her.

"Your illusions cannot harm me." she said . Her voice sounded different. It sounded more confident and far older. Reality around her once again shattered like glass. She was back in the circle of light surrounded by darkness. Again there was the laughter.

"The moral indignity, it never ceases to amuse me. What makes you think you are so special? What makes you think that you are the one? What makes you think that someone, something as pathetic as you could imagine making a difference!" the demon demanded. Qu'Tee scanned the darkness hoping to see her tormentor. She was about to reply when a pain stabbed at her head. She fell to her knees as images flooded her mind.

She looked at her hands they looked so small. How many times had she seen this, lived this? All around her she could hear fighting – a raid, a war, something she could not understand. She remembered her father grabbing her and rushing upstairs. There was shouting, and explosions. Everything happened so fast it was a blur of motion. She saw his face, it looked so grim. He was speaking but she couldn't understand the words. When ever things were bad; really bad, he would speak in the old language. She remembered vividly her mother hiding her in a secret room.

"Remember, we will always be with you," her mother whispered to her. She closed the door to the secret room and toppled a dresser in front of it. From a small crack in the wall she watched as her mother fought the intruders, armoured, masked soldiers. She wanted to help, but she was too smal, too helpless, too weak. She fell to her knees and closed her eyes. It was then that a stinging slap sent her rolling. She opened her eyes. She looked at her clothes, looked around like a cornered animal.

She was in that alley. She backed up until she was pressed up against a wall. She looked up and saw the bullies that picked on her. One of the girls grabbed her by the arm and then showed her cheek to the others.

"I told you she is a witch! Watch and see for yourself!" she ordered. The others watched as the bruise on her cheek healed before their eyes. Terror welled within her as the bully threw her down to the ground. "I heard her the other night. She was trying to cast a spell," she added.

"No! I swear I'm no witch!" she protested. The eldest of the bullies squatted down before her. There was a look there. A look between absolute hatred and disgust. "I was praying – I swear," she pleaded. The Bully grabbed her by the chin and glared at her.

"I remember what happened to the last whore who was tried as a witch. They burned the bitch in the town square. Do you remember?" she asked. Timidly Qu'Tee nodded. "It took her so long to die, and if you do not do everything, and I do mean everything we say; you will wish you were that lucky," the bully laughed as she threw her to the ground. Qu'Tee spaced out and curled up on the ground.

In the blink of an eye all of it was gone. She was back in the circle of light. There was laughter again – followed by unamused clapping.

"Behold! This – this is what seeks to defy me. Face the cold hard facts girl. You might have grown up a bit, but you are still the same weak, pitiful, worthless, pathetic girl." the raspy voice taunted. She was shaking. There was more laughter, it was coming from everywhere. So many people laughing, all laughing at her. She forced herself up to her knees as she remembered every humiliation every indignity she had to endure while she was at the orphanage. Tears escaped her eyes as she slammed her fists against the ground.

"Laugh if you will! I do not know why you torment me! I do not know why you are doing this to me, but I will not let you beat me!" she screamed defiantly. The fear was gone. In its place was rage. The laughter began to fade. She could feel it watching her circling her like a predator closing in on its prey. It was then that a pair of glowing red eyes blinked. They were not human; not remotely, and they focused on her.

"So brave. So defiant. You wish to fight? Your wish is granted my dear. Get her!" the raspy demonic voice ordered. She was about to move when another pair of eyes fixated on her. Then another set of eyes glared at her, then another, more and more eyes opened. There were thousands of them. They were everywhere, and they were all staring at her.

A starburst temporarily blinded her as something slammed into her face. Before she could react – they were on her. She could feel clawlike hands scratching at her and cutting her flesh. She screamed out as she backhanded the beasts or whatever they were off her. She spun around and managed to grab a weapon from another of them. Qu'Tee held the weapon and stood as if daring the creatures to try something. It was then that they pounced at her.

Instinct took over. Her movements were fluid and precise. None of the beasts could touch her. It was then that a pain stabbed at her leg. She dropped to a knee and looked over her shoulder. A crude spear was stabbed into the back of her leg. A mixture of frustration and rage began to consume her. She was a skilled fighter – but the numbers were getting the better of her. She jerked the spear from her leg and looked at her blood on the weapon. She was losing her focus and fast.

"Do I scare you so much that you need hide behind these pathetic beasts?" she hissed under her breath. The beasts were going to move in but stopped. They all looked away and stepped away from her.

"Scare? Fear? They are what I am. They are what I do. Believe me child, there is nothing in you worth fearing," the raspy voice taunted. Just then the darkness around her exploded. She shielded her eyes. Around her was fire. Lakes of molten red –

rocks burned and glowed red. There were thousands of goblins and other primitive beasts that were chanting and swaying in unison. It was then that the hair on the back of her neck stood on end. Slowly she turned around. She backed away as a wart covered reptilian hand reached out from behind a flaming rock.

"What are you?" she asked hesitantly as a repugnant mass – the demon Bo'Glin stepped out. His watermelon sized reptile eyes glared at her. His moth formed an unnatural looking smile revealing several yellow hued fangs. Of all the things the demon could look like – it would be a frog. She backed away.

"I thought you wanted to fight? Where is your courage child? Or is it that you forgot that I know you. I know every secret you wish remained hidden. I know your strength – but I am your weakness. Before she could move his arm shot over. The hand gripped her and mercilessly began to crush her. The weapons slipped from her hands. She couldn't focus. The fear and the pain were too much to deal with. "It ends – here and now," he finished. He flung her up. She wanted to move but all she could do was watch as the demon's mouth elongated showing hundreds of fangs. His tongue lashed out and coiled around her. She felt herself being jerked towards the pit of teeth. The frog demon leaped up and clamped his monstrous mouth shut.

The pain from the teeth was brief.
Then there was darkness…total unforgiving darkness

Qu'Tee the Cleric

It was around midday. Within a picturesque garden – Qu'Tee was twitching where she was sleeping. She gasped and sat up in a cold sweat. She had the dream many times, far too many for her liking. Each time it seemed and felt more real. After a few seconds she calmed down a bit.

It was just a dream. She sighed as she flopped back down onto the ground and looked up at the tranquil sky. A gentle breeze pushed clouds across a sea of blue.

"It was just a dream," she reassured herself. She looked over at the two intricately carved statues of Lady Angela, the angel that founded the Order of the Butterfly, that were standing to either side of her. In the past whenever she was scared, here she felt safe and secure. It was as though they were standing guard.

"Why do I keep having these nightmares and in the day time no less?" she groaned. "And why does it have to be," she began. Something moved in the grass beside her head. She looked over and saw a small frog hop out. Her eyes spaced out. "Frog," she muttered. The frog seemed to blink at her.

Throughout the temple…
Throughout the surrounding forest…
Even at the nearest village an echoing scream could be heard.

Back in the garden, one of the temple guardians raced in with weapon ready. His eyes quickly scanned the garden for signs of intruders. When he saw Qu'Tee clinging to the upper part of one of the statues he groaned and lowered his weapon.

"I should have known it was you," he walked over to where she was. He looked over at the stainedglass window that depicted an angel fighting off demons. "Where is it?" he asked rationally. Without even having to look her finger pointed down to where the confused looking frog was. The temple guardian squatted down. His hand then snapped down and grabbed the frog before it could get away. He walked over to where the nearest wall was and tossed the bewildered reptile over the wall and off temple grounds. "You can come down now. The monster has been dispatched. Qu'Tee glared at him.

"You know I hate frogs so shut up," she retorted indignantly

"Aren't you getting a little old to be acting like such a girl?' the temple guardian mocked. Her eyes narrowed. "I mean what could a frog do?" he began as he wiped his hands off. "Other than get you slimy," he added under his breath. He could feel the daggers coming from her eyes. He was an older looking Ken known as Leaf. He had a number of titles within the temple. He was the captain of the guards. He was the most skilled fighter in the area – the one that taught Qu'Tee how to fight. On top of that he had a natural gift of knowing exactly how to piss her off. She folded her arms across her chest and turned away from him.

"Leave me alone. I'm not in the mood for your attitude right now," she retorted. Leaf quietly shook his head and leaned against his spear.

"When are you in the mood for lessons? You skipped class –
again. I swear you are the most stubborn student I have had the
misfortune of having to train and teach," he added – he could
see her hands beginning to twitch. She looked over her shoulder
and glared at him. His face was always the same – impossible to
read – a perfect mask.

"Please spare me the speech. You were going over the same stuff
you did yesterday," she pointed out. He smirked.

"You skipped yesterday too," he pointed out.

"So what?" she fumed. Talking to him was like trying to talk
sense into a stone wall. "You know I work three times a hard as
any of the other students," she began but stopped. There was no
point. Justifying things equalled excuses and he would hear
none. She reached behind one of the statues and picked up her
staff. "You think I am slacking? You think I am not taking my
job here seriously?" she asked. He blinked and smirked.

"Did I say that?" he rebutted. Qu'Tee held her staff as though it
was an extension of her arm. "Any time you are ready," he said
– not moving – his eyes following her as she slowly circled
towards him. She was getting closer.

It was then that she attacked. In one fluid motion he blocked the
attack – got passed her defences and touched the tip of his staff
to her neck. For a few seconds the two stared each other down.
The young cleric made her move. Quickly, her body arched back
– a focused kick knocked his staff aside. She spun around

slamming her staff into the back of his knees sending him to the ground. She tried to press the attack but he was already to his feet. She fumed at how deceptively quick he was.

"You are too hungry. If you get like that your enemy will get the better of you – every – single – time," he stated seriously.

"And you talk too much," she retorted. Again she attacked. For someone so young – her skill with a staff was disturbingly advanced. But for all her skill – the teacher was one step ahead of her. None of her attacks could land their mark.

"You seem to forget that I know you," he began. He frowned. He side stepped one of her attacks and brought his staff down across her knuckles. "PAY attention," he added. She dropped her weapon and looked at the back of her hands. Never had she been disarmed so quickly. He sighed and shook his head. "Must have been a hell of a bad dream you had," he stated calmly. She looked over at him – he seemed calmer. "Your focus is way off. I don't know where you are but you are no where near here," he kicked her weapon up to his hand. "You able to continue?" he asked. She cracked her knuckles and shook her hands. He tossed the staff over to her. "Focus – it isn't everything – it is the only thing," he reminded.

Leaf watched as she cartwheeled backwards then flipped herself up so that she was balanced on the head of one of the angel statues. Slowly she balanced on one foot. She closed her eyes. She began to block it out. The dreams – the wind – the birds – the bugs – the beating of her heart. All she could see in her mind was where Leaf was. He blinked – she disappeared. Quickly he raised his staff as Qu'Tee brought her weapon down at him. It took all of his strength to keep her from overpowering him. Her staff wouldn't relent and his wasn't going to give. For a few long seconds she was balanced in the air where their weapons touched. It was then that Leaf stared in amazement. His staff – a metal staff at that, was beginning to warp.

He moved one side of his weapon up to redirect her potent strike. He staff slid down his and hit the ground. He struck where she fell or should have fallen – but she wasn't there! He rolled aside and stood defensively. He looked over and saw Qu'Tee perched in the branches of the tree above him.

"You going to be able to fight with your weapon like that?" she asked curiously. He smirked as he spun around and hit the trunk of the tree. Her eyes widened as she fell ungracefully from the tree and landed before him. "That hurt," she pointed out. Leaf looked at the warp in his weapon. A warp that she caused with a wooden staff.

"That was an impressive strike. A battle can be won with such a strike – not a war," he reminded. She groaned as she slowly got up. "Posturing can cost you more than wounded pride. It can cost lives. Yours and any you are fighting with or fighting to protect," he added – still focused on his weapon. Qu'Tee picked up her staff. "When ready," he reassured. She attacked.

Even with his weapon being in the state it was he was able to read her moves before she made them. She was too passionate with everything she did. It made her predictable. It was then that he made a mistake! The warp in his weapon threw his aim off! His metal staff slammed into the side of her head. Her weapon fell from her hands as she lolled and began to fall. Instinct took over. He caught her before she hit the ground. She was out cold. Her cheek bone looked broken and was bruised and bleeding – but slowly before his eyes the injury began to heal.

"Qu'Tee?" he whispered – patting her on the cheek with the back of his hand. Slowly her eyes fluttered open. In all of the sparring sessions she had been in since joining the Order of the Butterfly, never had she taken a hit that hard. She moved her head to the side. Her neck cracked. "You okay? You want me to get a healer?" he asked. Her eyes narrowed as she pulled away from him and glared at him. "Problem?' he asked.

"You treat all your students that way?" she asked. He groaned and shook his head. Of all her annoying attributes that aggravated him – her pride was at the top of the list. "A fight isn't about hitting – but about knowing how to take a hit and get back up," she quoted. He sighed and shook his head.

"I almost took your head off," he pointed out.

"I am a member of the Order of the Butterfly. The agents of the darkness Lady Angela fought didn't hold back. How am I supposed to be able to do the same if you pull your punches?" she protested. A reluctant tear escaped her eye.

"A dead student doesn't learn. So don't ask me to take this to a level that you can't follow. You are not ready for that," he stated seriously. "Now, am I bring a healer here – or am I taking you to the healer?" he asked.

"You above any here should know that I don't need a healer," she pointed out. She stood ready with her staff.

"Not all wounds are physical," he said. She blinked. "I know – you have been through hell – far more so than any of the other students. Stand down – lesson over," he said seriously. He noticed it. Her hands were twitching.

Slowly her eyes fixated on him. There was something she hated more than frogs – it was pity. She loathed it and anyone that targeted her with it. She almost flew at him. He seemed to be moving in slow motion but still seemed to be able to block every single one of her attacks.

He leaped away to regroup – but she wasn't letting that happen.

"I," she began. She spun around and landed a focused kick to his right hand. She blocked his attempt to counter her strike. She headbutted his helmet stunning him a bit. "will," her hand cracked against his knuckles. His staff fell to the ground. "not," she continued as she drilled her elbow into the right side of his head knocking his helmet off. "be pitied!" she shouted as she spun around and landed a strong kick to the left side of his head. He recoiled and fell to the ground. He shook his head and looked up at the cut that was already healing on her forehead. She was so focused that she couldn't feel pain. In all his years of teaching – never had he see someone with that much rage inside.

"Stand down!" he ordered. Her eyes were still fixated on him. She couldn't hear him. He hopped up to his feet and took on a fighting stance. His staff was behind her. "You leave me no choice. I had hoped I would never have to use this secret technique on a student," he stated seriously. His eyes fixated on her. She stood ready.

"Bring it," she hissed defiantly.

"So be it," Leaf moved his fists – his feet dug into the ground. "Behold a technique that leave all stunned!" he finished. He then turned and ran away. For a few seconds she stood stunned – true to his word – but it didn't last long.
"Get back here!" she shouted as she chased after him.

Destiny

From a window that overlooked the temple's garden two Ken priestesses were watching Qu'Tee chasing leaf around the garden. One seemed very amused by the display the other was quite the opposite.

"Two crowns says she'll catch him." one challenged. She was the Ken priestess known as Sugar. She, like Leaf, had numerous titles. She was a teacher, an alchemist/healer, she was also the temple's cook as well as being responsible for numerous other duties. Another task she was in charge of was travelling throughout the Veil in search of Ken that were scattered after the fall of the capital.

"You think this is funny?" the other asked. She was the head priestess known as Tee'Quilla the eldest of the warrior clerics within the Order of the Butterfly. "I swear he lets her get away with too much," she added shaking her head.

"You know as well as I that he knows what he is doing. Qu'Tee pushes herself too hard because she is different," Sugar added as she watched Leaf dodge several of Qu'Tee's attacks. "The reason you wanted to speak with me is because of her isn't it?" she asked.

"When you say different, why do I get the feeling that you are not talking about her healing gift?" Tee'Quilla asked curiously as she stepped away from the window and leaned against the wall.

"How many in the Order did we lose? How many tried as hard as her, and at her age no less?" Sugar asked. Tee'Quilla closed her eyes.

"That I knew personally?" she rebutted.

"You know what I mean," Sugar answered.

"Very few. They were old bloods. They served under the king himself. They had far more restraint though," Tee'Quilla pointed out. Sugar smiled as she watched her adopted daughter chasing Leaf.
"She is still very young. She may learn fast but she still has much to learn," she replied.

"How does she get along with the others? The students, teachers?" Tee'Quilla asked. Sugar sighed and stepped away from the window.

"She has been through more than any her age should have. Especially one as special as she is," she began. She took a deep breath to calm herself. "It is hard to say. Some days she seems like she gets along with everyone other days she is so withdrawn that others worry about her," she explained.

"She trusts you?" Tee'Quilla asked. The questioning was taking a twist that was starting to concern Sugar. "Be at peace sister she has been through much as you have said. People who have suffered tend to be hard to win over." she added.

"It took some time and a lot of hard work but yes," Sugar answered. The priestess walked over and closed the shudders to the window. Magically all the candles in the room lit up. "She is the reason you wanted to talk to me," she stated.

"You know me too well at times," Tee'Quilla stated. She walked over to a large desk and leaned against it. "I know you told me about her when you found her. Please refresh my memory," she requested politely.

"About six years ago I heard a rumour that that there was a girl in a village near to Pit Fighter territories. When I found her she was being beat up by several bullies. I found out later that she had been there for five years taking that same kind of abuse on a daily basis," Sugar stated as her hands clenched into fists.

"You cannot blame yourself sister. You did all you could," Tee'Quilla pointed out.

"You can say that, but you don't know how many times I went by that way. Anyway around the younger students she is so helpful and protective, but, because of what those bullies did to her, around some of the older students she is so timid," Sugar continued.

"Some?" Tee'Quilla asked.

"The girls. All of the bullies that tortured her those years she was at the orphanage were girls," Sugar answered.

"What about the boys?" she asked.

"Much of what she told me was in confidence," Sugar began.

"I am not asking you to betray any confidence," she reassured. Sugar closed her eyes.

"It is hard to put to words. I wouldn't say that she hates boys, but she doesn't trust them. I can say no more than that," she stated. Tee'Quilla nodded. "You evaded my question before. Qu'Tee is the reason you wanted to speak with me; yes?" she asked seriously.

"In a matter of speaking. She is still having the nightmares? In spite of the wards?" Tee'Quilla asked. Sugar placed her palm against the closed window and closed her eyes. In her mind she could see the two still running around in the garden area. "He is calling to her isn't he?" she asked.

"Why her?" Sugar asked.

"I do not know. I have searched through the ancient texts and scrolls seeking answers and found none; save one. I know what you and your daughter speak of is in confidence. But I need to know the nature of these dreams. What does she see?" she asked seriously.

"Is there no other way?" Sugar asked.

"Would I ask otherwise?" Tee'Quilla rebutted.

"Qu'Tee sees a great war. Ten nations standing, and falling as one. Whether it is history or prophecy I cannot say. But each dream is more graphic, more real than the last," she answered seriously.

"I see. I need you to be completely honest with me. I need to know. Her fear of frogs, her upbringing, her parents, her dreams all of it. Is there any chance that she is the one spoken of in our prophecy?" Tee'Quilla asked holding up a scroll.

"The signs would seem to say that but," Sugar began.

"Be at peace sister," Tee'Quilla reassured. "Does she know about her birth parents?" she asked curiously.

"She never asked, not once oddly enough. The memories must be painful," she said as she walked over to a shelf and picked up a bottle. "You want one?" she asked.

"Please," Tee'Quilla answered. Sugar poured two glasses and handed one to her sister. "Her parents were old bloods. They survived the fall of the capital. Their daughter survived the fall of that village. She has visions of both the wars the one that happened so long ago and the one that will happen. Bo'Glin himself fears her and is trying to destroy her. It can only mean that he is almost ready," she said as she took a sip from her glass. Sugar did the same.

"You believe her to be the one? The one that will unite nations? Piece together the broken mirror? She is just a child. Besides her horrific upbringing in that godawful orphanage she has not been outside of these temple walls. Every memory she has beyond these walls is stained by blood and hate," Sugar pointed out.

"You think I don't know that? You think I take any pleasure in speaking on this subject with you? As she is family to you she is to me. How much does she know? Of the prophecy?" she asked trying to keep her emotions in check.

"I do not like where this is going," Sugar began defensively.

"I like it less. What does she know?" Tee'Quilla repeated.

"She hasn't asked. All she knows is what any student her age knows through studies," Sugar answered through gritted teeth. Tee'Quilla finished her drink. "You want me to lie to her," she said seriously.

"If and I repeat IF she is the one spoken of in our ancient text. She must not know the full magnitude of her role. In spite of what she has endured she can not handle that burden.... yet," she began. Sugar moved to stand toe to toe with her sister.

"We both know how that story ends," she replied seriously.

"Yes unfortunately we do," she answered passively. Sugar

finished her drink and began pacing like a caged animal. "You think this is any easier for me?" she asked.

"How long has she known?" Sugar asked as she touched her forehead against the wall.

"Truthfully?" Tee'Quilla asked.

"Please?" Sugar replied.

"As soon as she saw her when you first brought her here. I would have told you but.." Tee'Quilla began but trailed off.

"You were afraid how I would react?" Sugar stated completing her sister's unfinished sentence.

"I know you sister. I know how you love her. How could I tell you when you were so happy?" she began but stopped. "Can you forgive me?" she asked seriously.

"It changes nothing. I had my suspicions. I could have asked but I didn't. I hoped, no, prayed that I was reading too much into things. Is she angry that I didn't come forward sooner? Before it came to this?" Sugar asked.

"Sister, she knows your love for her. And she knows why you didn't ask questions. Would any other mother do less?" Tee'Quilla asked with a friendly smile. Sugar tapped her head against the wall.

"She is just a child. I will go in her place," Sugar stated seriously.

"She said that you would say that. And you must know better than that. You cannot cheat fate. Such is the nature of destiny, do not doubt in your daughter's strength, character and potential. For if you of all people doubt her, how can she do otherwise?" Tee'Quilla rebutted.

"Never would I question her strength, character, or anything about her. But she is just a child. It is far too soon! You are as asking me to," Sugar began but stopped herself from finishing the sentence out loud. She managed to calm herself down, but it wasn't easy. She then looked over at her sister and relaxed a bit. "Okay, I will humour this. Let us say she is the one and that she must take this journey. So be it. You say she is the chosen one. That is a distinct possibility. You do not want me to tell her of the prophecy spoken of in the ancient text? That is a hard, but I can deal with it," Sugar stated.

"Sister," Tee'Quilla began.

"All I ask is that you allow me to go with her," she finished. Tee'Quilla closed her eyes and shook her head. "Is that so much to ask?" she added.

"We both know why you are saying such and we both know it won't work. Please sister, on this I will beg if I must, do not do this," she replied seriously.

"You are telling me that my daughter may need to go on a journey more dangerous than anything any her have faced. You would have me stand back and let her face it alone?" Sugar asked.

"She, she said that you would say this. I hoped she would be wrong. Please, do not do this," her sister requested seriously, but the look in Sugar's eyes told her that there was no give on this subject. "I do not want to see you get hurt sister not like this," she added.

"One does not go without the other," Sugar countered. Tee'Quilla groaned and shook her head. "What will it be?' she asked.

"You do not understand sister. I know where you are. I know why you are doing this just as our queen does. She told me you would do this. I hoped... I prayed she was wrong," Tee'Quilla began. "I hate that you are putting me in this position sister," she began. "Qu'Tee is a member of the Order," she pointed out.

"I'm not," Sugar reminded. Tee'Quilla fumed.

"You aren't going to listen to reason are you?" Tee'Quilla asked.

"She is my daughter. It is a package deal," Sugar replied.

"You are too close. You can't see it now. But you will. Two times over, you will regret your choice. I hate that you are doing this, but I will agree to your terms. I only hope – and pray that you know a measure of what you are getting yourself into," she relented.

"I'm a big girl. I can take care of myself," Sugar reassured. "When did the queen wish to speak with Qu'Tee?" she asked curiously.

"After I got the okay from you," her sister answered.

"The funny thing is, even if I forbade her to go," Sugar began but stopped. "But what if?" she started. Tee'Quilla raised her hands to cut her off.

"You are fishing sister. We both know it. You know her better than anyone here. She is not selfish by any stretch of the imagination. When she knows what is at stake, and what must be done?" Tee'Quilla rebutted. "So what say you sister? Shall we speak with her now or let her do a couple dozen more laps around the garden?" she asked. Sugar reluctantly smiled.

"That won't be necessary. Let's go," she replied as the two left the room.

Fate

Back in the garden area, Leaf was looking at the dent in his helmet. Qu'Tee had calmed down and was apologizing to her teacher.

"I said I was sorry," Qu'Tee pointed out. Leaf sighed and shook his head.

"You have to do something about your temper. If you lose your temper you lose your focus," Leaf began.

"Lose focus and you lose yourself. I know," Qu'Tee reassured. "I, I don't know what happened I just sort if lost control," she added. Leaf walked over and put his hand on her head and sighed.

"I am impressed that you are able to channel such emotion, such power, but if you do not control the power, the power controls you. Astute enemies will see this and use it against you. Rage is strong, but alone it will defeat you as surly as any enemy," Leaf pointed out, tossing his warped helmet and staff aside.

"I know. I know," Qu'Tee began. "You won't tell the others about this will you?" she asked hesitantly. Leaf sighed and shook his head. Just then the doors to the garden opened. Sugar and Tee'Quilla entered and looked around.

"Priestess Tee'Quilla? Mom? What are you doing here?' Qu'Tee asked hesitantly.

"We heard a cry from the garden area and came to see if everything was okay," Tee'Quilla replied with a friendly smile. Qu'Tee blushed and looked down at her feet.

"I, I'm sorry. It was me. I had a bad dream," the young cleric explained.

"A frog spooked her from her slacking," Leaf teased as he messed up her hair. "At times she is such a girl," he added with a smirk.

"Good thing as she so happens to be a girl and all," Sugar added with a smile. Qu'Tee blushed and looked away.

"Mom!" she protested.

"What happened to your staff and helmet?" Tee'Quilla asked. Qu'Tee quickly looked away. "Sister, could you take Qu'Tee over to the fountain? There are a few matters I need to speak with Leaf," she added. Sugar nodded and walked Qu'Tee away from the temple guardian and the priestess. "We have known each other for quite some time Leaf. Why do you let her get away with so much? I have seen you expel students for far less," she asked quietly. Leaf looked over to where Qu'Tee and Sugar were talking.

"I don't know. She works so hard – tries so hard," he began as he shook his head. "It is hard to put to words," he added seriously. Tee'Quilla stared at him for a few moments and then looked over to where Sugar and Qu'Tee were.

"Have any of the other students given her trouble?" Tee'Quilla asked.

"No. I would have noticed. Everything has been quiet as of late. Is something wrong?" he asked hesitantly. Tee'Quilla sighed and shook her head. Leaf sighed and looked over at Qu'Tee. "How serious is this?" he hesitantly asked.

"Only the queen knows for sure," she began as she motioned for him to pass the staff to her. "She did this?" she asked. He nodded. "I have sparred with you on numerous occasions and have seen you fight. Never, have I seen anyone get the better of you. How did she?" she asked curiously handing the weapon back to him.

"I was there, when the capital fell. I have faced enemies of all kinds foes of all types. When we set up here under the banner of the Order, I used what I knew, what I learned to teach. But, I have never seen anyone like her," he tried to explain.

"She is unique," Tee'Quilla admitted.

"That isn't what I meant. As a teacher – I hold back so that my students don't get hurt," he began.

"Control and discipline are necessary," Tee'Quilla admitted.

"As of late, I haven't been holding back," he stated. The reality of what he was saying sunk in.

"Are you telling me she has surpassed you?" Tee'Quilla asked.

"As you say; she is unique. You asked about her with the other students? May I ask why?" he asked seriously.

"I have my reasons. Is she interacting alright? Does she get along?" she asked.

"Hard to say. She is a very quiet person. More often than not she tends to her studies and chores. Truth be told I haven't seen her with the others save for during lessons," he replied. Tee'Quilla looked over at Qu'Tee and shook her head.

"She doesn't feel like she fits in. I hoped that would change. How is she during lessons ?" she asked seriously.

"She has trouble paying attention. Her mind wanders and she has a tendency to daydream. Typical for someone her age. I have noticed her watching the other students on some occasions," he added remembering back.

"Was there a reason?" she asked.

"Hard to say. I noticed it shortly after you asked me to keep an eye on her. She knows that she is different than the others here," he answered.

"Are they jealous? Envious?" Tee'Quilla asked.

"There was one time. Qu'Tee managed to perfect a technique several of the older students were having trouble with, and they didn't take it well. Knowing how she is I worried she might lose her temper and hurt them, but instead she just shut down. I never saw her like that before." he recounted.

"What happened?" Tee'Quilla asked

"I was going to step in, but one of the youngest students stepped in and told them to leave Qu'Tee alone. Strange thing, they backed down, even apologized," he answered. For six years she has been here. I believe she has learned five times as much as any I have taught," he added shaking his head.

"This is a bad thing?" Tee'Quilla asked.

"She judges herself too harshly on everything she does. If it isn't perfect by her standards she will start over and try again until it is yet, she doesn't expect that from those around her. She doesn't judge anyone save herself," he explained. "But I wager you know that much, her being family and all," he added.

"I have seen that. Her, upbringing, prior to her arrival here was a harsh one. Many of the scars have not healed yet. I will be blunt about this. From what you know of her seen of her, could she be the one spoken of in our ancient text?" she asked. All color drained from his face as he looked over at the young woman laughing with her mother.

"The chosen one? I do not like the direction this is going," he began defensively.

"She is family. You think I like it anymore that you? I need to know," she rebutted. Leaf sighed and closed his eyes.

"I myself never put much faith in prophecies. I believe that the road ahead is made with the hands of today – not the promises offered from tomorrow," he began. "But, I will say this. There is something special in her and I don't mean her healing gift. There is a presence about her," he admitted.

"Were she to lead the cause, to take up our fallen banner?" Tee'Quilla asked.

"I don't think there would be a voice that would challenge it. I still don't like any of this. I know the prophecy you are speaking of. She doesn't deserve that," he added seriously. Tee'Quilla placed her hand on his shoulder and passively nodded. "If any one person could do the task you are subtly dancing around, I would put money on her being that one," he stated confidently.

"All of this may be moot," she reassured.

"The queen hasn't spoken with her yet?" he asked.

"Today," she answered.

"If, she is the one," he began. "When would she have to leave?" he asked hesitantly.

"The omens are ill. There is a dark cloud forming where the demon fell. He will make his move very soon and we are nowhere near ready to stop him," Tee'Quilla replied grimly. He wanted to deny it, but he could feel it too. He felt it once before and that was moments before the capital fell.

"If she is to go – I will go with her. She may be strong but her age still betrays her. She lets her feelings and emotions get the better of her. Out there," he began but she raised a hand. He stopped.

"I know how you feel. I feel it too. And you know as well as I, why we can't go," she pointed out. He wanted to argue the issue, but he knew she was right.

"I will pray for her safe return," he said politely. "If you will excuse me, I have an appointment with a soon to be very cross blacksmith," he said with a smile as he walked away.

"Is everything okay?" Qu'Tee asked as she and her mother walked over to where Tee'Quilla was. "If you are upset about his staff," she began.

"Be at peace," Tee'Quilla reassured. "I was just talking to him about your studies. Anything you wish to explain?" she asked curiously. Qu'Tee began to fidget and looked away.

"That would depend on what he told you," she replied.

"I'm teasing. He said you were unlike any student he has every had the good fortune to train," she reassured. Qu'Tee blinked in modest disbelief.

"He said that?" she asked.

"I might have paraphrased. Your mother told me that you are still having bad dreams, in spite of the wards we put up?" Tee'Quilla asked curiously.

"Not every day," Qu'Tee answered lowering her eyes. "I know that they are just dreams but still…at times they are so real," she added.

"This, is it part of the reason for your fear of frogs?" Tee'Quilla asked.

"Could be. I guess. I've always been scared of frogs. Even before the dreams started happening," she began as she looked at her mother and her aunt. "Am I in some sort of trouble?" she asked hesitantly.

"No. so if you are thinking you will disciplined because of this, please get that thought out of your head okay? None of us are perfect. Do try to remember that," she added as she sat down by the fountain.

"I'll try," Qu'Tee said as she sat down beside her aunt.

"What can you tell me, about Bo'Glin?" Tee'Quilla asked.

"Just what I learned from class. He is a demon; a powerful one. It took the combined might of the nations to stop him. Other than that," she began.

"What does he look like?" Tee'Quilla asked. Qu'Tee looked over at her mother, then back at her aunt. "The dreams? The beast you see the monster that you have been seeing?" she added.

"That that is Bo'Glin? Why? But why would he be after me?" she asked timidly. Tee'Quilla placed her hand on her niece's cheek.

"Tell me about the nations," Tee'Quilla asked.

"After the demon was gone. Doubt, envy, anger caused a rift to form between the allied nations. Ever since they have never been the same," the young cleric answered, still unsure where this was going.

"You, asked why? Bo'Glin fears you are the one spoken of in our ancient texts. He fears that you will unite the nations. He fears that you have in you – the power to undo everything he seeks to accomplish," Tee'Quilla explained.

"Okay. That is a little out there. Why would anything as powerful as a demon be afraid of me? How would I be able to unite the nations? Who would follow someone like me?" Qu'Tee asked emotionally.

"I would," Sugar answered seriously. Qu'Tee was going to interrupt.

"So would I," Tee'Quilla added seriously. "As would Leaf. You do not give yourself enough credit," she said with a smile as she got up. Qu'Tee was mildly stunned. Coming from her mother was one thing – she knew her aunt was not prone to saying such things lightly. "I know this is a lot to take in all at once. Shall we?" she asked.

"Shall we what?" Qu'Tee asked.

"There are things that need to be said about things that may or may not be," she began as she helped her daughter up to her feet. "The Queen herself wants to speak with you," she added with a wink.

"She wants to talk to me? Why?" she asked defensively, trying to think of anything she might have done or said to merit that kind of attention.

"Be at peace. She heard about how special you are. She knows that you have many questions. Not just about this. She may not have the all the answers you seek or have sought but she will be able to start you to a place where those answers will be," Tee'Quilla reassured.

"I'm not in trouble?" she repeated. Sugar messed up her hair.

"You will be if you keep being so stubborn you brat," Sugar retorted. "You didn't do anything wrong. The queen is proud of your accomplishments just as the rest of us are so get it through your skull already," she added.

"Are you ready?" Tee'Quilla asked.

"I guess so," Qu'Tee replied hesitantly as they made their way back into the temple.

History

In all the years that Qu'Tee had called the temple grounds her home, there were many places that were off limits. Some because she was too young, some were for her safety, some were for other reasons.

"I completely forgot that you have never been here before," Tee'Quilla remarked, noticing Qu'Tee captivated by the intricate sculptures that lined the hallway. "Do you know what this place is?" she asked. Qu'Tee shook her head. "It goes by many names. The one that best suits it though is the Hall of Heroes," she said proudly.

"There are so many statues," Qu'Tee began. She paused as a realization hit her. "They, they all died didn't they?" she asked

"No, most of them died though. They died protecting the Veil," Tee'Quilla answered. It was then that Qu'Tee made her way towards a set of sculptures. Behind them was a painting of a couple standing beside a king. "Do, do you remember them?" she asked.

"They, they look familiar," Qu'Tee began. It was then that memories flashed in her mind. Sugar placed her hand on her daughter's shoulder. "They, they died when I was little," she remembered.

"They were your parents. They served under the one true king and they were instrumental in turning Bo'Glin away when he sought to taint our lands," Sugar said proudly. Qu'Tee placed her hand on the painting.

"Is he after me because of them?" she asked.

"I do not pretend to know the will of demons. It could be revenge against those that were instrumental to his fall, but I feel it goes beyond that. He sincerely fears you," Tee'Quilla answered, taking a few moments to admire the picture. Eve'Lyn, Ma'Tore. I wish that you could have known them as we did. They were noble, strong, and compassionate. They almost singlehanded kept the forces of the goblins and orcs and undead at bay as the hero challenged the demon. It was so foolish. He was human but he would not give in. they battled though the mountains. It was then that the unthinkable happened. Bo'Glin stabbed his grotesque fist through the hero's armour. Undaunted, with the last of his strength he stabbed his sword into that demonic beast. The two fell into the ocean below. The Pirates and the Knights of Porpoise Bay searched for days for any sign of either of them, but all they found was the hero's broken mask," she concluded.

"Did you know them? My mom and dad?" Qu'Tee asked curiously.

"Between myself, your aunt here and Leaf, we know and have known most of the Ken population. Your mother had an affinity for poetry. Your father was a solder in the Order of the

Butterfly," Sugar stated.

"How do you know?" Qu'Tee asked.

"I have friends all over the place. Plus my sister is privy to all sorts of juicy gossip," Sugar added with a smile.

"What she says is true, although I wouldn't have worded it quite that way. Eve'Lyn and Ma'Tore were resourceful, brave and loyal. Many of these I things I see in you," Tee'Quilla stated. Qu'Tee looked over at Sugar. Her mother seemed a touch distant.

"Are you okay?" Qu'Tee asked. Sugar snapped herself out of it and smiled.

"It, it has just been a while since I have been here. It brings back so many memories," she reassured. She shook her head. "Don't worry so much about me. It is my job to worry about you remember?" Sugar teased.

The trio made their way through the winding Hall of Heroes. As the walked, Qu'Tee noticed that the walls were covered in ancient glyphs. Some looked familiar to her oddly enough.

After what felt like an hour of walking the three found themselves outside of two large iron doors. Embossed into the surface of the metal doors was an elaborate picture of an angel fighting off the demonic forces led by a demon shaped like frog. Above it was a message written in ancient text. Qu'Tee looked at it for a few moments. It was then that she could understand it.

"The doors to the future are bound by yesterday's tomorrow," Tee'Quilla and Qu'Tee said at the same time. Sugar and Tee'Quilla looked over at the young cleric. The large iron doors began to open inward.

"You, how did you know that?" Tee'Quilla asked hesitantly.

"I don't know. I just sort of did," she answered.

"Come, the queen lies beyond these doors," Tee'Quilla stated, letting the issue drop. Qu'Tee followed her mother and aunt beyond the large doors. The room beyond was shaped like a dome that seemed to be as big as the temple itself. A pillar of rippling light illuminated a statue of Lady Angela.

Qu'Tee looked up at the source of the light and saw a skylight covered by rippling water. It was then that she realized where they were.

"We are under the garden," she realized.

"Indeed we are," a friendly voice affirmed. The three looked over to the far side of the room. Sugar and Tee'Quilla slowly knelt. For a few seconds Qu'Tee was stunned, but she then quickly knelt as well. "Welcome young Qu'Tee. I have heard a great deal about you," the queen of all Ken added motioning for them to rise. "You have a great deal of questions I would imagine," she added. The three walked towards the table where the queen was sitting at. To either side of her were her most trusted guardians.

"You could say that. Why did you want to see me?" Qu'Tee hesitantly asked.

"You are not in trouble. Be at peace," the queen reassured. "There, there are dark times approaching. A wave of darkness is coming and if all are not ready, it will consume us all. Do you understand?" the queen asked.

"I don't," Qu'Tee began.

"You do," the queen interrupted calmly. Qu'Tee sighed and lowered her eyes. "The demon has returned. Bo'Glin, has returned," she added.

"Are you sure?" Tee'Quilla asked.

"The signs are there. His presence cannot be ignored. His taint has divided the nations, turning one against the other. His foul agents and minions are calling for his return. The goblins and orc tribes are starting to rally. The undead are rising from the ground. Since his defeat so long ago, he has been planning this day, the day his vengeance would be within his dark grasp," the queen replied seriously. "The rift between the nations, the fall of our capital, the scattering of our people, all of it was his doing. Of that there is no doubt," she added solemnly.

"I don't understand. What does all this have to do with me?"

Qu'Tee asked.

"Everything and nothing I am afraid. The path through darkness is narrow. It is forged through pain and fire. All that walk there return. There is danger, sacrifice, fear, hopelessness, despair. If the need was there, if you were called to walk this path in the name of Lady Angela, could you walk such a path?" the queen asked.

"If the need was great, I could and would, my queen," Qu'Tee reassured.

"I am both happy and sad by your answer my dear. Tell me, what do you know of the war and the demon lord's fall?" the queen asked seriously.

"Had I known you would ask about this stuff I would have brought notes," Qu'Tee remarked passively.

"Just do your best," the queen reassured.

"Okay. There was a time, a very long time ago, when the nations were at war with each other. Even the human nations didn't trust each other. Around that time the demon came. His minions and armies attacked the divided nations. It was then that the first king, Talas'All appeared. He rallied the nations and forced the demon and his dark agents into the sea. After that the Age of Unity began. All the wars between the nations ended," Qu'Tee began. "But, the demon wasn't gone as everyone had believed. The sea where he retreated turned foul. The goblins and orc tribes started acting up again. The nations readied for another war, but, a spell, a powerful one destroyed the king's citadel and the mountain it once stood on. The Knights of Porpoise Bay and the Pirate nation searched the remnants of the ravaged island. All they could find was the king's broken sword," Qu'Tee closed her eyes. Another war began. The nations were able to stave off the evil invasion, but at a great cost. Without our king, the unity that kept the allied nations so strong began to buckle. It was shortly after the alliance fell apart that our ancestral home, the Ken Capital was attacked. Our people were scattered throughout the Veil. No nations came to our aid in that dark hour. Not long after that dark day, the demon returned. The nations still opposed the demon, but divided all were doomed to defeat. In this dark time, a hero arose. Against the dark tide, he stood. To this day no one knows who he was. He was a symbol that reminded the nations of the great fall king," she continued.

"Do you know the rest of that story?" the queen asked.

"I know that the hero led a small force into the mountains where the demon's armies were strongest and in that fight both the hero and the demon fell from the mountain and into the sea," she answered.

"There is more to it than that. The hero you speak of, he challenged the demon and faced the demon alone. Goblins, orcs and undead sought to aid their master but were kept at bay, kept from interfering by two great Ken heroes, Eve'Lyn and Ma'Tore," the queen stated with pride.

"My, mom and dad were there?" Qu'Tee asked in mild awe.

"Were it not for them, the outcome would have been very different. As it was, both were never seen again. A few weeks later, a skeleton washed up on the western shore. On it was the hero's mask. His sword and shield were never found. The unity that bound the goblins and orcs dissolved and were no longer a viable threat to any nation let alone the Veil. The undead, bound by their master's magic crumbled," the queen continued.

"If that is so, how did this demon's evil pollute the land still?" Qu'Tee asked.

"Bo'Glin, he is a crafty one. Even in defeat he had sown seeds to taint and corrupt. Since the fall of our capital, desperately have we tried to remake what was destroyed. We who served the king closest were targeted for a reason. Prophecy and ancient text spoke of the one who would herald the demon's final defeat," the queen began. Qu'Tee began to giggle nervously.

"This is a joke right? You aren't trying to tell me," Qu'Tee began.

"The chosen one spoken of is you," the queen clarified.

"Are you sure?" Tee'Quilla asked.

"I have no doubt. Her gift of healing, the demon's fear of her, the blood that courses through her veins. She is the one; the only one that can do this task," the queen stated seriously. Qu'Tee looked at the queen, then her mother, then her aunt.

"You people are losing me here. What are you talking about?" she hesitantly asked.

"If the ten nations do not stand as one before the dark tide, all will be lost. The Veil as we know it will cease to exist and an age of darkness and blood will begin. The chosen one, you, must unite the nations," the queen explained.

"How exactly am I supposed to do that? Last I heard everyone was barely speaking and in some cases some nations were on the brink of war with each other. Why would anyone listen to me?" Qu'Tee asked timidly.

"You are young, your time her has been secluded. But do not sell yourself short. Your are very resourceful and passionate. Such is the reason the demon fears you so," the queen reassured.

"Why do you say he fears me? The monster I have seen does not fear me," Qu'Tee interrupted. She quickly regained her composure. "I am sorry," she added passively.

"Bo'Glin, he is not immortal, not yet. All of the pieces are not in place. You my dear, are key to this. You will either be the key to his immortality, or his final defeat. He may torment you, but have no doubt that his fear of you is real. You are the one thing, the one person in the Veil he does fear," the queen reiterated.

"But, even if all of this is true. I do not know where to begin. How am I supposed to thwart a demon so powerful? How will my voice change the hearts of bitter enemies?' Qu'Tee asked.

"Be at peace. Where you go may be filled by shadows, but there will also be light. Kindred spirits will hear your voice and will listen. As for defeating this demon, all your time here that you spent training and studying has been leading to such a moment. When the time comes, you will know what will need to be done," the queen began as she looked over at Sugar. She sighed and shook her head. "Know that, you will not be alone in this dark time. Your mother will be by your side," she added. Qu'Tee looked over at Sugar, her eyes almost lit up.

"Is this true?" Qu'Tee asked optimistically.

"Do you think I would let you do anything this dangerous on your own? Silly girl," her mother mused, she then turned and face the queen. "I thank you for allowing me to do this," she added with a bow. The queen sighed.

"You are her mother. How could I stand in your way? Regardless, I must ask you if you are up to such a task?" the queen asked.

"She will not face this darkness alone," Sugar answered.

"Very well. I will say no more. I only hope, nay, pray, you know what you are doing. Qu'Tee," the queen said getting the young cleric's attention. "Can you do this?" she asked seriously.

Qu'Tee knelt before the queen and bowed her head.

"Failure is not an option. Not only are you counting on me, but the Veil as well. I will not let you down," she replied confidently. When she looked up at the queen, she could swear that the queen was glowing.

"Daughter? Go to our room. We have a journey to prepare for. I will join you shortly," Sugar instructed. Qu'Tee got up and hurried out of the room. Once she was gone, Sugar closed her eyes. "You left a little bit out of your story highness," she added.

"You know what is at stake. Does she need to know?" the queen asked. "That being said, you of all people should know that fate and destiny cannot be cheated. Are you sure this is wise? You can not make the choice for her. You cannot take her place," the queen stated seriously.

"Perhaps if I am there, that, choice, may not need to be made," Sugar rebutted.

"You have committed yourself to this. I cannot talk you out of this. I will not even try. I am saddened though. You can not see it now as you are far too close. But twice over, you will regret your choice. The pain you feel now, is nothing compared to what lies ahead," the queen said passively.

"Time will tell," Sugar replied. She bowed to the queen and hurried away.

"Do you want me to follow them?" Tee'Quilla asked.

"No. She has made her choice. It changes nothing. We must prepare for what will be," the queen said with a sigh.

"Why can we not tell her?" Tee'Quilla asked stubbornly.

"She would not listen to reason. Even if we did, it would change nothing," the queen replied as she rose to her feet. "The future is bound by yesterday's tomorrow. Perhaps, it will be different. Perhaps we are wrong. In this dark time nothing is certain," she continued as she looked at the ruby ring on her hand. "I have a favour to ask of you," she began, placing her hand over the ring.

"I don't like the sound of this," Tee'Quilla hesitantly began.

"Be at peace. A darkness is coming. Bright though Qu'Tee is, alone she may not be seen. Even with her mother's aid I fear it may not be enough," the queen began as she removed the ring and handed it to Tee'Quilla. "However, if she has the voice of all Ken, she will be seen," she added.

"Are you sure this is wise my queen?" Tee'Quilla asked looking at the ring.

"Would you not follow her should her hand raise our fallen banner?" the queen asked with an enigmatic smile.

"But even so, she is still so young," Tee'Quilla pointed out.

"The hope of all nations, including the Ken rest with her. Young or no, this is what must be. Young or no, she may be a child, but, she is a child that may not return. She needs all the help we can give her. Just as you and your sister believe in her, so too do I," the queen replied. Tee'Quilla sighed and clenched the ring in her hand.

"When should I inform the others of this, change?" Tee'Quilla asked.

"When the Butterfly opens her wings, not a moment before," the queen answered. Tee'Quilla knelt and bowed to the queen she had served for so many years.

"From the wisest to the youngest. These are interesting times highness. Your will shall be done," the head of the Order of the Butterfly concluded as she rose and left the chamber. The queen sighed as she sat back down in her chair.

"Be brave young Qu'Tee. Be strong. Know that wherever you go, all Ken are with you," the queen whispered as she closed her eyes.

<u>Beginning</u>

In their modest room in the temple, Sugar and Qu'Tee were packing for their journey. Sugar was almost ready to leave. Her daughter on the other hand was looking at a large pile of clutter.

"At time like this you learn just how much stuff you have," Qu'Tee remarked.

"Or need?" Sugar suggested.

"That too. How were you able to be ready so quick?" she asked.

"I've done a bit of travelling. You know that," Sugar rebutted. "I will warn you though. If you want to take all of that, you are carrying it," she warned. Qu'Tee pouted. "Do you want some help?" she offered.

"Please?" Qu'Tee admitted. Sugar sat down beside her and looked at the pile. "It's kind of funny. I, I don't really remember much of my life before here. Other than my experiences at that orphanage," she added.

"So in a sense, this will be your first real outing?" Sugar asked with a half smile.

"I guess so," Qu'Tee replied.

"Then let's make this fun," Sugar began as she pondered for a moment. "What will you need?" she asked.

"My staff, my armour, some clothes, some food?" Qu'Tee guessed.

"Good start. How far is the nearest village?" Sugar asked.

"I don't remember. A couple days?" Qu'Tee guessed.

"About that far. Don't weigh yourself down with clothes. We'll pick up stuff on the way," Sugar suggested.

"Doesn't that get expensive?" Qu'Tee asked.

"Special outing, you let me worry about that. That being said, what clothes do you need?" Sugar asked. Qu'Tee thought for a moment then began sifting through the pile before her. "Take your time," she reassured. The pile before Qu'Tee shrunk exponentially. "Good start. What else do we need?" she asked.

"I already mentioned my armour. Food?" she asked.

"So how much do you really need? If the nearest village is about two days away?" Sugar asked. Qu'Tee looked at the provisions she had before her.

"Less than what I have?" she asked.

"I'll show you how to survive on long journeys," Sugar reassured. The pile before her daughter could now almost fit into one pack. "Not bad. Bear in mind, that not all journeys will be quite as luxurious. But for this one we won't hold back," she added with a smile.

"All I know, remember of my experiences beyond these temple walls," Qu'Tee began.

"All of the world isn't like that. In your studies of the other nations, you must have wondered what they are like first hand. For some of them, text does not do them justice," Sugar reassured.

"Really?" Qu'Tee asked entranced.

"Elves, dwarves, merfolk, even the humans, wizards and mages. They really are unique," Sugar said with a smile.

"Even the humans?" Qu'Tee asked passively. Sugar sighed.

"Not all are like those creeps at that foul orphanage. Many are dedicated, passionate and creative," Sugar reassured as she put her arm around her daughter. "And if they are anything less I will be there to put them in their place," she said making her daughter laugh. "But I doubt that will be necessary," she added.

"Why?" Qu'Tee asked.

"Because, I know the kind of woman you are. Do you have a

knife?" she asked.

"My staff is my weapon," Qu'Tee answered.

"Noble sentiment, really. But there are some occasions where a dagger will get the point across faster than a staff," Sugar began as she handed a slim dagger to her daughter. Qu'Tee was going to argue the issue. "Daughter, please, trust me on this," she reassured. Qu'Tee relented and added the dagger to her possessions. Sugar watched as her daughter managed to fit all of the things before her into one pack. "Welcoming to the fun art of being an adventurer. Fun stuff huh?" Sugar teased.

"You do this sort of thing a lot? I mean, you've gone off quite a bit since I've known you," Qu'Tee asked.

"Not that much," Sugar rebutted.

"I didn't mean that. Not that way," Qu'Tee reassured.

"I'm teasing. Remember? I do that sort of thing," Sugar reassured. "This kind of scary?" she asked.

"A little bit," Qu'Tee admitted.

"You will do just fine. Trust me on that," Sugar reassured.

"Out of curiosity, where will we sleep?" Qu'Tee asked.

"More often than not we will be camping. Not as glamorous as the bards make it sound, trust me," Sugar mused.

"But, you still go?" Qu'Tee pointed out.

"It is hard to put to words. When we get back, you'll understand," Sugar stated. Qu'Tee sighed. "Any second thoughts?" she asked.

"No. Everyone is counting on me," Qu'Tee said with a smile. Sugar knew that it was a front. She was always like that when she was scared.

"Need any help with your armour?" Sugar offered.

"I think I can do that by myself mom," Qu'Tee rebutted, shooing her mother from the room.

A short while later...

The two were standing outside of the temple gates.

"Looks different from out here," Qu'Tee remarked.

"It does. Are you ready?" Sugar asked. Her daughter nodded. They began to walk when the temple gates opened. They looked and saw Tee'Quilla exiting the temple. She said something to the guard at the gate. The guard nodded and entered, closing the gate behind him. "This is new," she added under her breath.

"I am glad I caught you before you left," Tee'Quilla said, taking a moment to catch her breath. "Let me guess, you helped her pack?" she added.

"You could say that," Sugar said with a smirk. Her sister walked over to where they were and smiled. "You know I hate it when you smile like that," she added under her breath.

"It is good news this time. Promise," Tee'Quilla said with a wink. She focused on her niece and sighed. "There is a matter that the queen herself wanted to talk to you about before you left," she said seriously.

"Was this some sort of test?" Qu'Tee hesitantly asked.

"Yes and no. The queen asked me to give this to you before you left," Tee'Quilla said with pride as she extended the ring she had been given. Both Sugar and Qu'Tee were shocked by the display.

"If that is what I think it is, there is no way I can accept that," Qu'Tee replied stepping away from the ring as though it was toxic.

"Why?" Tee'Quilla asked.

"I am no priestess! I am not worthy of such a thing!" Qu'Tee protested. Tee'Quilla smiled as she knelt before her niece and smiled. "Why are you doing that?" she asked defensively.

"Truth be told, I was hesitant when the queen told me to do this. I see now, she was right," Tee'Quilla stated seriously. Qu'Tee looked over to her mother and watched as she too dropped to one knee. "But, she was right," she added.

"What are you talking about?" Qu'Tee protested.

"The journey ahead is frocked with danger and adversity. Even with my sister as a travelling companion it will be, testing to say the least. I had my doubts at first but I see now that she was right, as always," Tee'Quilla said proudly.

"Okay. What exactly are you talking about?" Qu'Tee repeated.

"Tell me what I am offering. Then tell me why, you are refusing," Tee'Quilla requested.

"That is the ring of the queen. I recognize it from class and know what it being offered means. I am not worthy of such a thing," she protested.

"I have known you since you arrived. You are worthy. All of this proves such," Tee'Quilla reassured.

"But that would mean," Qu'Tee began.

"That you are now queen of all Ken," Sugar completely proudly.

"I know this is a lot to take in. Believe me, I understand. I myself was hesitant when the queen told me to do this. But, after hearing you just now, I understand," Tee'Quilla stated proudly with a smile.

"I cannot accept," Qu'Tee protested. "They will think I am a thief, a pretender," she added adamantly.

"This ring is enchanted. It cannot be stolen. It cannot be taken. It can only be given. It is the will of the queen, a power higher than the Order that you be given this ring. Will you refuse the will of our queen?" Tee'Quilla seriously asked.

"I am a child. The fact that I am on a quest of THIS magnitude is one thing," Qu'Tee began. Her aunt raised her hand, stopping her train of thought.

"Why?" Tee'Quilla asked.

"What?" Qu'Tee asked, seriously puzzled by the direction this was taking.

"Tell me why you think you are not worthy of this?" Tee'Quilla asked.

"Like I said, I'm still a child. How am I supposed to be responsible for all Ken?" she explained. Both Sugar and Tee'Quilla smiled. "What? Why are you smiling like that?" she hesitantly asked.

"If any in your class were offered this, what would they have said?" Tee'Quilla asked.

"They would have jumped on it," Qu'Tee admitted.

"Yet, you refuse. Why?" Tee'Quilla asked curiously.

"If I accept and make a mistake, all Ken will suffer. It is a most generous offer but I cannot accept," Qu'Tee explained.

"With every word you use to protest this, you prove how right the queen was. Tell me, if any in your class were offered this, what would they have said?" Tee'Quilla rebutted.

"They probably would have accepted," Qu'Tee admitted.

"Yet, you refuse. Why?" Tee'Quilla rebutted.

"I do not want any mistake I make to harm a nation," Qu'Tee replied honestly.

"Sounds to me like the will of a queen. Your journey will be harsh. Would that I could travel with you but I cannot. Even with my sister's aid it will be a trial that few could pass. With this ring though, with the backing of a nation, it could make a world of difference. You are the only woman who can wear this ring. Do so proudly, as the woman before you did," Tee'Quilla requested.
"Mom?" Qu'Tee hesitantly asked.

"This is your choice daughter. But, my sister is known to speak her mind. She would not say anything lightly. She is a cleric priestess," Sugar replied seriously.

"I know! I mean, you know what I mean," Qu'Tee flustered. "But this is too much," she added defensively.

"You are on a quest to save the world niece. What is another title?" Tee'Quilla mused. "Are you saying that you know more than the queen?" she challenged.

"No! I would never," Qu'Tee began.

"Then accept this. Never let anyone or anything question that this is your destiny and birthright. You are a worthy successor. The queen herself believes in you, would you do less?" Tee'Quilla asked extending the ring to her niece.

"I don't like this, but if she says I must," Qu'Tee began.

"She did," Tee'Quilla reassured. Both she and Sugar watched as the reluctant queen put the ring on her finger. "May the Order guide you and Lady Angela protect you on your journey," Tee'Quilla said as she knelt and bowed to her niece.

"Please tell her that I will not let her down," Qu'Tee requested, staring at the ring on her finger. "Do I look any different?" she asked modestly,

"Not really, why?" Sugar asked.

"I don't know. The queen was sort of glowing. I thought it was the ring," Qu'Tee answered. "I don't feel any different either," she added. Sugar and Tee'Quilla were quiet for a moment. "Did I say something wrong?" she asked.

"If I may ask, have you seen any other people glowing in such a fashion?" Tee'Quilla asked. Qu'Tee thought back.

"I don't know. A few times I think. Why?" she answered. It was then that both Sugar and Tee'Quilla understood why the queen chose a successor. "You two are starting to scare me," she pointed out.

"Be at peace. We will talk about it later. Will you be able to handle things here without me?" Sugar asked her sister.

"We'll muddle through," Tee'Quilla said as she hugged her sister. She then knelt and bowed to her niece, the new queen of the Ken. "And you, know that wherever your journey takes you, the Order and all Ken stand with you, my queen," she added.

"Stop talking like that. You are embarrassing me," Qu'Tee protested.

"Regardless, it is true. You have come a long way since that fateful day when you arrived here," Tee'Quilla admitted as she hugged her niece. "I'm very proud of you," she whispered as she got up. "If either of you need help, you have but to call. Now if you will excuse me, I have some chores that need attending. Good journey," she concluded as she returned to the temple gates. Sugar and Qu'Tee watched as the gates opened for her and prompt closed after she was in.

"Quite the auspicious start wouldn't you say?" Sugar asked.

"That is one way of putting it," Qu'Tee admitted, looking at the ring on her finger. "You know, yesterday, I was an adopted orphan studying in a temple trying hard just to stay out of trouble. Now everyone in the Veil is counting on me, OH, and I'm a queen now," she added. Her mother smiled.

"Is this going somewhere?" Sugar asked.

"If this much can happen in just one day it makes me wonder what tomorrow will bring, or the day after that," Qu'Tee pointed out. Her mother quietly laughed and shook her head. "Don't laugh! I'm being serious," she added. Sugar messed up her hair. "Don't do that to your queen," she protested.

"I'm still your mother, nice try though," Sugar mused as they walked down the forest path and out of view of the temple.

Enter the Hero?

It had been one day into their epic journey. Nothing of notable importance touched the two travellers, a pleasant surprise for the new queen of the Ken, who was expecting the worst. One thing that did surprise her, unpleasantly so, was that her mother was continuing her studies as though they were still back at the temple.

"You know," Qu'Tee began. "When we left the temple, I presumed that I would get a break from this sort of thing as I am trying to save the world and all," she pointed out. Her mother quietly laughed.

"How would you feel if you fell behind the rest of the students?" Sugar pointed out.

"I'm sure I could live with it or fake it if need be," she answered. Her mother closed the book she had been reading from and smiled.

"You're precious. Have I told you that today?" Sugar asked, putting the book away.

"Not today, if memory serves me," Qu'Tee sarcastically replied.

"How are you holding up so far?" Sugar asked curiously.

"Still seems unreal," Qu'Tee admitted.

"First time out can be like that. It's almost time to eat. There was a stream down by where the path twists. Could you get some water for me?" Sugar asked. Qu'Tee took the small pot and hurried away. She stopped and looked over at her mother.

"Mom?" she said getting her attention. Sugar looked over at her. "I'm glad you're here. I don't think I could do this sort of thing on my own," she added as she vanished into the forest.

Moments later the young cleric queen was by the trickling stream. She sat down on a rock and hugged her knees. She didn't want to admit it, but she was starting to miss home, the temple.

"I have to do this," she sighed. She looked at the ring on her finger. "But what if I screw up? What if I can't do it?" she added. Her monologue was interrupt. She heard something moving in the branches above her! In one fluid motion she leaped from where she was sitting, rolled, and grabbed her staff. She stood ready for whatever might be there, spying on her or worse! "Who is there?" she demanded. There was no answer. "You do not want me repeating myself.

A few, very slow seconds passed. A blur of motion shot down from the branches. Qu'Tee spun around, brought her staff down but stopped before finishing the strike, MUCH to the relief of a small squirrel that was now staring saucer eyed at the weapon that almost brained him

"You scared me half to death," Qu'Tee muttered, lowering her weapon. "Why did you do that?" she asked the still shaking tree rat. "Sorry for almost whacking you. I guess I'm a little tense," she admitted as she sat down. The squirrel began to calm down. She reached into her pocket and pulled out a small handful of seeds. "Peace offering?" she said, she slowly placed a couple seeds between them. Hesitantly the squirrel looked at the seeds, then at her. "I won't hurt you," she reassured. Timidly the squirrel inched forward, not taking his eyes off her. It then grabbed the seeds and began to eat them. "Want more?" she offered, holding her hand out. The squirrel inched forward and began to eat the seeds from her hand. "Oh, I almost forgot. Mom is waiting for me!" she remembered. She placed the small handful of seeds on the ground and filled the pot with water. "You be good and don't scare people okay?" she said with a smile, forgetting her staff.

The squirrel blinked as though trying to make sense of what just happened. It seemed to shrug its shoulders and resumed eating the yummy seeds. It was then that a man silently dropped from the same tree and stood behind the squirrel. A few seconds passed before the squirrel realized he was there.

"Don't you have a job to do?" he asked he wore a mask that hid all of his face, save his eyes and wore numerous weapons. The squirrel squeaked and hurried up a tree. The man shook his head. "Why couldn't they give me a familiar that didn't have its brain in its stomach?" he muttered shaking his head. It was then that he noticed the staff by the stream. "She forgot her weapon," he added. It was then that he heard a squirrel cry out. "Damn it," he hissed as he ran into the forest. It was a few seconds later that he saw his squirrel frantically trying to depict what he saw. After a few seconds, the man understood. "They got here faster than I anticipated. Go! I will be there in a moment," he reassured, drawing his sword.

Back at the campsite, Qu'Tee and her mother were standing back to back armed with only two knives. Surrounding them like circling predators was an exceptionally surly looking group of bandits. Ten of them.

"I forgot my staff by the stream," Qu'Tee cursed her forgetfulness.

"Say nothing," Sugar said under her breath, not taking her eyes from and of the ruffians before her. "We have nothing worth stealing. Leave in peace," she stated seriously. The leader of the group and his brethren laughed.

"Value my dear, is in the eye of the beholder," he remarking looking over at Qu'Tee.

"If your filthy, vagrant eyes look at her again I will carve them from your depraved skull," Sugar warned. The leader pretended to be scared. She was going to continue the train of thought when she sensed another presence nearby. "More company," she said under her breath, unsure if there were more ruffians. It was then that one of the bandits groaned and dropped to his knees.

All eyes looked to the gasping bandit. He fell, face first to the ground, a throwing dagger embedded squarely in his back. The would be murderous thieves looked around for the attacker but could not see him.

"Who would dare be so bold as to attack my band in its element?" the leader almost spat.

Qu'Tee sensed something flying towards her. Her hand lashed out and caught her staff.

"You forgot this by the stream. Thought you might need it," the masked man pointed out. Sugar looked over her shoulder at the man that had reunited her daughter with her weapon of choice.

"Friend of yours?" Sugar asked.

"He is now," Qu'Tee replied.

"Son, you made a big mistake. Gort, Harn, Tawo, beat some sense into that waif of a boy," the leader began, returning is attention to Sugar. "After they have their fun with the boy, then we will focus on treating you lasses right properly we will," he mocked. Sugar looked over at the three heavy set bandits on route to deal with their would be ally.

"Help our new friend dear. I will keep these ones busy," Sugar stated seriously.

"You sure?" Qu'Tee asked, her mother nodded. "As you say,"

she affirmed.

"Neither of you are going anywhere," the leader reminded. Just then, Qu'Tee hopped up landed on one bandit's head then leaped away from the circle. The bandit she used as a means of escape stumbled off balance knocking another thief to the ground. Frustration was beginning to set in. "Get her!" the leader ordered. This simple exercise was going no where near as smoothly as he wanted.

The masked man watched as the three bandits made their way towards him. Each outweighed him by nearly a hundred pounds if that, but they were undisciplined. He could tell by they way they moved, held their weapons. They were used to fighting prey that did not, or could not fight back. He was neither.

Qu'Tee watched as her new ally fended off the attacks of the bigger ruffians. The way he used his weapons, the way he used his surrounding to keep his enemies off balance impressed her.

"Need any help?" Qu'Tee asked. The masked man stabbed a sword into the belly of one man. He released the weapon and drew another blade. The bandit gasped and keeled over.

"I wouldn't turn it away if offered," he admitted. Qu'Tee spun around. Her staff cracked into the side of one bandit's head. Much to her shock it seemed to have no affect. "Don't rightly think he uses that much," he pointed out.

"More than one way to take a tree down," Qu'Tee rebutted. She hopped up, placing a foot on the angry bandit's chest. Before he could react, she slammed the end into his face as though her weapon was a spear. He screamed out as he lashed out knocking the cleric face first into a tree. She was out cold. The masked man looked at where she lied motionless then glared at the bloody face of the man that had struck her.

"You will pay for that," he hissed. There was a rage in his eyes. An aura began to pulse around him. The bandits tried to back away, but it was too late. The masked man exploded towards them. His twin swords flashed five times as he came to a screeching halt behind the stunned ruffians. "Die," he added in disgust, looking at his swords. Blood poured from the deep cuts he had landed. Then like a feral animal he turned his attention to the remaining thieves.

"Who the hell are you boy? How the hell can you move like that?" the leader demanded. The masked man sheathed one of his swords. He removed five throwing daggers and fanned them out in his hand as though they were playing cards.

"Today is your lucky day wench. Let's get out of here boys," he stated. Before he could move, Sugar lashed out and cut his cheek. Before he could say another word, the masked man threw the handful of daggers at the remaining bandits. The leader watched, unable to move as five bandits fell dead. Of the group, now only two were left standing. The other bandit began to run. The masked man threw his sword as though it was a spear and impaled the man to a tree.

"How are you feeling?" Sugar asked the unmoving leader. He tried to move but couldn't. "The blade I cut you with had a mixture on it. Quite harmless really. Not poisonous or anything like that, but it paralyzes very quickly, but I'd imagine you gathered that much," she said as she looked over her shoulder. "Is she okay?" she asked. The masked man nodded and helped Qu'Tee regain her footing.

"Just a little dazed. What did you do to him?" he answered and asked, noticing the remaining thief standing so perfectly still.

"Just a little something to get his attention. Wait here. I'll be right back," she said to the unmoving prisoner. "How are you feeling daughter?" she asked quietly.

"Little woozy. I've dealt with worse," she answered as she looked over at the masked man. "I don't think I've seen anyone fight like you," she commented. It was then that she noticed his eyes. She blinked as she walked over and began to study the masked face more closely, so much so that he backed up.

"You okay?" he asked hesitantly.

"I know you, don't I?" she said more than asked.

"I seriously doubt it. I am rarely in these parts," he answered backing away. She stepped forward, not giving him room to escape. "I really should be going," he muttered nervously.

"Don't be silly. I don't know where you come from stranger,

but I would be personally insulted if you didn't at least stay and have a meal with us," Sugar said politely.

"Why do I get the impression that I wouldn't want to do that?" he remarked. Sugar walked over and patted him on the cheek.

"Clever boy, Qu'Tee? As our rude guests spilled the water you so thoughtfully got for me, could you be a dear and fetch some more? There are some things I need to discuss with our friend," she requested. Qu'Tee nodded and began to walk away. As she did she looked over her shoulder at the person that helped them. "I never much liked masks. Is there a reason for yours?" she asked calmly.

"It's, it's kind of personal," he replied.

"You've been following us. Is there a reason?" Sugar asked. The man looked away, in the direction Qu'Tee had gone. "You know her? An old friend perhaps?" she asked. The masked man sighed and shook his head.

"I'm no friend," he replied.

"But you do know her. Interesting as your markings show you are from Pit Fighter territory," Sugar remarked as she walked over to where her fire was. "She has never been by that way. So tell me how it is that she would know a barbarian?" she mused. The masked man sat down before her.

"You must be mistaken then. How could I know her?" he

rebutted. Sugar smiled as she sat down. He was being elusive.

"Then we would seem to be at an impasse. You see, if you don't know her – or me, that would mean that you were following us for, what reason?" she asked curiously. They looked over and saw Qu'Tee had returned.

"Have you finished interrogating him yet?" Qu'Tee asked. Sugar giggled as she took the pot from her daughter.

"You can be so silly at times. We were just discussing some things, right?" Sugar asked. The man looked over at the bandit that was still motionless. The only thing he seemed to be able to move was his eyes.

"What she said," he affirmed.

"I like this boy," Sugar said with a smile as she began to put things into the pot. "Be at peace. Only people who are at odds with my daughter need worry about me," she reassured with a wink.

"She gets like that," Qu'Tee admitted. She studied him some more. She was positive that she knew him. There was something so, familiar about him. It was only when he looked over at her that she realized she was staring. "I'm sorry," she added blushing. "May I ask who you are?" she asked.

"I, I'm just a shadow," he replied passively. Qu'Tee sighed as she got up and walked away. Sugar shook her head.

"My daughter tends to be shy around new people. Don't take it too personal," Sugar reassured as she dipped a small bowl into the pot. "And one for you," she added as she dipped another bowl into the pot. "Could you be a dear and bring this to her? She will be hungry later if she doesn't eat now," she requested. The masked man nodded as he took the two bowls and walked off in the direction Qu'Tee had gone. "He must be the one she told me about," she said to herself.

Back by the stream, Qu'Tee was sitting on a rock hugging her knees.

"Why did you come here?" she asked, not moving. The masked man stepped out from the bushes. She looked over her shoulder at him. He looked away. There was something in her eyes that he could not explain. "Why now?" she asked. He sighed as he sat down before her.

"How did you know it was me?" he quietly asked. He remained still as she reached forward and slowly removed his mask. It really was him.

"Evallion," she whispered, unable to look away.

The Hero

By the stream, time seemed to stand still.

"It, it really is you? This isn't a dream?" Qu'Tee hesitantly asked. Evallion sighed and looked away. There were so many things he wanted, no, needed to say to her, but he couldn't seem to utter a sound. He looked over at her just in time to be slapped across the face. He had been hit before, but for some reason this hurt more.

"What was that for?" he exclaimed. It was then that he saw that her eyes were watering. There was a mixture of hurt mixed with anger looking back at him. Qu'Tee closed her eyes as it all came back to her.

Qu'Tee was in a village. She never knew the name. All she knew is that it was where the orphanage was. She was a child again, hiding from the bullies that tormented her. This time was different from the numerous times before though.

"She couldn't have gotten far! Find her!" the eldest of the bullies ordered as they hurried by the alley. Qu'Tee closed her eyes and just wished she could disappear.

"What are you doing?" a friendly voice asked. She looked over and saw a boy looking at her. He couldn't have been much older than her. She did her best to stop shaking, but she was still so scared. "Why are you crying?" he asked.

"Some girls are picking on me. They always do," she answered.

"But why?" he asked.

"Because the little piece of trash is a witch," a voice answered. They looked over and saw them. The bullies found her. "How cute, she found a little friend," she mocked, her friends laughed. The boy stood up and frowned at them.

"Leave her alone," he stated seriously. The bullies laughed. He was going to say something when he felt a gentle tugging on his pant leg. He looked down and saw such a hurt, defeated look on Qu'Tee's face.

"Please don't do this. I'm not worth it," she said passively. He watched as she walked over to where the bullies were. "I'm sorry I ran away," she added timidly. The boy watched as a strong backhand sent Qu'Tee to the ground.

"You little bitch. You wasted our time making us chase you," the eldest of the bullies said as they all began hitting the defenceless girl. The boy could feel a rage inside as he watched the display. His hands clenched into fists.

"Stop that," he said under his breath. But they couldn't hear him over the hitting and mocking. He grabbed a piece of wood from a broken crate and charged towards the lynching. Three of the bullies saw his charge and moved out of the way. The eldest of the bullies looked up just in time to have her vision clouded by a burst of stars. She recoiled, staggered back several paces before falling backwards. The boy swung the piece of wood viciously at any of the bullies that were remotely near Qu'Tee. "If you go near her I swear I'll kill you!" he threatened. Two of her friends helped the lead bully up.

"You little shit," she cursed spitting out a bloody tooth. "You are really going to regret that," she added as they began to circle in on him like ravenous wolves circling wounded prey. The boy lashed out with his weapon at any that got too close. It was then that one of them managed to get the board from him. Qu'Tee watched as the bullies jumped him and beat him. It worse than any of the times they beat her up because it was all her fault. The only reason he was being hurt was because he tried to help her. She wanted to do something, say something, but all she could do was cry.

"Maybe next time you will mind your own business," the eldest bully taunted spitting on him. "Let's go," she said to her friends as they hurried away. Qu'Tee looked at the boy. He seemed to be glowing. The light was fading, growing more dim with each passing moment. She crawled over to where he was. She was mildly startled when he put his hand on hers.

"Why did you do that?" she sobbed. "It's all my fault you got hurt," she added.

"Sorry," he strained. Each breath was a laboured effort.

"What? Why are you sorry?" she asked in modest disbelief.

"I wasn't strong enough to stop them. Next time," he said coughing up some blood. "Why is it getting so dark?" he asked passively. It was then that she noticed the light in him that was glowing seemed to be flowing upward from him. She didn't know what it meant, but she knew it couldn't be good.

"No! Don't leave me!" she pleaded. She placed her hands on his chest and concentrated. Her hands began to glow as a magical aura encompassed them both. "Please god. Do not let him die because of helping me," she pleaded. She closed her eyes as all of his wounds began to heal. Within minutes, it was as though he hadn't been hurt at all.

Qu'Tee sniffled and opened her eyes. He was okay. He was going to be okay. She got up and started to walk away. The boy slowly sat up and looked around.

"Where are you going?" he asked. She stopped.

"It is better if I go. I don't want you getting hurt because of me," she answered. He crawled over and leaned against a broken crate.

"You made me better," he said looking at his hands and arms. "How did you do that?" he asked curiously. Qu'Tee sighed. She walked back and sat down beside him.

"They say it is because I am a witch," she answered passively.

"I don't think you are," he rebutted confidently. She blinked in modest disbelief.

"You don't think so?" she asked hesitantly.

"You, you really mean that?" she asked.

"Yeah. I mean if you were a witch you would have a funny hat, a broom and you would have turned those creepy girls into toads, then again they were already kind of toad-like," he said. For the first time in her life, she laughed. "Want some candy? My mom gave me some," he offered. He reached into his pocket and handed a candy to her. She looked at it as though it was made of precious metal.

"You aren't scared of me?" she asked.

"Not really. You scared of me?" He answered and asked popping a candy into his mouth.

"A little bit," she admitted as she nibbled on her piece of candy. He reached in his pocket and offered her another candy. She took it and smiled at him. "Not as much," she said with a smile. He laughed as he offered her another candy. "Thank you," she said politely, holding the candy close to her heart.

"Why don't you tell your mom and dad about those toads?" he asked. Qu'Tee nibbled on her candy and sighed.

"I, don't have a mom or dad. I'm from the orphanage," she answered passively.

"I don't have a dad. My mom is pretty nice though," he began as he looked up at the sky. "It is getting late. Want me to walk you home?" he offered. She shook her head.

"I can do it myself," she reassured.

"I'm sorry. I'm kind of slow some times. My name is Evallion. What is your name?" he asked curiously as he helped her up.

"Qu'Tee," she replied.

"Do you want to be friends?" he asked. She could feel herself blush. All she could remember was people hating her, despising her, picking on her. No one ever wanted to befriend her.

"No one wanted to be my friend before," she said modestly. He walked over to where she was and made a silly face at her. She couldn't help but laugh.

"Was that a yes?" he asked with a smile.

"Okay," she said as he began to hurry away. "Can I see you again?" she asked. He stopped and waved to her.

"We'll play tomorrow," he said happily as he ran towards his home. She closed her eyes. She was back in the present looking at Evallion. He had grown up in a lot of ways, but his eyes looked exactly the same. She sighed and lowered her eyes.

"You wouldn't understand," she passively answered.

"Try me. I know I'm not a scholar or anything like that, but I'm not stupid," he retorted, rubbing his swollen throbbing cheek. Qu'Tee looked down at the trickling stream.

"Do you, remember when we first met?" she asked.

"That would have been around when we were five or six," he replied.

"Before that day, I didn't care if I lived or died. I didn't have any family. I had no friends. I was being picked on everyday. I was different from everyone. Do you know what it is like to be hated by everyone?" she asked looking over at him. "That was the first time since my parents died that I didn't feel so alone," she added.

"I know what that is like," he admitted.

"Do you?" she asked.

"Meeting you there, playing with you, cheering you up, it was something I looked forward to each day," he said as he lowered his eyes. "I just wish I could have done more," he said, remembering all the failed times he tried to protect her. She looked over at him and shook her head.

"You really don't understand," she said in modest disbelief.

"What are you talking about? How many times did those creeps beat you up because I couldn't stop them?" he asked.

"I didn't care," she replied, the answer surprised him.

"What?" he asked.

"I was used to it. I could take everything they did to me so long as I wasn't alone. I, I think I could handle it. I could understand that you wanted to go away. But, why didn't you tell me? Did you hate me so much?" she asked. Evallion's eyes spaced out as he fell to his hands and knees. His mind was racing at what he had heard.

"Hate? You thought? Oh god," he muttered. He took a few seconds to collect his thoughts. He was shaking still, but it wasn't as bad as it was a few moments ago. He sat down and looked up at her. "Do you know, the reason I left?" he asked.

"You got tired of being around someone like me?" she guessed. He slammed his fist into the ground. Though it was dark, she could see that a tear had escaped from his reluctant eye.

"Because I didn't want you of all people thinking I was weak!" he explained as he looked at his fists. "Ever since that day when those bullies were picking on you. There was, a voice, something inside me saying that I had to protect you. Do you have any idea what it feels like? Knowing that no matter what I did or tried they would just go through me and do the same to you," he said almost hissing as he remembered each time the bullies hurt Qu'Tee right in front of him.

That feeling of helplessness – hopelessness left a bad taste in his mouth even now.

"After that last time, I swore an oath to myself. It was the last time those animals would do that to you. But, I needed to be better, I needed to be stronger. That was why I went to train in the Pit Fighter territories," he explained. He shook his head. "I trained so hard, worked so hard so that when I returned, I could make a difference. But, when I got back, you were already gone. The bullies were gone too. I asked around, but nobody had any answers," he said as he picked up the mask. "Since that day – the day I failed you so completely, I donned this mask," he explained.

"Why? I don't understand," she asked.

"I couldn't stand to look at myself. Nor did I want others to see the failure I had become," he said, studying the features of the smooth mask. He looked over at her. "I never stopped looking for you. Be it chance, good fortune or luck, I don't know which, and I learned that you had been adopted and that you were living among the Ken. It took some time finding anyone that would speak of where the Ken were located," he said shaking his head. "Then about a week ago, if I had to guess, I found the temple. I don't know how long I stood in the forest staring at the outer wall. I knew you were in there, but I couldn't bring myself to take that final step," he said shamefully.

"Why?' she asked curiously.

"What right did I have? You said yourself that you thought I hated you," he began.

"You thought, I hated you?" she asked hesitantly.

"You had a new life, a family, you seemed so happy from what rumours I managed to hear from the Ken that were in the village. I realized it would be selfish to just appear and expect you to forgive me. Regardless, I swore an oath to aid you and protect you. Even it was from the shadows, for me that would have been enough," he said as he slowly got up and put the mask back on.

"Why are you putting that back on?" she asked.

"Little has changed. I still failed you when you need me. I have much that I still need to atone for," he said as he extended his hand to her. "Your mother must be worried about you by now. We should head back," he pointed out.

"There is one thing," Qu'Tee began. He looked over at her. "You said that you wanted to protect me from the moment we first met? Why?" she asked.

"You do that sort of thing for people you love," he replied. She blushed. He winked and hurried back towards the campsite. She fumed. Behind that mask he could say anything and she couldn't tell if he was being serious or just teasing.

"Wait for me," she protested as she chased after him.

The Gathered

Around the campfire an uneasy silence had grown between Qu'Tee and Evallion. Sugar could tell that something had happened between the two just by the way they made such laboured efforts not to look at each other.

"You two were gone for a while. Anything a mother should know of?" she teased. Qu'Tee and Evallion blushed.

"Mom!" she protested.

"Nothing like that!" he reassured. Sugar giggled as she handed both of the flustered youths another bowl of stew.

"I'm just teasing. By her flustered silence, I guess that would make you Evallion?" Sugar asked, he nodded. "She spoke very fondly of you and how much you did for her during that, dark chapter of her life. Thank you," she added sincerely.

"Your thanks and praise is not deserving. I was stupid for leaving as I did and she was hurt because of it," he stated seriously lowering his eyes.

"He does play a good martyr," Sugar remarked making Evallion twitch.

"Yeah, one would almost think he gets off on it," Qu'Tee added indignantly, Evallion fell over as though struck by a weapon.

"What is this? Pick on the new guy day?" he rebutted. Sugar giggled and motioned for him to calm down.

"I'm teasing. Be at peace. I do that sort of thing. I am glad you are here Evallion. I presume then, it was you then that was asking questions about her in Ga'Lelle?" she asked curiously. He nodded. "I had a hunch it was you," she added.

"Why?" he asked.

"Who else would be asking about her?" she pointed out.

"You knew he was there and didn't tell me?" Qu'Tee asked in modest disbelief.

"At peace daughter. Your happiness is mine, but so too is your sorrow. All I knew of him is what you told me. I was worried that you might be hurt, besides, if you went to the village to do those errands I asked you to do as I asked you too you might have learned this for yourself," she pointed out. Qu'Tee pouted. "Does she not look adorable when she does that?" she teased making Qu'Tee blush.

"Definitely very cute," Evallion admitted. Qu'Tee fumed. She KOed her childhood friend with her staff and stormed away.

"Good form, needs more control though," Sugar remarked as

she did what she could to revive him. "Sorry about her temper," she said with a friendly smile.

"I deserved it," he reassured. "Did you mean what you said? About worrying about me hurting her?" he asked.

"I would be lying and badly at that if I said the thought hadn't crossed my mind," she admitted seriously.

"I understand. You have no reason to trust me," he admitted.

"Remove the mask and I might," Sugar offered. She could tell he was reluctant about that issue, but much to her surprise he took the mask off. "Wow, I'm impressed. You are a cutie," she teased making him blush. "My concern is my daughter. Do right by her, you do right by me. You say you want to help her, truth be told we could use all the help we can get," she admitted seriously.

"This is why she left the temple?" he asked.

"The path we are going down is a very dangerous one. Without help, I am unsure if we will succeed," she explained.

"Does this have to do with the goblin and orc infestations increasing?" he asked.

"That, is the smaller part of the problem we seek to avert," she replied.

"The age of blood and darkness?" he asked.

"You are well versed for one so young," Sugar remarked.

"I don't know much about it, just that the goblins and orcs shall herald his return. Truth be told my training took priority over my studies," he said as Sugar handed him a small potion. "What is this?" he asked.

"Minor heal potion of sorts," she answered. He looked over at the bandit who was still paralyzed – then looked at the potion hesitantly. Sugar giggled. "Oh you are too precious. It isn't poisoned. My daughter doesn't know her own strength some times," she pointed out. He sighed and down the potion. Sure enough he felt much better. He then tensed up and froze. She smirked. "Very funny," she mused. Evallion smiled as he handed the empty vial back to her. "Be a dear and make sure the queen is okay?" she requested. Evallion put his mask on and got up. It was then that the words suck in.

"Queen? She is a queen? Like, ruler of a nation?" he asked hesitantly.

"You know of another type of queen?" she rebutted. He hurried away.

A fair distance away, Qu'Tee was sitting beneath a tree looking up at the stars. She felt bad about lashing out at him as she did.

"Want some company?" Evallion asked.

"You okay?" she asked.

"Yeah, your mom gave me a heal potion and I'm good as new," he reassured. "I heard that you are a queen," he said. She smiled and looked at the ring on her finger. "Quite the step up from when we were kids huh?" he added.

"At times I fear that all of this is a dream and I'll wake up back in that awful orphanage," she admitted.

"I had no idea your mom and dad were royalty," he remarked.

"They weren't. after our capital fell, all of the Ken royals were killed. It was decreed at that time that ruling power would be given with the blessing of the Order of the Butterfly, to the one who wears this ring," she explained.

"Must be a lot for you to take in all at once," he admitted.

"You could say that." She fumed as she looked at him. "You know I feel ridiculous talking to a mask," she pointed out.

"You knew it was me in spite of it," he rebutted. "Don't know how you managed that," he added. She looked up at the stars.

"I remembered your eyes. I could never forget them," she said shaking her head. "I know what you said about your mask and all," she began.

"But?" he hesitantly asked.

"How am I supposed to talk openly with you hiding behind that thing. Take it off now," she said indignantly.

"What?" he asked.

"You heard me. Take it off or I will take it off for you,' she threatened.

"You can't be serious," he replied.

"I am very serious. A or B," she warned.

"I am a lot stronger than I used to be," he warned back.

"That does it! Gimme that mask!" she said as she tackled him to the ground. So caught up in their play fighting were they that they failed to notice Sugar watching the display with mild amusement. "Take it off now!" she repeated.

"Oh my, how forward," Sugar remarked. Instantly the two were aware of where they were, what they were doing and who had just walked over and caught them. "On a first date no less, shameful I say," Sugar teased. Instantly the two were up to their feet.

"It isn't what you think!" he reassured.

"What he said," Qu'Tee added. Sugar believed them but

couldn't resist.

"So I didn't find you two groping each other in the dark saying take it off?" she teased. Qu'Tee could feel her face turning beet red.

"I was talking about his mask mom," she reassured. "It is driving me batty," she added.

"Is that all that happened Evallion?" Sugar asked standing before him.

"Word for word," he replied. Sugar sighed and turned her back on the two. For a few long seconds a silence hung over them. "I believe you," she added with a wink. The two youths fell over.

"You could have just said that in the first place," Qu'Tee pointed out.

"What fun would that be?" Sugar mused as she walked over to where Evallion was. "I understand why you wear the mask, but when speaking with the queen of all Ken, please be respectful and remove it, okay?" she requested. He nodded as he removed his mask.

"As you say," he said politely.

"So proper and behaved. Hard to believe you are the same man who not a few moments ago was rolling around in the dark with my daughter," Sugar teased making them blush.

"Stop teasing me," Qu'Tee protested. Sugar patted her on the cheek.

"Go back to the campsite. Get some rest you two. We have a lot of ground to make up for," Sugar suggested. Qu'Tee nodded and hurried away. Evallion looked over at Sugar.

"How is our guest?" he asked.

"The bandit? He is staying put," she answered.

"Need any help keeping an eye on him?" he offered.

"Get some rest, let me worry about him," she reassured. She headed back towards the campsite and saw the two youths resting by the fire. She then focused on the bandit who was still paralyzed. She walked over and stood toe to toe with him. "Memory is a funny thing. The potion I used on you. It could last days – or might be permanent. Have I got your undivided attention?" she asked – the look in his eyes spoke volumes. She tapped him on the forehead. He crumpled to the ground. "Walk with me and be quiet. The children need their rest after all," she remarked motioning for him to follow her. Once they were a fair distance away from the campsite – they stopped. "Curious as to why we are talking?" she asked seriously.

"You could say that," he admitted.

"One, I am very, displeased at how you spoke in my daughter's presence, but, I may be willing to overlook it," she hinted.

"What do you want?" he hesitantly asked.

"You seem like a rather resourceful lad. The kind that has a knack for hearing things and stuff like that. There are, some circles I cannot travel in, some places I cannot go. I trust you can fathom where this is going," she pointed out.

"You want me to scout around for information? Why should I?" he asked – before he could get an answer he doubled up. It felt as though his stomach was on fire. Sugar sat down beside where he was curled up and placed a potion in front of him.

"The paralysis drug I used on you has a nasty side affect. The potion in front of you deals with the symptoms – for a while," she explained. He quickly downed the potion. True to her word – the pain was gone.

"What information are you hunting for?" he asked indignantly.

"Nothing quite yet. Right now we are on route to Lyte Wood," she explained.

"The Elf capital?" he asked.

"The same. I need you to scout ahead to make sure that, other, forest dwelling entrepreneurs do not give us any static," she explained.

"If they don't listen?" he asked.

"Make sure they do," she said as she handed him a small pouch.

"What is this for?" he asked hesitantly.

"Expenses. I don't want any trouble between here and the Elf capital, and I don't want excuses. Questions?" she asked. He shook his head. "Good journey to you then. We will be in touch," she reassured as the thief vanished into the night. "So it begins," she said to herself as she made her way back to the campsite.

Unlikely Ally

Dawn came surprising quick. Qu'Tee and Evallion slowly woke up and saw that Sugar was awake and working on breakfast. Qu'Tee stretched out.

"I don't think I will get used to sleeping on the ground. I miss my warm comfy bed," Qu'Tee remarked. Her mother smiled as she handed her a bowl. "Thank you," she added.

"Just wait until the weather gets bad dear. You will miss it even more," Sugar teased.

"You are not helping mom," Qu'Tee remarked. She looked away from her mother and focused on her breakfast. Sugar giggled as she handed a bowl to Evallion.

"Out of curiosity, where did that guy go?" he asked, noticing he was absent.

"He was too small so I cut him loose," Sugar mused. She could see the answer didn't sit well with their knew travelling companion. "We came to an understanding of sorts. He won't be bothering us anymore," she reassured.

"By the way mom? Where exactly are we going?" Qu'Tee asked.

"Our nearest neighbour is the Elves so I thought that would be a good place to start. Her daughter's eyes lit up at the prospect. "I thought you might like," she added.

"Am I missing something?" Evallion asked hesitantly.

"Not really. I just always wanted to visit the elves. I've read about them since I started schooling among the Order. Their customs, their dress, their people, everything sounds so dreamy," she answered happily. Evallion sighed and shook his head.

"Reality and fantasy rarely cross over. When they do the outcome is rarely good," he remarked calmly taking a sip from his bowl. Qu'Tee looked away from him.

"Hmph! Boy someone sounds jaded," she pointed out. He blinked and looked over at his angry travelling companion.

"What is that supposed to mean?" he asked.

"You're just jealous because they are so dreamy," she remarked. He almost went cross-eyed at the statement.

"Have you even met an elf?" he asked.

"Of course I have! They would visit the temple from time to time," she rebutted.

"They? I only remember you talking about that archery

instructor," Sugar pointed out. Qu'Tee blushed. "Come to think of it he was kind of cute," she admitted.

"So in other words you had a crush on this guy?" Evallion remarked. Sugar winced as Qu'Tee landed a punch to the side of his head that sent him rolling away into the forest.

"Nice hit," Sugar mused. Qu'Tee pouted. Evallion slowly made his way back towards where the camp was. "You okay Eva?" she asked with a smile. Evallion frowned, Qu'Tee snickered.

"Don't call me that. I got enough of that growing up," he said as he sat down beside Qu'Tee and looked away from her. "Just so you know, most documentation about the elves is written by elves as such it is hardly impartial," he pointed out. "Not that I care if you get your expectations up and wind up disappointed," he added.

"You two almost have pouting turned into a sport," Sugar mused.

"I am not pouting," Qu'Tee and Evallion said together. They looked at each other, then quickly turned away. Qu'Tee got up and started to walk away.

"I'm going for a walk," she said as she vanished into the forest. Evallion sighed and shook his head.

"So what was this instructor like?" he asked curiously.

"Jealousy doesn't suit you," Sugar commented as she handed him another bowl. She could see that he didn't like the joke. "I suppose he was a pleasant enough fellow. Kind of a distant sort, you know the type. Very disciplined, very patient. If I had to say, I would say Qu'Tee admired him more than liked him," she added.

"Are the Ken and the Elves close?" he asked. She was mildly surprised by the question. "I'm just curious. I know that the Ken and the Humans haven't always been eye to eye," he added. Sugar nodded.

"Many humans see the Ken as stuck up?" she asked.

"I wouldn't say that," he reassured.

"I know. The Ken are known as the Chosen nation. Do you know why?" she asked. He shook his head. "In the days of the king," she began.

"Talas'All," he added.

"Yes. The Ken were his people. Some believe he was a dwarf because his weapon was a Rune carved axe. Some say he was Elf because of his diplomacy skills. Even the mages and wizards have reasons to believe he was of their nation, and yes, I am sure that there are records among the human nations saying he is human," she began.

"The Ken were always the soldiers closest to the king in times of war," Evallion added.

"Do you know why?" she asked.

"Not really," he admitted.

"Being Ken and all, this will sound quite impartial, but of the nations at the time, the Ken, the Chosen, were the only nation who looked solely to the king. Even our monarchy was fiercely loyal to his decrees," she explained.

"Do not stand between the Ken and the Crown," he remarked. "Is that what that saying means?" he asked curiously.

"More or less," she answered.

"I always thought it meant that the Ken wanted to rule the Veil," he admitted.

"The sad reality is, many of the other nations think that as well. Anyway, I think the reason she is so enamoured by the elves is because of how she was treated by the humans," she pointed out. Evallion sighed and nodded. It was then that Qu'Tee came back. She seemed a little more agreeable. "Welcome back daughter," she added.

"So what were you talking about?" Qu'Tee asked untrustingly.

"Nothing all that interesting. We will be leaving soon. Qu'Tee, why don't you practice with Evallion and please go easy on him," she requested. Evallion blinked, there was something moderately disturbing in the way she said that.

"What if I don't want to?" Qu'Tee rebutted stubbornly. Sugar smiled at her daughter in a way that made her mildly nervous. Sugar tapped her fingers together and looked over at Evallion.

"That would be your choice dear, you are the queen and all. But, if you don't do as you are told I will tell Eva some deliciously embarrassing stories about you when you were younger," she began as her eyes lit up. "Oh! Like that time you," she began. A mortified look crossed her daughter's face. Qu'Tee grabbed Evallion by the arm.

"Time to train!" Qu'Tee interrupted as she all but dragged Evallion away. Sugar giggled at the display and focused on packing up their supplies.

A short distance away, Qu'Tee stopped and took a few moments to catch her breath. She then grabbed Evallion by the collar of his leather armour and scowled at him.

"What did she tell you about me?" she demanded.

"Nothing! Honest!" he reassured. She let him go. "So what was that display about?" he asked. She flustered a bit but managed to regain her composure.

"Never mind! She said I needed to train so let's get this over with," she replied holding her staff defensively. "Draw your weapons," she instructed. He did not.

"I hear the training the Ken go through is pretty intense," he stated.

"Our nation was decimated. Our people scattered throughout the Veil. In order to survive, we need to be strong. Draw your weapons," she repeated, again he did not. "Did you not hear me?" she asked sternly.

"I heard you the first time. I do not train with weapons," he challenged as he took out his mask and put it on. She watched as he began to slowly circle her, his eyes fixated on her. "Any time you are ready," he offered. She seemed to vanish. Evallion arched his body to the side avoiding her strike. A focused kick just barely missed the side of his head. A flurry of punches came at him from all angles – but every one of them was blocked or dodged as though he knew what she was doing before she did. In frustration she leaped away from him.

"Why aren't you fighting back?" she demanded between gasps

"You train your way, I do mine," he rebutted seriously.

"Are you holding back?" she almost hissed.

"I am a Pit Fighter, a gladiator or as many nations call us barbarians. Fighting isn't what we do. It is who we are," he rebutted. "So to answer your question – yes, I am holding back. If I didn't you would be getting seriously hurt," he admitted. She fumed at the level of arrogance she believed he was giving off. She began spinning her staff around as she made her way towards him. As soon as she was within reach her weapon and her body moved as one. Still he seemed able to evade her strikes. It was then that his arm snaked out around her staff and trapped it next to his side. Before she could react he flicked her forehead. She was mildly stunned as he released her weapon and rolled away.

He's toying with me! She fumed. She began another barrage of attacks against her opponent. Again he seemed to be one step ahead of her. Nothing she did seemed to connect. Her timing was off – worse, his wasn't!

Just then he seemed to vanish!

"What the?" she muttered. She looked up just in time to see the bottom of his foot. He landed on her forehead and leaped away. Qu'Tee fell off balance. Evallion sighed and removed his mask.

"You're really good," he admitted. "I don't think I've ever seen someone move like that," he added with a smile. Her fists were shaking as a rage began to build within her.

"Are you making fun of me?" she almost growled. He blinked in modest disbelief as she slowly rose to her feet. She held out her hand, her staff seemed to fly up from the ground and into her hand.

"No, I was being serious," he said as he could see a powerful aura throbbing around her. "Not good," he said lowering the mask. He stood ready. Qu'Tee began to seemingly move in slow motion. Her movements were hypnotic like an elegant dance. He tried to read her movements but it was impossible. She danced her way towards him. He prepared to dodge her staff and was rewarded with a kick to the side of the head. He rolled away and looked over and saw her balanced on one foot. Wherever she was, she wasn't there.

"Prepare to fall," she said coldly. Her voice sounded older. She seemed to vanish. Instinctively he dived forward. The ground exploded where he was standing. He looked over at the smoke and saw Qu'Tee leap from the smoke.

"Did I mention how cute you are?" he asked. She blinked. Her focus was gone. He leaped up, coiled his arm around her staff and clamped his legs around hers. Before she could react, before she knew what was happening the two hit the ground hard. The way he had her hand trapped with her staff, the way he positioned her staff she could not move.

"That was not fair!" she protested. She tried to get free, but he was having none of that. She fumed as she looked over at him.

"You get kind of scary when you get intense," he remarked. She scowled at him.

"Let me go," she stated through gritted teeth. Instantly he let her go. He expected that she was going to hit him, instead she bowed politely. "I'm sorry," she added seriously.

"Why?" he asked.

"I lost control," she answered passively. "You could have been hurt," she added. Evallion was going argue the that, but when he looked over at the still-smoking hole in the ground he opted to keep his mouth shut. He removed his mask.

"Happens to the best of us. I was kind of showing off a bit. Sorry about that," he replied. It was then that she walked over and stared into his eyes. "What?" he hesitantly asked.

"Did you mean it?" she asked curiously.

"Mean what?" he asked. She fumed as she bopped him on the head sending him face first into the ground. "That kind of hurt," he slurred. It was then he tensed up. It didn't go unnoticed. Evallion stayed close to the ground.

"Something wrong?" she hesitantly asked.

"Trouble, stay close," he answered quietly. He put his mask back on and drew his weapons. Quietly he stalked through the forest. There it was! Qu'Tee could hear it too. There was something ahead on the other side of the hill.

"What is it?" she whispered.

"Sounds like goblins," he answered. He moved a bush aside. They looked over and saw a small clearing littered with dead traders and numerous slain goblins. From what he saw, the traders were ambushed. They put up a bit of a fight, but they didn't stand a chance. His eyes panned the carnage for the goblin or goblins that were still alive. Qu'Tee peeked out from around him.

"Those are goblins?" she asked curiously.

"You've never seen them before?" he asked. She shook her head. "Yeah," he answered. Qu'Tee was surprised at how different the goblins seemed. Some were tiny like little kids. Some were the same size as they were, a few were bigger. They were definitely not what she expected. It was then that something moved by one of the dead goblins. Her eyes widened as a goblin no bigger than a cat poked its head around. It looked similar to the other goblins, only this one was a hundred times more cute. "There it is," he affirmed. Qu'Tee smiled and managed to stifle a giggle as the tiny goblin scurried around as though looking for something or someone. "I'll be back in a moment," he reassured. He stepped forward and fell face first to the ground. He looked back and saw a frowning Qu'Tee holding his ankle staring at him. "What did you do that for?" he asked under his breath. He looked over to see if the goblin heard them. Luckily it seemed too lost in its own thoughts.

"What do you think you are doing?" she protested smiling as she watched the tiny goblin almost dancing around.

"I was going to kill that thing before it brings more goblins here?" he answered. A punch sent him face first into a tree.

"How could you think of hurting such a poor little thing?" she asked. He shook off the effect of the punch and stared at her in disbelief.

"Poor little thing? That is a goblin not a stray kitten," he pointed out. It was then that they became aware that they were being watched. The goblin was looking over at the two, as though trying to make sense of what they were doing.

"Put your weapon away Eva or I will bop you," she warned. Evallion groaned as he reluctantly put his swords away and stared at the goblin. The goblin seemed to mimic him. Qu'Tee smiled as she squatted down and smiled at the adorable looking creature. The goblin looked over at her and mimicked her expression. "That is so cute," she said. She reached in her pocket and pulled out some seeds. She began to extend her hand, timidly the goblin backed away. "It's okay. I won't hurt you," she reassured. Evallion shook his head in disbelief. She ate a seed then opened her hand showing more seeds there. The goblin looked at her then the seeds. Slowly it made its way over and plucked one from her hand.

"Do you have any idea how ridiculous this is?" Evallion asked.

"Shut up Eva," she retorted.

"Sh'up Eva," the goblin repeated. Qu'Tee almost went saucer eyed. Evallion found the display less than amusing. "You no hurt?" it strained to say. She nodded as she placed the seeds on the ground before the tiny goblin.

"I didn't know goblins could speak," she said amazed.

"Most don't. they don't need to. Their actions speak for them," Evallion answered.

"Do you have a name?" she asked, ignoring him.

"Name?' the goblin repeated, confused by the word.

"Me, Qu'Tee," she introduced. The goblin nibbled on another seed. It seemed to think for a moment. It then pointed at her.

"Coo'Tee!" it repeated. Qu'Tee almost squealed. The goblin then began to dance around before her. "Coo'Tee! Coo'Tee! Coo'Tee!" the goblin almost song.

"He is calling you a cootie you know," Evallion pointed out. She threw him a nasty look unlike anything he had seen before. "Qu'Tee, that, is a goblin. It is a monster – not a pet or some cute wayward creature. Goblins attack people, ravage villages. That, thing, was one of the beasts that ambushed these traders," he explained seriously . but his words were falling of deaf ears. She was too entranced by the tiny goblin doing a little dance.

"A waif goblin," Sugar remarked calmly. The three looked over and saw Sugar watching her daughter quite amused by the goblin. "You don't see those very often, at least on their own," she began as she looked over at the carnage nearby. "Ah, he was with them," she realized. Evallion stood up and clapped his hands together.

"A voice of reason! Please, tell her," he requested. Qu'Tee picked up the goblin and showed it to her mother. The goblin made a cute face at the elder of the group.

"Isn't he the cutest?" she asked, once again ignoring Evallion.

"They are adorable at that age," Sugar admitted.

"Can we keep him? I promise I'll take care of him,' she reassured. Evallion almost went cross-eyed again.

"I don't know," Sugar began.

"Please?" Qu'Tee pleaded making a pouty face. The goblin looked over at Qu'Tee then mimicked the expression.

"Peas?" the goblin tried to repeat.

"Impressionable little critter," Sugar remarked.

"Coo'Tee nice. He Eva meanie," the goblin said sticking his tongue out at Evallion. Sugar and Qu'Tee giggled. The goblin smiled proudly. Evallion shook his head in modest disbelief.

"I haven't seen many goblins like him. Few his age speak or can speak," Sugar remarked. Evallion didn't like the direction things were going.

"No, you aren't serious," he protested. Qu'Tee and the goblin squealed with glee. "Oh my god," he muttered under his breath. Qu'Tee put the goblin down and studied him for a moment.

"Now what shall we call you?" Qu'Tee asked.

"I have a few suggestions," Evallion began. The three looked back at him. He threw his hands up. "I give up!" he said shaking his head.

"Me, Qu'Tee," she began pointing to herself. "You?" she asked. The goblin thought for a moment. "How about, Boo?" she asked. The goblin danced around before the three adventurers.

"Boo!" he repeated happily.

"Looks like our party got a little bigger," Sugar remarked.

"This is going to be a long, long journey," Evallion said under his breath, still unable to wrap his head around this turn of events.

The Scout

It had been a couple of days since the small party exited recognized Ken territory. Things had been quiet, no bandits, no goblins, even the weather was favourable for them. Sugar checked her map and smiled. They were making good time.

"We might as well set up camp here," she suggested.

"Set up camp," the goblin Boo repeated with a smile. Evallion groaned.

"Be nice," Qu'Tee requested as she put Boo down. "Say Boo, do you want to help?" she asked the goblin seemed to think about the words.

"Boo help Coo'Tee?" he repeated. She smiled and nodded. "Boo help Coo'Tee!" it said happily. Evallion sighed and shook his head.

"I'm going to train. If I am needed," he said, unable to take the goblin's antics. Sugar sighed as she knelt down before Boo. Timidly it backed away.

"Boo, could you help me out for a bit?" she requested. The goblin looked over at Qu'Tee, as if to see if it was okay.

"Coo?" it asked passively.

"It's okay," Qu'Tee reassured. The goblin hopped up and sat down on Sugar's shoulder.

"Boo!" the goblin said happily. Sugar smiled and shook her head.

"Be a dear and see if Evallion is okay," Sugar requested.

"Why? He seems fine to me," Qu'Tee asked curiously.

"He hasn't been acting like himself the last couple of days. I am worried that he is not used to sharing your time with precious here," Sugar pointed out. It took a few moments for the words to sink in.

"Are you saying?" Qu'Tee began. "Are you trying to tell me Evallion is jealous of Boo? You must be joking," she asked in modest disbelief. Sugar looked over at Boo who seemed oblivious to what they were talking about.

"Be that as it may, check on him," she stated more than asked. Qu'Tee sighed and walked away. The thought was ridiculous. Why would he be jealous of a goblin, granted an adorably cute little goblin, but still!

Qu'Tee tried not to think about it. She made her way through the woods, following the path Evallion had taken. Within moments she found him. She was going to call out to him, but there was something in seeing how he moved, did each strike that was so disciplined and controlled, that all she could seem to do was watch. It was then that the fighter had become aware he was being watched.

"Is something wrong?" he asked hesitantly.

"Not really. Do you train like that everyday?" she asked.

"When I can," he admitted. "Now what did you really come her for?" he answered and asked. Qu'Tee walked over to where he was and looked him in the eye.

"Mom was worried about you," she answered. He looked at her as though she had sprouted a second head.

"Worried about me? Why?" he asked hesitantly.

"For some reason she thinks you might be jealous of Boo," she remarked. Evallion almost fell over laughing.

"That is the most ridiculous thing I ever heard. Where would she get such a ludicrous idea?" he asked in disbelief.

"Because you started acting all funny after he joined us maybe?" she suggested.

"You think?" he began as he shook his head. "Listen, I don't like the fact that we are travelling with that little monster. I'll openly admit that. I don't like the fact that you are treating like some lost puppy," he began. He could sense that she was going to argue the issue. "Hear me out before you jump in!" he added seriously. Qu'Tee sighed.

"He is not a little monster. His name is Boo," she reminded.

"Fair enough. Boo, as you so affectionately call him is a monster. As surely if you found a baby dragon or any other such beast. You haven't encountered goblins before have you?" he asked. She nodded. "I thought as much. I had a friend a while back. His niece found a goblin, much like Boo. She took him in and treated him like a pet," he began.

"What happened?" she hesitantly asked.

"Long of the short of it? It grew up. It killed her, my friend and four other villagers before we managed to kill the beast," he answered seriously. She looked away.

"Boo isn't like that," she reassured. Evallion sighed and shook his head. He walked over and placed his hand on her shoulder.

"Believe me, I really hope you are right. Know this though, if it comes to a choice, it will be no choice at all. If I see it becoming a beast, it dies," he warned seriously. She looked over at him, clearly unhappy at that idea. "I can live with you hating me more than I could living with the thought of knowing I let a monster kill you when I could have stopped it," he added seriously.

"No," she replied equally serious. She could sense his protest. "If, If it comes to that, the responsibility is mine and mine alone," she added. He sighed. She heard him out, that would have to be enough for now. "But you will see, Boo is different. He will surprise you in a good way if you give him a chance," she pointed out.

"Why is this so important to you?" he asked curiously.

"It, it just does," she sighed. "There, there is something about Boo that reminds me of me. When I was growing up, everyone treated me like I was evil because I was different. No one wanted to give me a chance, they would have preferred if I just died. What if, someone did to me, what you, what everyone wants to do to Boo?" she asked quietly.

"That is hardly the same," he argued.

"I know it must sound silly, but I believe in Boo, kind of like how you believed in me. You are so sure he will turn into a monster, but I don't see that," she added. He could see how serious she was about this. "This isn't about me not trusting you or your judgement. I hope you know that I do. Will you at least give him a chance?" she asked. He groaned and shook his head. He knew she wasn't going to let the issue die. She was just going to twist and spin it until she got the result she wanted.

"If I say yes will you let this issue drop?" he asked tiredly. Qu'Tee smiled and held onto his arm. "You don't fight fair," he added. She smiled at him. She seemed to glow as he looked at her.

"This means a lot to me," she said happily as she hurried back towards the campsite. He waved at her then slumped down to the ground. He really hoped that he wasn't going to regret this concession. It was then that a familiar looking squirrel hopped from the branches above and landed before him. He wasn't surprised. "You are early. Does that mean?" he began, the squirrel nodded. "So, we are being followed," he whispered as he looked around at the surrounding forest. "Is he near?" he asked. The squirrel nodded. "I shouldn't be surprised. We are in elf territory. Keep an eye on him. If it looks like trouble, you know what to do," he instructed. The squirrel nodded and ran away up the nearest tree. "Whoever you are, I really hope you are friendly," he muttered as he headed back towards the campsite.

Day uneventfully passed on into night.

The party was sitting around the campfire. Evallion looked over at how Qu'Tee was feeding Boo as though he was a child. It was still too much for him to wrap his mind around, but he told Qu'Tee he would give the little monster a chance. He took a sip from his bowl and looked around at the shadows that danced off the branches and leaves.

"You seem on edge," Sugar remarked getting his attention. "Expecting someone?" she asked curiously. Qu'Tee was too absorbed with Boo to hear her words. Evallion took another sip.

"Couple days ago, give or take, a friend, confirmed, a suspicion," he began.

"We're being followed?" Sugar asked, refilling his bowl.

"His markings are Elf, that much I know. If he is friendly or not I have no idea. But he has been watching us a little more closely than I would prefer," he added, taking another sip from his bowl.

"And here I thought it was because of Boo," she mused.

"Right now he is the lesser of two evils. By now he knows I am aware of his presence. He will either act tonight or invite friends tomorrow. Both options leave a bad taste in my mouth," he stated seriously. Sugar nodded. She reached into her robes and pulled out a small green vial.

"Drink this," she instructed. He took the item from her and studied it. "If our friend is making his move tonight, you will need it," she added. He quickly downed the potion and almost gagged.

"That was vile!" he groaned.

"Yes, it tends to be that way, but it works," Sugar admitted. He was going to complain more, but the potion started to take effect. His senses seemed sharper. He could hear almost every creature in the bushes and trees around them. He heard a sound! A familiar sound from the darkness, a bow string was being drawn back. His eyes rapidly panned through the shadows. He saw an acorn bounce off something in the shadows, no, not something, someone. He heard a whistle.

Everything seemed to be in slow motion to Evallion. Instinct took over as his hand snapped over towards Qu'Tee. She was stunned by the action, thinking he was trying to scare Boo. But it was then that both she and Boo noticed the arrow in Evallion's clenched fist. An arrow that was less than an inch away from Boo's chest. Truth be told, Evallion wouldn't have cared if the goblin took an arrow, but Qu'Tee was holding him. She could have been hurt!

"Over there!" Sugar pointed. Evallion saw someone leap from his perch.

"I'm on him!" he replied. He threw the arrow aside and leaped into the surrounding forest. He quickly put the mask on. For some reason he felt lighter. He was moving faster than normal. Evallion saw the arrow's owner running from the trees to the ground and back again with Elf-like grace and agility. "You are mine!" he growled. He leaped at the attacker who was trying to escape. Evallion's blade flashed in the moonlight, cutting in half the tree they were in. ungracefully the two fell from the tree, catching every branch on the way down. The two rolled down a hill. Evallion was to his feet first. He had his sword at the neck of his attacker. It was then that he became aware that the elf had another arrow ready and aimed at his chest.

"You are pretty quick for a barbarian," the elf remarked.

"You got pretty fast hands yourself," Evallion admitted.

"Quite the situation we have here. I doubt you could cut me before I let loose my arrow and I doubt I could shoot before you cut me," he pointed out. It was then that the rest of the party caught up with them.

"Hey! He's an Elf," Qu'Tee remarked. The Elf blinked, not taking his eyes off Evallion.

"You sound surprised. You are kind of deep in Elf territory," he pointed out. From the corner of his eye he could see the tiny goblin perched on Qu'Tee's shoulder.

"What is the meaning of all this? Why have you been spying on us and why did you attack us?" Sugar asked seriously.

"If I lower my weapon will your pet barbarian attack?" the Elf seriously asked.

"Don't tempt me to find out who is quicker sharp ear," Evallion warned.

"Can't say I like that remark," Sugar pointed out. Evallion sighed. Slowly he moved his weapon away from the trapped Elf. Slowly the Elf lowered his weapon and slowly sat up.

"You are in Elf Territory, travelling with a goblin, at a time when the goblins have been laying siege to our capital. I believe you have to answer some questions first," the Elf rebutted seriously.

"You tried to hurt Boo?" Qu'Tee began. The Elf was going to remark when he noticed the ring on her finger. He sighed and shook his head.

"It seems that the Queen of all Ken is keeping strange company these days," he remarked surprising Qu'Tee. "Is there a reason that the Ken queen, a barbarian and a goblin are on route to the Elf capital?" he asked curiously.

"You could say that," Sugar admitted.

"I think we need to have a long talk," the Elf said, clearly unhappy with this turn of events. Sugar nodded and motioned for him to follow them back to their campsite.

The Wayward Prince

At the campsite, the party of four watched as the elf took a sip from his bowl.

"Rumour of Ken hospitality does not do it justice," he remarked.

"You are too kind," Sugar politely replied. She looked over at her travelling companions who were still frowning at the Elf. It did not go unnoticed by their guest.

"As much I as I hate to impose, I feel the need to ask. Why are you travelling to the capital unguarded? If this was diplomatic a messenger would have been sent announcing your journey," the Elf pointed out.

"These, are uncertain times. If too many knew who we were and what we sought to do, other parties might become aware and seek to hinder our progress," Sugar pointed out. "While on the subject, you mentioned that the goblins were attacking the capital? That sounds like a foolish venture," she added.

"You would think that. But for the last couple of months they have been disturbingly relentless. Worse, they have been organized. They are not merely rushing the wall like beasts like the odd ones have in the past," he answered seriously.

"Could it be Bo'Glin?" Sugar asked. The Elf shook his head.

"No, it is not his magic that empowers these beasts," he answered as he looked over at Evallion. "No disrespect to your barbarian friend here, but, the way they fight is disturbingly human," he explained.

"None taken," Evallion remarked casually.

"How bad is it?" Sugar asked. The Elf sighed and shook his head.

"Bad. The near by villages were hit hard before we could turn them back. It all happened so fast, so suddenly that we never even saw it coming. All villages under the banner were ordered back to the capital. Since this siege, this war began, we have been cut off from the outside. We don't know if there are any elves still in the trees east of the capital," he added seriously. "So when I saw you travelling with a goblin in your midst," he added. Sugar motioned for him to let the issue go.

"No harm was done, fortunately. Consider it forgotten," Sugar reassured.

"But that still doesn't explain its presence,' the Elf pointed out.

"He has a name. It is Boo, not that little monster, that thing or it," Qu'Tee rebutted.

"Boo?" the Elf repeated in modest disbelief. He looked over at Evallion, hoping it was some sort of inside joke, the fighter shrugged his shoulders. "I take it she hasn't been exposed to may goblins," he added.

"You could say that," Qu'Tee admitted.

"That would explain much. But regardless, if you are seeking to speak with the ruling power in Lyte Wood, travelling with a goblin and a barbarian might be a hindrance," he pointed out.

"Keep calling me that and I may start acting the part," Evallion warned.

"Apologies if I offended. Dealings with your nation have been, trite, to say the least. Especially in these, unpleasant times," the Elf replied politely.

"That is because the Forest Nation is encroaching in our territory," Evallion rebutted almost instantly the two men were to their feet. Qu'Tee quickly got up and stood between the two men that were glaring at each other.

"No fighting," she said, hoping to defuse the situation a potentially volatile situation.

"Coo'Tee say no fight!" Boo repeated sternly, standing by Qu'Tee's leg. Both Evallion and the Elf were stunned.

"As you might have noticed, Boo, he is a bit unique for a

goblin," Sugar remarked, motioning for everyone to sit down. The tension began to fade. Everyone slowly sat back down. The Elf reached into his cloak and pulled out a small flask. He took a sip from it and shook his head.

"So it would seem," the Elf commented. He looked to the east and sighed. "Perhaps, I was wrong about all of this," he said pensively. He extended the flask to Evallion. The fighter looked at it for a moment then accepted.

"Sorry for losing my temper," he replied taking a sip. Whatever it was, it was a touch sweet for his liking.

"May I ask why the barbarians…forgive me, the Pit Fighters, have an interest in traveling with the Ken?" the Elf asked curiously. Evallion looked over at Qu'Tee.

"They do not know I am here," Evallion answered.

"I see," the Elf remarked.

"My reasons for being party to this, are personal," Evallion added.

"That would explain, you and the goblin. What part do you play in this little drama?" the Elf asked curiously.

"Other than being a courteous host?" Sugar mused.

"You know what I mean," he answered with a smirk.

"I am her mother," she answered with a smile.

"Then, I would just have one more question for the young queen. Why do you travel to the capital?" he asked curiously.

"You know of Bo'Glin?" she asked.

"Few do not, although not many know him by name. Most merely know him as the demon or other such titles. You have my undivided attention," he answered calmly. Qu'Tee looked into the fire, remembering what she learned, remembering what she was told, remembering the dreams.

"He is getting ready to strike out at all life in the Veil," Qu'Tee continued.

"How do you know this?" he asked seriously.

"I have seen it. In my dreams," she answered. He studied her face for a few long moments before looking away.

"You believe that?" he asked. She nodded. "You believe you are the one spoken of in ancient text? The one that shall stop the age of Shadow and Blood? How will you get the nations to listen to you now of all times? Speaking as an Elf we have other more pressing concerns to address," he pointed out.

"Even if the Elves survive the war with the goblins, will there be enough to stop Bo'Glin and his minions? Will there be enough men on the wall? Will there be enough arrows to keep him away?" Qu'Tee asked. The Elf blinked in modest disbelief. Her words were profoundly deep for one so young.

"Continue, please," The elf requested sincerely.

"I know things are bad for the Elves right now, but if it is just the shadow of the wave that is coming, can you, as an Elf, ignore it?" she asked with a reassuring smile. He studied her for a few seconds and then looked away. "I know I am asking a lot, especially with me being so young, but you must know, that the Elves cannot stand alone. Especially now. No nation can," she added passively as she scratched a spot behind Boo's ear.

"She will speak with a voice that cannot be ignored," The Elf sighed. "So, this, war we are trapped in, it could be a ploy to keep us isolated?" he asked.

"You said that the elves had other concerns. It could be part of a bigger tapestry. I don't know. All I do know is that the nations, all of them need to be as one if we are to stand a chance against the demon," she replied, smiling at Boo. The Elf leaned back against the tree behind him.

"The road to the capital is quite perilous as of late. I will escort you there. Whether or not the king will listen, I cannot say. But, I believe in you. Perhaps that will be enough," he offered sincerely.

"A chance is all we can ask for in these dark times," Sugar

admitted.

"Then that chance you will have," the Elf affirmed as he looked to the east.

"If there is a war going on like you say, what are you doing so far from home?" Evallion asked curiously. His words startled the Elf a bit. He looked over at the fighter and sighed.

"Personal reasons," he answered quietly.

"How are we supposed to get into the capital if they are at war?" Qu'Tee asked.

"Whatever value my voice holds should prove enough. You should rest now while you are able. We have a lot of ground to travel tomorrow and not a lot of time to cover it," the Elf pointed out. Qu'Tee and Boo curled up near to the fire.

"You too Evallion. You will have plenty of opportunities to stand watch and you will envy this offer," Sugar mused. Reluctantly he relaxed by the fire. Sugar and the Elf got up and walked a short distance from the others.

"He seems different from the others," the Elf remarked.

"Humans or barbarians?" she rebutted.

"Both," he admitted.

"he tries hard, too hard at times. I think it is his strength and weakness. A trait my daughter shares unfortunately," Sugar mused.

"Is he trying to prove something?' he asked.

"In a manner of speaking. His heart is in the right place," she replied looking back at the sleeping youths. "May I ask the reason you are out here? You have a sharp eye," she pointed out.

"As I said, it is personal. The king, he wouldn't approve of my being out here, and he will be less than pleased when I return," he said with a sigh.

"So, you weren't following us, you just happened onto us?" Sugar asked.

"Quite by chance. On was on my way elsewhere when, I noticed your odd party heading down a path that led to the capital," he admitted. "You get some rest. I'll keep watch," he offered sincerely.

"As you say, and thank you Arrow," she replied politely, surprising him.

"You know who I am?" he asked. She smiled and waved to him as she walked back to the campsite. He sighed and shook his head.

Early the next morning…

Everything was packed up, the fire was put out and once again the party was on their way to the capital. The Elf was looking over at Sugar. She knew who he was, did the others?

"It must have been a while since you came by this way. How different everything must look," Arrow said with a sigh. Qu'Tee and Evallion looked around. Everything looked normal enough.

"I can't see anything," she remarked.

"Same here," Evallion added.
"Boo!" the goblin chimed in.

"I can. The forest is dying. When did this begin?" Sugar asked curiously.

"The war taints the land with blood. The old trees are being ravaged. Powerful magic, old magic is fighting with the forest, and the forest I fear is losing," Arrow answered grimly. "Some say the land is strong when the king is strong. If so, the same holds true now," he added sadly.

"Is the king ill?" Sugar asked.

"I am sorry. This is something I am not really comfortable speaking of just now," Arrow replied, the subject was clearly not something he wanted to be thinking about.

As they got nearer to the capital, the state of the forest's decay grew more and more visible. Trees that were hundreds of years old looked ill to the point where a strong wind could topple them. The plants looked poisoned and dying. The grass was brown, black and yellow. The party had a hard time believing that they were in the forest of the Elves.

"The capital lies beyond this ridge. Be warned, it isn't a pretty sight," Arrow warned. Cautiously they made their way to the ridge and stopped. All of them were stunned by what laid before them.

The forest surrounding Lyte Wood was clear cut burned and ravaged. The bodies of thousands upon thousands of goblins littered the ground. Broken tribal banners fluttered as a morbid breeze wafted across the battlefield. The remnants of dozens of broken war machines laid , still smoking.

"How many tribes?" Evallion hesitantly asked, mentally taking in the number of banners.

"So far, or that we know of?" Arrow replied. He looked over at Boo and saw how the goblin was clinging timidly to Qu'Tee's leg. He had encountered numerous goblins before and during the war. Never had he seen a waif goblin act like Boo. "Lyte Wood in all its glory," he added. It was then that the party noticed that there were several Elf banners among the carnage. "A lot of good Elves died. When they started this siege, we underestimated them. They lured many away from the capital. Thousands of them rose up from hidden pits. They fought bravely, but their numbers were too much," he recounted.

"Did any survive?" Evallion asked.

"Not that we know of. I was on the wall. It was like watching ants swarming. We couldn't do anything about it either. If we fired, we would have hit our own. By the time we organized a retaliatory strike, the damage was done. We forced them to retreat," Arrow answered. In his mind he remembered being there. Seeing the bodies of friends. Those that weren't dead were dying slowly. No medicine, no potion, no healer could save them. Four days after that dark day, the last of those that were recovered slowly, painfully died. He shook his head. "The coast appears to be clear. Come on," he said as he led the way through the carnage. Qu'Tee picked Boo up and hid his eyes. In the back of her mind, she couldn't help but see something familiar about all of this. It was like her dream. The stench of death and burning flesh. Through her boots she could feel the heat coming from the still smouldering ground. The smoke that wafted across the land made it almost seem like a horrific dream.

As they walked, as they got closer, the Elves on the wall instantly became active.

"Looks like they noticed us," Evallion remarked. His eyes locked onto about twenty bows that were aimed at them. The gates of Lyte Wood opened and a small unit of Elf soldiers made their way to intercept them.

"They don't look very friendly," Sugar remarked. Arrow stood before the gathering and motioned for them to wait. The Elf soldiers stopped and looked around, as though looking for a trap. Once they were sure that the area was secure they focused on the people before them.

"I do not know why you would come here now," the Elf soldier in charge began. Arrow lowered his hood and stared at him. "Crown Prince Arrow? What are you doing out here?" he asked in modest disbelief. Qu'Tee and Evallion were mildly stunned by the revelation. Sugar smiled and remained silent.

"Crown," Evallion began.

"Prince?" Qu'Tee finished.

Lyte Wood

A few long seconds seemed to pause as Arrow talked with the Elf soldiers. Qu'Tee looked over at her mother. She alone did not seem shocked with the news that the rogue Elf that had encountered them was in fact a prince.

"Why didn't he tell us he was a prince?" Qu'Tee whispered to her mother.

"I am sure he had his reasons," Sugar reassured.

"My prince, when we heard that you were gone we feared the worst," one Elf remarked. Arrow sighed and shook his head. "The king was worried," he added.

"I am sure father had other matters to contend with," Arrow rebutted.

"Sire?" another Elf hesitantly began.

"Enough! I'll go speak with him," Arrow interrupted.

"Uhm, highness? About your, ah, travelling companions?" another Elf hesitantly brought up. The Elves looked over at Qu'Tee, Evallion, Sugar and Boo. Qu'Tee frowned at the Elves that seemed fixated on the goblin.

"You say one word about Boo and I will clobber you," she warned. The Elves blinked in modest disbelief, returning their attention to Arrow.

"The Goblin is under the protection of the Ken queen. And so long as she is within Elf territory she is under my protection. Is that clear?" Arrow pointed out. A minor ripple of confusion perplexed the Elves. "If it is too much of a burden, I am sure that you can tell my father that you refused his son access to Lyte Wood. I am sure he will understand," he added cynically. The ripple instantly vanished. The Elf in charge of the soldiers walked over to where Sugar was and politely bowed.

"I apologize," he began.

"That is sweet. But my daughter is the queen, not me," Sugar pointed out.

"I thought the Ken queen was older," another Elf remarked.

"Taller too," another piped in. Qu'Tee began to fume. Evallion, Arrow and Sugar winced as Qu'Tee quickly pummelled the Elves that seemed to be insulting her.

"Any more comments?" Qu'Tee almost hissed. The Elves backed away towards Arrow. "Hmph! How rude." She added indignantly.

"Rude!" Boo piped in

"Highness? She needs protecting?" one of the battered Elf soldiers asked, still in a mild daze from the hits he had taken.

"Ahem? Qu'Tee? We are not at home remember? It is rude to pummel people in their own back yard," Sugar pointed out. Qu'Tee was about to protest, but there was that look in Sugar's eyes. She knew better than to question it. She walked over to where the Elf soldiers were and bowed politely.

"I, I'm sorry. Some times my temper gets the better of me," she apologized.

"Okay," one Elf began. "Why is the Ken queen here?" he asked the young queen. Qu'Tee closed her eyes and tried to chose her words carefully. She took a deep breath and looked at the Elves. There was something in her eyes, her posture that seemed older.

"Bo'Glin, is coming," Qu'Tee summed it up.

"I see. This is a bad time, a very bad time," an Elf began.

"It will get far worse if we do not stand ready," Qu'Tee pointed out.
"The prophecy, it is coming to pass," Arrow added.

"We need to speak with the king as soon as possible," Sugar reminded, offering health potions to the Elves. "And it would be nice if your friends on the wall would stop aiming their arrows at us," she suggested with a smile. One of the Elf soldiers did a sharp whistle and signalled to the archers on the wall. Slowly the weapons lowered and they resumed patrolling the wall. "Thanks a bunch," she added with a smile.

"I don't know if the king will like hearing this right now. The goblins are readying themselves for another attack. Our scouts predict the next wave will make the last two look like skirmishes. Worse, the goblins have been breaking all the arrows they find out here," one Elf stated grimly.

"If we have to go toe to toe with them, they will wash over us like a green tide," another Elf added as he placed his hand on Arrow's shoulder. "All that aside though, it is good to see you again," he added seriously.

"Myself, I would feel far more comfortable speaking about this further? Inside?" another Elf suggested. Arrow nodded and motioned for his companions to follow him. The Elves escorted the party towards the gates. As they neared, the large gates, they opened inward. Qu'Tee couldn't help but feel humbled at the scale of the massive doors. Once inside she gasped. She had read about the splendour of the Elf capital. About structures hundreds of years old, of bards and scholars and other such wonders, yet, all of what was before her was different.

In the streets and alleys near to the wall were Elf camps. Hundreds of wounded, tired Elf soldiers stood ready to ascend the wall should the alarm sound.

In the village that surrounded the Elf Citadel, many of the

structures looked poorly maintained. In Qu'Tee's mind's eye, she could see how things were before the war. Merchants and foreign traders walking the streets. There was a lot of people walking and speaking and trading. She blinked. The reality of the situation was before her. There were more people here now.

"This is bad," Qu'Tee remarked. "How can a city sustain a nation?" she asked.

"I know," one of their Elf escorts began. "To answer your question, it can't," he added.

"How long?" Sugar asked hesitantly.

"Food and water is being rationed, again. Even so, there is barely enough. We can provide for the capital under normal circumstances, but a nation?" the Elf replied grimly. "Even so, the people haven't lost hope. They believe in us, that we can protect them from the goblin hordes. We will not betray that. We will not take that away from them. They have lost enough," he added seriously.

"I understand," Qu'Tee began. It was then that her eyes lit up. Before another word could be said she raced over to where a few vendors were. The party was mildly stunned at how the Ken queen seemed so entranced by the fabrics, bobbles and trinkets.

"She doesn't get out much does she?" an Elf said more than asked.

"Mom! Look at this!" Qu'Tee called out. The gathering walked over to where she was. Her attention wandered from item to item with an eager innocence.

"It seems like an age since outsiders have visited," the merchant remarked with a smile. "First time to our humble city?" the merchant asked. Qu'Tee nodded happily. "I regret that it had to be under such circumstances, but welcome nonetheless," the merchant added politely with a bow.

"Curiosity, why is she so enamoured with Elves?" Arrow quietly asked. Sugar watched as her daughter and merchant continued to talk.

"She was raised by humans. They treated her poorly to say the least. I think she hoped, believed that she would find more acceptance among the Elves," she rationalized quietly.

"I see. I will go with my friends here to the Citadel. It will be better if someone announces some measure of," Arrow began as he struggled with the way to diplomatically say it.

"It would be a lot to take in under the best of circumstances. I am sure if he received advanced warning about Evallion and Boo it might defuse a situation before it happens?" Sugar offered, Arrow smiled and nodded. "Go, we will wait here for your return," she reassured.

"Come on boys, I am sure father must be dying to see me," Arrow said to the Elves escorting them. One of the Elves looked at Sugar. "They will wait here and will cause no trouble," the Elves relented and followed Arrow through the crowded streets towards the Citadel. It was only then that Qu'Tee became aware that Arrow and the Elves had left.

"Where did they go?" she asked modelling an elegant looking dress. The sleeves were too long. Sugar giggled, she looked like a kid playing dress up in her mother's closet. It had been ages since she had seen that look in her daughter.

"He is going ahead to announce us," Sugar answered as she pulled the sleeves up a bit. "Definitely a new look for you," she mused.

"Why would he need to do that?" Qu'Tee asked curiously.

"Because if you showed up with a goblin and a barbarian it might take some explaining," Evallion pointed out.

"They would have a problem with Boo?" she asked, Evallion almost fell over.

"What about me?" he pointed out.

"What about you?" she rebutted indignantly. Sugar shook her head as the two playfully argued. She turned her attention to the amused merchant.

"How much for the dress?" she asked.

"In these times? Please," the merchant answered quietly.

"What do you mean?" Sugar asked.

"Look around. The entire Elf nation is here. The forest is dying. Where will that leave us?" the merchant tiredly asked. "The soldiers, they bravely guard that wall, but, soon it will be a moot issue. The fight will be brought into the city – or it will have to be taken to them. Either way, we will be much like the Ken, a people without a home," he added. He instantly regretted the choice of words. "I meant no disrespect," he reassured.

"I understand, and no worries, no offence taken," Sugar reassured with a wink. "Although if the goblins were foolish enough to try to take the fight in here, I doubt any would be able to fall back. I find that Elves tend to be as stubborn as Dwarfs when protecting their homes," she mused. The merchant smirked and shook his head. Few people would speak of Dwarfs and Elves in the same sentence.

"Your daughter, she is the queen of the Ken?" the merchant asked. Sugar nodded. "I thought as much. I remembered the last time the Ken came by this way. I remembered the ring. What happened to the old queen if I may ask?" he asked curiously.

"Not more curious as to why the queen is here?" Sugar mused.

"A bit. I know it isn't about our current plight. That only leaves a few possibilities I can think of and they are ones I would rather not speak out loud in such tense times," he replied seriously.

"True enough. But, if completely surrounded by darkness, any light seems brighter," Sugar commented.

"I suppose. I don't know how much longer we can wait for such a light though, or if there will be any left to see if," the merchant remarked trying not to dwell on the subject. "Any how, seeing the light in your daughter, seeing that youthful enthusiasm reminded me of how things used to be here," he added with a sigh.

"And how they will be again," Sugar rebutted with a wink. She looked over at her daughter who was now looking at rings, talismans and necklaces. "See anything you want dear?" she asked. Qu'Tee motioned for her mother to hurry.

"Look at that one," she said pointing to a ring with some old Elf runes carved on it.

"That is a boy's ring," she pointed out.
"I know, but look, doesn't it look like it says Boo?" Qu'Tee asked. Sugar studied the Runes and how they seemed to look like the word Boo.

"It is an ancient Elf dialect. The that rune means luck," the merchant pointed out.

"Can I get it mom? I wanted to get something for Boo," Qu'Tee playfully begged.

"I suppose it couldn't hurt," Sugar said as she examined the ring. It was a beautiful ring. "I must insist sir," she began. The merchant was going to protest. "I have many potions that can do many different things. They may not be able to set right everything that is wrong right now, but they may help," she pointed out.

"You are quite persuasive," the merchant relented.

"Really? Some would call it bossy," Sugar mused. She reached into her robes and seemed to fish around for a few moments. She then took out three vials and handed them to him. "This, is a heal potion," she began handing it to him.

"How much will it heal?" the merchant asked.

"Quite a bit. This one," sugar answered as she removed the cork from the second one and sniffed it. "This one will turn any pot of water into a yummy soup. A little goes a long way," she added. "And this one," she began but stopped she motioned for the merchant to lean forward. She whispered what the potion would do. His eyes widened. "Fair trade?" she asked with a smile.

"More than," he reassured with a smile as he put the potions behind the counter.

"Boo, I got a present for you," Qu'Tee said to the goblin on her shoulder. The eyes of the tiny goblin seemed to light up.

"It understands her?" the merchant asked.

"Peasant for Boo?" Boo tried to repeat.

"Boo is a special goblin," Sugar admitted as she handed the ring to her daughter. She watched as her daughter showed the shiny ring to the goblin. "At least, I really hope he is," she added seriously. Qu'Tee nodded as she placed the ring in Boo's hands.

"Peasant is for Boo?" it asked holding the ring close to his chest.

"You got it Boo," Qu'Tee reassured. Boo hesitantly looked at the ring then smiled at Qu'Tee. "I think he likes," she added happily. Sugar walked over and smiled at the goblin that was entranced with his gift.

"I think he does. May I see that for a moment Boo?" Sugar asked. Boo was hesitant. O promise I will give it right back," she reassured. Boo thought for a moment, looking from the ring to Sugar to Qu'Tee then back to the ring.

"Pomiss?" Boo hesitantly asked.

"I promise," she affirmed. The goblin extended the ring to Sugar. Sugar studied it for a moment then reached into her pouch and pulled out a small cord. "As this is your first present I would hate for you to lose it," she pointed out. She laced the cord through the ring. She then carefully secured the cord around boo's neck. She then moved back. Boo looked down at the ring that was resting against his chest and smiled.

"Thanks mom," Qu'Tee said with a smile.

"I still can't believe you are making such a fuss over a goblin," Evallion remarked. Mere seconds later he was on the ground with a hand mark on the side of his face. Qu'Tee turned her back on him. Sugar giggled as she helped Evallion up.

"You should have seen that one coming," she pointed out. It was then that she noticed a small delegation of Elves baring the royal banner heading their way. "That was fast," she admitted. The crowds moved as the royal guards stopped before them. Arrow smiled as he stepped before them and bowed.

"On behalf of the king, my father I welcome you to Lyte Wood," Arrow said diplomatically. "He insisted, that you spend the night and that he would hear you early tomorrow," he added.

"You must have a lot of silver on that tongue of yours," Sugar mused.

"Well, let us talk about such things later. Shall we go?" he offered.

"Does the offer extend to Boo?" Qu'Tee asked. The goblin on her shoulder was still entranced by his present. "Because if not," she began defensively. Arrow motioned for her to calm down.

"Be at peace. It wasn't easy getting him to allow a goblin in the Citadel, but I explained that, these are odd times and that, Boo, is a unique goblin," Arrow reassured. Sugar could tell that it was a forced effort to keep a straight face saying such things. Qu'Tee politely to the Elf prince.

"Thank you Arrow," she replied. The merchant shook his head as he watched the odd gathering, in the company of the royal guard heading towards the Citadel.

"Odd times? That is putting it mildly," the merchant mused as he examined the potions he had been given.

The Empty Quiver

For the first time since she left her home, the temple grounds, Qu'Tee had a chance to relax in a hot bath. She had a cloth over her eyes as she tried to mentally absorb everything that had happened. Running into her long lost childhood friend, becoming queen of the Ken, taking part in a journey to save the Veil. Part of her wanted to go back home. It was simpler there. If she made a mistake there, she would be scolded, punished at worst. Out here, a mistake could affect the Ken nation, no, all lives in the Veil. She shook her head. Now was not the time to think of such things. Focus on the bath. After spending however many days in the wilderness she honestly forgot how good something as simple as a hot bath could feel.

"I could stay in here for hours," she sighed. The door creaked open. She moved the cloth and smiled as she saw the goblin Boo peeking in to see if she was okay. "Hey Boo. Everything okay?" she asked.

"Boo guard!" the goblin said proudly.

"That's right. I feel safer already," she said with a wink. She smiled as Boo looked down at the ring he had been given.

"Peasant say Boo?" he asked looking at the carvings on the ring.

"You are so smart," she said proudly. Boo seemed to beam at the praise. "Can I have some more alone time Boo? I promise we will play when I am done in here okay?" she requested. The goblin smiled and nodded as he hurried out of the room. "I don't understand. Why does everyone think he will turn out bad?" she asked herself as she put the cloth back over her eyes and leaned back against the tub.

A chill breeze blew against her, sending a shiver down her spine. The door slammed shut.

"Boo? Did you do that?" she asked. There was no answer. "Boo?" she repeated hesitantly. She removed the cloth. All color drained from her face. She wasn't in her room in the Elf Citadel. She was in a dark, unholy place. A wave of terror washed over her. She wasn't in a bath, she was in a pool of blood!

In a panic she scampered out of the pool. It was then that she fell face first to the dirty stone floor. She looked back at the pool and saw a chain binding her ankle to the pool of blood. She tried to wipe the blood from her skin, but nothing seemed to work.

"This can't be real," she muttered timidly.

"But it is," an all too familiar voice croaked. Her eyes quickly scanned the shadows and saw a pair of red reptilian eyes fixated on her. "It has been too long since we spoke young Qu'Tee," the demon of her nightmares taunted. She almost gagged. There was a stench in the air. A foul mixture of swamp rancour, disease and death. "I remember well, my first taste of blood. It was, intoxicating. Tell me, how does it taste for you?" the demon mused. Qu'Tee did her best to cover herself up with her arms. She glared at the demon.

"You are sick!" she almost screamed. The demon laughed, sincerely amused by her indignation. Her eyes widened as the demonic reptile slowly rose up from his throne. "Stay away from me!" she ordered.

"My dear, you are in no position to tell anyone anything. Have you any notion just how vulnerable you are? How helpless?" the demon taunted. Part of her was telling her, screaming at her that it was a dream, a horrific dream like all the others she had. But part of her could feel the blood, feel the pinching of the manacle on her ankle, smell the rancid scent of the demon. What if it wasn't a dream? What if it was real? "I see it in your eyes," the demon stated with a hint of pride. "You are understanding, learning. That is a good thing. Look back at the pool you are bound to," he ordered. Qu'Tee tried not to look back at the pool of blood she had been in. "Do not, make me repeat myself," the demon warned. Hesitantly she looked over her shoulder at the pool of blood. "The blood that stains your skin, the blood of that pool, is unending, it is limitless. It is filled by the broken lives of the people you are condemning. Family, friends, even that boy Evallion," the demon remarked she rose to her feet and glared at the demon. "Touched a nerve?" he mocked. She lunged towards the demon but ended up slamming face first into an unforgiving stone floor. "Seems like someone is forgetting who is master here," he croaked. Qu'Tee forced herself up to her hands and knees.

"You are not my master you filthy monster!" she rebutted. He head was swimming from hitting her head against the floor. "We'll stop you! You won't win!" she protested. The demon laughed, sincerely amused by the statement. "What is so funny?" she asked angrily. She watched as the demon picked up a skull, then crushed it effortlessly within his hand.

"You have been dreaming again? Have you forgotten already?" he asked with a wicked smile. An uneasy feeling washed over her. "Oh dear, you have. Qu'Tee, my pet, you and your friends already tried to stop me. You rallied the nations in a grand attempt to thwart my will," he began as his eyes widened. "You fought me, with everything you had, allies from every nation. Weapons, spells and you lost," he hissed. All color drained from her face hearing him say such things.

"You, you are lying," she stuttered. The demon quietly laughed.

"How do you think it is that you are here?" the demon challenged. She tried to find an answer, but her mind was swimming. Nothing was making any sense. She looked over at the demonic frog that was making his way towards where four forms were bound to the wall. "How precious. You must have been daydreaming again, back to that time when you were free. How painful such dreams must be. Remembering how things were and having to return here, to your morbid reality," the demon mocked. An orange flame danced from his reptilian hand and lit up the torch on the wall. "You and your foolish friends tried to stop me, and failed,' he reminded. She would have screamed at the sight, but something bound her voice in her throat.

On the wall before the demon Bo'Glin, were the broken remains of Evallion, her childhood friend, Sugar, her mother, Arrow, the Elf Prince, and Boo, the goblin. Her hands were shaking as her eyes began to water.

"Poor baby," the demon mocked. It traced the back of his putrid hand against the decaying bloody face of Sugar. "It took them almost two months to die. Evallion held out the longest," the demon remarked with a giggle. "He clung to that thin thread of hope right until the end. It was pathetic," he said, clearly disgusted. Effortlessly he ripped the head off her childhood friend and lobbed it towards her. She watched mortified as she saw the face Evallion looking up at her. "I tire of these games. I tire of your daydreaming. I tire of your delusions of hope," he croaked. His arm elongated towards her. Before she could react his hand tightly clamped around her neck. She gasped as the hand began to crush her throat. "Time to die," he hissed as he threw her back into the pool of blood. Qu'Tee could feel her strength leaving her. The air was leaving her body. She couldn't breathe. She tried to get away, but couldn't. her vision began to fade. She felt as though she was falling. Everything felt fuzzy. It was as though she was floating. Floating away from the memories, the pain. It was all going away.

Just then, the door to Qu'Tee's bathroom all but exploded from its frame as Evallion leapt in with weapon ready. All color drained from his face as he saw Qu'Tee under the water. She wasn't breathing and looked so peaceful. He threw his weapon aside as he fished her out of the tub.

"Sugar! Arrow! Anyone help!" he shouted out. He carried the unmoving body over to her bed as guards and those he called for rushed into the room. Sugar hurried over to where her daughter was.

"What happened?" she asked seriously.

"I was looking out the window when Boo rushed into my room acting all crazy. I couldn't make sense of what he was saying," he explained. Sugar placed her hand on her daughter's chest and closed her eyes. "He then said that Qu'Tee was in trouble. When I came in," he began. She motioned for him to calm down. "Calm," Sugar ordered. She quickly took out some potions. She opened one of Qu'Tee's eyes and saw the expression looking back. "His magic is present. She is trapped by a spell," she said as she opened her daughter's mouth and carefully, slowly poured the potion into her daughter. "Fight it," she whispered as she took a deep breath and began to pray. Hope was fleeting for those present. It was then that they noticed her hand twitch.

"How did a spell reach her?" Arrow angrily asked on of the guards.

"They are not at fault," Sugar reassured as she held her daughter's hand. Slowly she was coming back. She placed a hand on her daughter's cheek. She began to breathe again. It was a laboured effort though. She sighed and put a blanket over her daughter. "If anything happens, alert me," Sugar instructed as she made her way towards the bathroom.

"Where are you going?" Evallion asked. She didn't reply. Sugar fumed as her eyes panned around the room. Something was not right. Something did not belong. Something was out of place. It was then that she saw something moving from under where Qu'Tee had left her clothes. Sugar walked over and jerked the clothes aside and saw a dumb looking frog sitting there.

"You are the cause," Sugar almost growled. Before the frog could hop away her hand shot down and grabbed the slimy reptile. "What would a rare breed of frog be doing so far from home?" she asked the frog. Arrow walked over to see who or what Sugar was talking to.

"A frog?" he asked curiously.

"Don't touch it. It's skin is quite toxic," she warned.

"Is that what?" he began.

"No. My daughter is quite resistant to poisons. It is part of her gift. But with her fear of frogs, mixed with dark magic, the result is just as bad. This Citadel is warded?" she asked seriously. As she took a potion out from her robes.

"Of course. They are constantly maintained and checked," Arrow reassured.

"Then we have a problem," she began as she poured the contents of the vial into the bathtub. Arrow was going to ask what she meant when she dropped the frog into the water. A high pitch whine came from the frog as though something was ripping it slowly apart. "He found a way in. A way that cannot be warded. Even back at the temple of the Order of the Butterfly," she stated. They watched as a black liquid seeped out from the dissolving frog, turning the water black. "He possesses a simple beast and uses is like an avatar, a talisman or the like. He focuses his power through the host and is able to cast his spells as though he is here," she explained. The inky waters began to boil. A demonic face formed in the inky substance then dissipated.

"But, if he can do that," Arrow began.

"Why now? He couldn't he do this before? I don't know. All I know is that, every time he did this before she was able to pull herself out of it. She was able to," she began but stopped, unable to say such things out loud. Arrow put his hand on her shoulder.

"She hasn't given up yet. I don't think we should either, do you?" he suggested. Sugar sighed and nodded as they rejoined the others. "Any change?" he asked. Evallion shook his head. He held her hand and watched, waited, hoped that she would wake up. It was then that her eyes slowly opened.

"I don't," she strained. Her voice was raspy and hurt. "What happened?" she timidly asked. She looked around at the concerned people that were around her. Sugar sat down on the bed and smiled.

"You scared us," she replied. Qu'Tee tried to sit up, but it felt like there was a lead weight on her chest. "Stay where you are please. The potion I used takes a little while to fully work. Qu'Tee looked over at Evallion.

"Listen to her. I thought I lost you, I don't want that to happen again," he began. It was then that he was aware how that might sound. He blushed and looked away. "I meant we," he added. Qu'Tee sighed and closed her eyes. She squeezed his hand. "Is she?" he hesitantly asked.

"She is just sleeping," Sugar reassured. "I have a favour to ask of you," she added.

"Name it," Evallion answered, not looking away from Qu'Tee's face. When she was sleeping she looked like an angel.

"The road ahead will not be any easier. The fact that Bo'Glin is able to use frogs as demonic extensions of himself," Sugar began.

"You want me to squish anything froglike with extreme prejudice?" Evallion interrupted.

"Nicely worded. Can you make that happen?" Sugar affirmed.

"I'll keep alert," he reassured. Sugar looked over at Boo who was still quite worried. Sugar cleared her throat, getting the attention of the tiny waif goblin.

"It seems that a certain young goblin is a hero," she pointed out.

"Boo do good?" the goblin asked hesitantly.

"If you didn't act as you did. If you didn't act so brave, my daughter might not have survived. You saved her life Boo," she added, winking at Evallion. He rolled his eyes. He didn't want to admit it, but she was right.

"She's right. If you weren't here, none of us would have known she was in trouble until it was too late," Evallion added. The goblin looked surprised and confused. It crawled over the sleeping cleric and looked up at him.

"Eva no hate Boo?" he asked saucer eyed. Evallion smirked, a few of the those present managed to stifle a laugh. The young fighter shook his head.

"If you stop calling me that I might," he relented. The goblin smiled happily.

"Eva like Boo!" the goblin sang. Boo crawled back over Qu'Tee and hurried over to where Sugar was sitting. "Eva like Boo!" he said proudly. Sugar giggled as she picked Boo up and winked at Evallion.

"I think we should get Boo something to eat. All of this must have made him hungry," she suggested. The goblin was still entranced by the idea of Evallion not hating him and that Qu'Tee was okay and that everyone was praising him. "What do you think Boo? Want us to get you something yummy?" she asked.

"Boo likes yummies," the goblin answered.

"I had a hunch," she admitted as she stood up. "Evallion?" she began he looked over at the Ken with a goblin sitting on her shoulder. "I will trust that you will behave yourself while we are away," she teased. Evallion blushed and lowered his eyes. "If anything happens that seems amiss, do not hesitate to call for help, okay?" she added softly. He nodded. "Arrow, can you escort us to the kitchen?" she asked. The Elf prince nodded and motioned for her to follow him.

Invasion

In one of the many common areas within the Citadel, Qu'Tee was playing with Boo. Sugar and Evallion were more focused on the reason they were there. Arrow had parted company to help plead their cause. Since then, neither of them were able to get any answers save, that the king will see you shortly.

"The waiting is starting to get under my skin," Evallion said, looking at his mask. Sugar put her hand on his shoulder.

"Getting angry won't help us, or her," she pointed out.

"Arrow must have told his father about why we are here, and the attack that," Evallion began as an aura began to pulse around him. Sugar placed her hand on his cheek. "She could have died, and I have to wonder if the king cares," he said under his breath as he glared at the Elf guards that were watching them.

"What is that supposed to mean?" Sugar asked curiously. Evallion motioned for Sugar to walk with him towards the window. Once there, he looked out at the hundreds of Elves that were in the streets surrounding the Elf stronghold.

"I am not without means. I heard that the king lost his wife recently, a sickness, no cure. Three sons, all died of, strange occurrences. His daughter went missing a while back, was lured out of the city. His only family left is Arrow. Now that he has him back, he might be content to leave us to rot here," he whispered.

"That doesn't sound like him," Sugar rebutted.

"I know. The Elves and Pit Fighters were never on the best of terms, but he has changed. I know why we are here, but if I think that the king is against us, against Qu'Tee, I will not hold back," he stated. It was only then that they were aware that Qu'Tee and Boo were behind them.

"What are you two talking about? And why do you look so serious?" she asked hesitantly. Evallion looked at Sugar and then over at the apathetic guards.

"I am just questioning where the Elves stand. This waiting is getting to me," he admitted.

"This sort of thing can't be rushed. I have a good feeling about this," Qu'Tee reassured. Evallion smiled as he took his mask out.

"I believe in you, but if they keep us waiting much longer, I will go through those pale faced guards and whoever else who wants to ignore the seriousness of all this," he said as he put his mask on and began pacing. She was going to follow him, but Sugar placed her hand on Qu'Tee's shoulder.

"Give him some space. He is a little wound up," she pointed out.

"Why?" Qu'Tee asked.

"He hasn't gotten any sleep since we got here," she answered. Qu'Tee lowered her eyes as she began to put the pieces together.

"Because of what happened to me?" she asked.

"Do not blame yourself. He is worried that there are, other reasons why we have been kept waiting. Truth be told, he does have a point, but I will not go into that with you right now. You have to be focused on what is important," Sugar reassured. "Remember, we believe in you. If you believe in yourself, others will have little choice but to believe as well," Sugar reassured. It was then that the doors to the throne room opened. A robed noble entered and politely bowed. "Where is Arrow?" she asked curiously.

"The king wished to thank you in returning his son to him," the Elf noble began. Evallion groaned. He walked over and grabbed the noble by his robes and lifted him up.

"That is not the reason we are here damn it!" he exclaimed. Almost instantly the guards reached for their weapons. "Now we will see the king. If you announce us or if we have to go over you is entirely up to you," he warned.

"That won't be necessary," a familiar voice pointed out. Evallion looked over and saw Arrow and the Elf king. "I am sincerely sorry about the wait, please accept my apology," he added.

Evallion looked at the noble and then at Arrow. He groaned and released the noble. "I was explaining to my father about the seriousness of the situation. Especially in light of what happened to queen Qu'Tee," he added. Evallion dropped the noble and removed his mask.

"I, apologize for my outburst, highness," Evallion said politely, kneeling and bowing to the Elf king. The king was surprised by the act. He looked to the Elf guards who were just waiting for the order to act.

"Stand down. I have never seen any from the Pit Fight nation apologize. My son was right about you. You are different," the Elf king began as he walked over to where Qu'Tee was and seemed to study her for a few moments. "You must be the new queen I have heard my son speak of. I bid you welcome to my humble home, and a apologize for your ordeal," he said sincerely, bowing to her.

"It wasn't your fault. Mom told me that there was nothing that could have been done to stop it. I'm just lucky that I had good friends to help me," she replied. The king smiled and then looked at the goblin perched on her shoulder. "Oh, this is my friend Boo," she introduced.

"Arrow said much about your pet. If my son says your goblin is different," the king began as a messenger rushed in.

"Highness! The goblins are attacking!" the messenger exclaimed.

"How many?" the king asked.

"Unsure sire. They are standing on the ridge. It is impossible to determine their numbers," the messenger answered. The king looked over at his guests and then at the messenger.

"Tell the archers to stand ready. If it seems like this is the final wave of goblins, tell them to hold nothing back. If it is just another wave to soften us up, they are to hold their fire, and have the ground forces ready," he explained. The messenger nodded and hurried away. The king then looked over at Qu'Tee. "If I were to ask the aid of the Ken, would they come?" he asked curiously. Qu'Tee was surprised by the question. She closed her eyes and sighed.

"I am afraid that I could not sire. Even if all the Ken rallied to stand here, what difference does it make if there are ten, or a hundred people standing on a falling wall?" Qu'Tee asked passively.

"You would leave us to our own in such a time?" the king asked.

"I never said that. Mom, look after Boo," she rebutted.

"Where are you going?" Arrow hesitantly asked.

"If the goblins attack, I will be there with your people. I may not be good with a bow, but I may be able to help those that try to stop them from reaching the gates," she answered seriously. The statement surprised many.

"I will go with her," Evallion added.

"So will I," Arrow followed suit.

"Arrow," the king began.

"Father, if the queen of the Ken is fighting for us, how can I not?" the prince challenged.

"Would you not be better suited on the wall though?" the king pointed out. Arrow thought for a moment. "You are a good fighter son, but you are an exceptional shot. Your true potential to help will not be served on the ground," he pointed out.

"You have a point. Sugar, don't worry, I won't let anything get near her. You two, with me," Arrow ordered, motioning for two guards to follow him.

"May we go highness?" Qu'Tee asked. The king sighed and nodded. The young cleric and fighter then hurried out of the room. The king walked over to where another guard was standing.

"Send word out. All citizens able to do so should be armed and ready. If this is their final wave and the wall falls, I want them ready," he instructed seriously. The guard nodded and hurried away. "She surprised me," the king admitted.

"My daughter tends to do that," Sugar admitted.

"I have known many that led nations. Most would willing offer the aid of their nation, few would offer their aid. She is quite young," the king mused.

"I fear it isn't youth. It is how she is," Sugar rebutted. The king smiled.

"Then, much of how she is must be because of you," he began as he looked over at the goblin. "Are you sure this is wise? Many goblins seem and act friendly as waifs," the king pointed out.

"I know. I will be keeping an eye on Boo," she remarked as she scratched a spot behind Boo's ear. "But, I got a weird feeling about this one. I really do think he is different," she added seriously.

"For your sake and hers, I hope you are right," the king replied.

A short while later, Evallion and Qu'Tee were standing among the Elves by the gate. In spite of everything that the Elves had endured, no matter how tired or hurt, every single one of them that stood there seemed so focused.
"Looks like you have been in quite a few battles," Evallion remarked. The Elf nearest to him looked over at the masked Pit Fighter.

"I will be in many more should those foul animals think they will get past me," he began seriously as he walked over and stood before Evallion. "I will be honest barbarian, I have never been overly fond of your kind, but, the fact that you are willing to stand here says much about your character," the Elf added.

"That almost sounded like a compliment," Evallion mused.

"It was. None here know if this is the final stand of Lyte Wood. This day, the Forest nation may suffer as the Ken have. The fact that you are standing here, willing to risk your life protecting our home means much," the Elf admitted.

"There is a saying among my people," Evallion began as he extended his hand to the Elf. "May courage and strength carry us forward," he added. The Elf smiled and shook Evallion's hand.

"There are fifteen banners!" a voice from the wall shouted out.

"Looks like this is our fight," another Elf said as he groaned.

"Fifteen banners?" Qu'Tee asked curiously.

"This isn't their final offensive. They are just trying to weaken the wall and any that try to protect it," an Elf explained.

"How many banners do they have?" Qu'Tee asked.

"No one knows for sure, but we know there are far more than fifteen. Open the gates!" another Elf answered. Qu'Tee took a deep breath and sighed. She had never been in a real fight before. Not a fight like this. She watched as the Elves marched in unison and matched their pace. She looked over at Evallion . he was beside her, but she could not see his eyes because of his mask. She looked to the distance and saw the banners the Elf mentioned. On the ridge before them stood a wall of feral looking goblins. They were chanting in one voice. It was unsettling, but the Elves around her remained focused, unmoved by the distant enemy.

"Spearmen stand ready!" an Elf shouted out. Qu'Tee watched as hundreds of Elves stepped forward to the front of the army's lines and held their spears up. In the distance the goblins seemed to be moving around. "Staggered formation!" the same voice ordered. The lines of spearmen spread out to cover more ground. They watched as several horrific looking war machines began to rise to the goblin lines.

"What are those things?" Qu'Tee asked hesitantly.

"Whatever they are, it is our job to keep them from reaching the wall," an Elf answered. The distant goblins screamed out and began their charge. From where she was, it looked as though a green tide was washing from the ridge towards them.

"Spears! Three ranks!" an Elf ordered. Instantly the Elves readied their weapons, making a wall of unreceptive spears to receive the invaders. The ground began to shake as the hundreds upon hundreds of goblins and their massive machines drew closer. "Stand ready!" the Elf ordered. The goblins were still charging, undeterred by the Elf defensive. Some of the war machines loomed closer, like foreboding towers. "Arms ready!" the Elf shouted out as the goblin screams got louder. They were a mere hundred yards away. All the Elves readied their weapons for when the goblins broke through the fist line. Qu'Tee and Evallion readied their weapons.

Qu'Tee closed her eyes. She could hear the goblins baring down on them. She could hear the massive war machines rumbling forward. More commands were being issued by the Elves but she couldn't make out what was being said. Little by little she blocked out every sound until she could hear only the beating of her heart. It was then that she opened her eyes. All she could see were the goblins charging towards her. They seemed to be moving in slow motion.

The first wave of goblins slammed into the wall of spears. The remaining goblins raced over the ones that had sacrificed themselves.

The fight began.

The Elves screamed out and relentlessly attacked at any goblin and beast that had crossed the line. Qu'Tee leaped up and over several of the Elves around her and landed among the goblins. Thought and action were fluid and one. Nothing any goblin seemed to do could get close enough to touch her. Her staff, like an extension of her arm struck enemies down and aside. These goblins were so different from Boo, they were like wild animals that had been starved and set loose.

A goblin stabbed a spear towards her. She spun around, coiled her arm around the weapon and punched the seemingly rabid goblin in the face until he dropped the weapon. Just then four goblins jumped her! And began to club at her with their crude weapons.

She managed to roll free of them, but then she looked up and saw a goblin getting ready to bring its crude rusty axe down on her. There was no time to defend! But the strike fell short as an arrow slammed into its chest. She looked up and over at the wall and saw Arrow waving to her. She nodded and leaped back up to her feet.

Over where Evallion was, he and several Elves were doing their best to stop a war machine and the dozens of goblins that were trying to make it go forward. When the wave of goblins hit, he had been separated from Qu'Tee. In the chaos he almost couldn't see her. But he could. She wasn't far, but there was a sea of goblins between them.

There is no way I am going to be able to go through them. No matter how many I kill dozens more will fill the gap. Evallion thought. He spun around and sliced his sword through the axle of one of the war machines. If through or around isn't an option, over! He thought. The towering monstrosity began to teeter. He leaped out from the chaos and ran along the toppling machine. The tower crashed into the ground crushing dozens of goblins. He leaped over and savagely bisected four goblins by Qu'Tee.

"I was wondering where you disappeared too," she remarked.

The two stood back to back and fought the savage monsters that sought to swarm them.

"The wall!" a voice screamed out. The two looked over. One of the monstrous machines had breached the Elf lines. Several goblins screamed out as the monstrous device exploded. Seconds later the goblins began to retreat. Qu'Tee and Evallion looked over at the smoking wall. It wasn't compromised, but it was badly damaged.

"Why did they run?" Qu'Tee asked hesitantly.

"They did what they wanted to do. They hurt us badly and almost breached the wall," a wounded Elf replied. They looked around and saw that almost a third of the Elves had fallen. Either to the fury of the goblins or the explosion. The remaining two thirds were badly wounded.

"What were those things?" Qu'Tee asked, pointing to one of the toppled war machines.

"None of us know. The goblins have been making them. They seem to be a cross between a siege tower and a battering ram," an Elf answered.

"Why are they glowing?" she asked. The Elf looked over at her.

"What?" the Elf asked curiously. Qu'Tee pointed to three of the damaged war machines.

"They are glowing. Can't you see it?" she asked. It was clear by the expression on his face that he couldn't. she then pointed to one that had been damaged near to the wall. "That was is pulsing even," she added calmly. A look of panic consumed the Elf.

"Get away from there!" the Elf shouted to the Elves that were trying to help the wounded near the device. The warning came too late. The monstrous thing exploded killing all that were near it. The Elf groaned and looked around at the dozens of other machines that littered the grounds around the outer walls. "This is bad, very bad," he muttered. Moments later, Arrow hurried over to where they were.

"What is going on out here?" Arrow asked, looking over at the smoking hole in the ground and the bodies that were scattered around it.

"Their objective wasn't to damage the walls sire. They are trapping us. Those – things we thought we stopped, they are enchanted. The Ken queen noticed it," the Elf began. Arrow looked over at Qu'Tee.

"How?" he asked curiously.

"They were glowing. Some more brightly than others," she pointed out looking at the remnants of the shattered war machines that littered the battlefield.

"They explode. There are hundreds of them," Arrow remarked.

"And we don't know what triggers them. If we try to bring the fight to them, if we try to march," the Elf began.

"They could kill us just the same. And without knowing the trigger," Arrow began.

"No way to defuse them," Evallion added.

"All these times we thought they were trying to breach the wall, they were just putting those pieces in place. Letting us think we stopped them," Arrow began. He looked to the distant ridge. For just an instant he thought he saw a cloaked woman. He shook his head, she was gone if there in fact was anyone there. "I think we need to speak with father, now," he added seriously as he motioned for Qu'Tee and Evallion to follow him.

The Plight of Elves

In the throne room of the Elf king. Arrow was pointing out on a map the locations of the decimated war machines that surrounded Lyte Wood. The situation was a grim one. The king clenched his fists and slammed them against the table.

"They played us. They let us believe we were safe within the walls, all the while trapping us," the king said as the frustration began to set in. his mistake could cost the Elves everything.

"If Qu'Tee wasn't there, we wouldn't have even known," Arrow pointed out. The king looked over at her.

"How?" he asked curiously.

"They were glowing. It is kind of hard to explain. Some were brighter than others though," she replied. The king looked over at Sugar and then walked over to where his throne was.

"I see," the king began. "The magic that surrounds us, how could Bo'Glin do so much without us knowing?" the king asked, hitting his throne.

"Sire?" Qu'Tee said getting his attention. "If I may speak, I do not think it is his magic at work here. His work has, a different feel to it," she pointed out.

"You, can see the difference?" the king asked.

"Not really, but, it is just a feeling," she admitted.

"Father, if what she is saying, is remotely possible," Arrow began.

"I know where this is going and the answer is no," the king interrupted. "It is bad enough that you sneaked out once," he added seriously.

"I'm missing something here," Evallion remarked.

"My sister, she was lured out by magic. Puppet magic. Some of my more trusted people abroad informed me that a coven had taken root in one of our outermost villages," Arrow explained. Evallion leaned against the table and looked at the map of the territory around Lyte Wood.

"Puppet magic? The Order of the Hand? I didn't think there were any left," the fighter remarked. Qu'Tee looked at the people who were talking and fumed at how she was being left out.

"Can someone explain this to me?" she requested. Evallion looked over and saw her scowling at him.

"The Order of the Hand was a circle of covens. They viewed themselves as a nation and took, quite a few liberties," Evallion began.

"Needless to say, the nations came down hard on them. They were hunted down and killed for their, manipulations and machinations," Arrow added.

"All of that is history son! There is no evidence that she was lured out by puppet magic. Chasing this ghost will not save her, if in fact she is still alive," the king said grimly.

"She is alive!" Arrow protested.

There were a few long, tense moments of silence as the king and Arrow stared at each other. Qu'Tee walked over and stood between them, focusing her attention on the distraught king.

"You have lost much. I can see why you are afraid," she began.

"Afraid?" the king asked.

"That is how he wants us to be. He wants us to worry. He wants us to be afraid, so much so that we can not help but cling to what little we still possess," she added. The king wanted to argue the fact, but the statement was disturbingly accurate.

"I do not know if there is puppet magic at work here, but I do know that there is magic working against the Elves. It aids the goblins and weakens your people. If it is not stopped, there will not even be a structure here to remind people of your once great nation," she warned.

"What would you have me do? We are trapped here. We cannot," he began but frustration stopped him from saying more.

"I do not think it was chance that brought Arrow to us, or him bringing us to you at this time. I offered my help before. If you wish, I can do so now as well," she offered sincerely. The king smiled and shook his head.

"Can you stop the coming invasion?" the king asked.

"Alone, no. from what I saw of these goblins, there were like feral beasts, yet were remarkably focused and driven. Is that common?" she asked curiously.

"No, usually they are like feral beasts," Arrow replied.

"Then, it stands to reason that someone or something is uniting these goblins. I cannot say how or why, but I do know that magic is playing a big part in this," Qu'Tee pointed out, as she looked over at Boo.

"What exactly are you proposing?" the king asked. She was going to answer when she noticed something about Arrow. She studied him for a moment. It wasn't her imagination. There was something glowing on the side of the Elf prince's neck. "Why are you looking at my son like that?" he hesitantly asked.

"Arrow, this may sound strange but, could you lower your collar please?" she requested. The statement confused all present.

"Okay? I guess," Arrow replied as he pulled the collar of his shirt down a bit exposing his neck. Her eyes widened. On his neck was a glowing circle with a glyph in the center. The color was the same as the glow that surrounded the war machines.

"You left here before? You left because you heard her voice? Your sister?" she asked passively. The eyes of all Elves fixated on the Ken queen.

"Is this true?" the king asked looking over at his son.

"Yes, but, how did you know?" Arrow asked seriously. Qu'Tee closed her eyes. In her mind she could hear whispers. She could see what he saw as though the voice was calling to her. Only she saw a cloaked woman beaconing to him, not an Elf!

"I, don't know. All I do know is that it wasn't your sister you heard," she tried to explain.

"I know my sister," Arrow protested.
"I do not pretend to know how puppet magic works or what it is. But who you saw, who you heard, she was no Elf. The same glow that was on those machines around Lyte Wood is on your neck," she stated pointing to the spot on his neck where the mark was.

"That is impossible!" the king protested. Arrow moved his hand to his neck and tried to absorb the possibility, the remote possibility that what she was saying was true.

"Why would she lie?" Evallion rebutted.

"Guard! Get my mage advisor here at once!" the king ordered. The guard nodded and hurried away. The king got up and walked over to where Qu'Tee was. "I will be blunt, are you implying, that on some level, that my son is in league with the forces trying to destroy us?" he asked seriously.

"No sire," she reassured. The king calmed down a bit.

"I, am sorry, I thought," he began.

"I worded it poorly. I am sort of new at this sort of thing," Qu'Tee admitted. "What I meant to say was that, the same magic that touched those devices outside the walls, has also touched him. It is hard to explain," she added. It was then that a robed Elf entered the room. When he saw Qu'Tee he seemed to tense up for but a mere second. It did not go unnoticed by the Ken queen.

"Diplomacy is an art that takes decades to master under the most ideal of circumstances," the king reassured as he motioned for the cloaked Elf to step forward. "This is my advisor Taleur. One of the people responsible for the maintaining of the protective wards and other such duties," he introduced.

"I do what I can to serve highness," the robed Elf said eloquently with a bow.

"Taleur, our guest here, the Ken queen, she seems sensitive to the ways of magic. The broken war machines that surround us are enchanted, worse, she says that the same magic that touched those machines touched my son," he added. The robed Elf nodded.

"I see," Taleur began as he walked over to where Arrow was. Part of him seem surprised that he was there, but he did not let it show, but Qu'Tee could see it. "I cannot see any magic on him. Are you sure?" he asked. Qu'Tee knew he was lying, but could not say so, not yet.

"Yes, on his neck?" she pointed out. The Elf smiled and looked over at Arrow's exposed neck. He could see the mark she was speaking of but shrugged his shoulders.

"What exactly is it that you see there? Some magic is harder to detect and notice than others. Any magic enchanting the broken machines around us would be quite bright," the Elf pointed out. Qu'Tee could sense something about this Elf, something dark. "Mother? Do you have some paper?' she requested. The eyes of the Elf seemed to perk up, as though trying to guess her next move.

"I might," Sugar began as she reached into her pouch and pulled out a blank scroll. "This suffice?" she asked. Qu'Tee nodded. She took the scroll and walked over to where the map of Elf territory was. She picked up a quill and looked over at the mage advisor and the neck of the Elf prince, she then lowered her eyes and began to write on the paper.

"Something wrong?" Evallion hesitantly asked.

"No. Perhaps I was mistaken," she replied. The Elf advisor smiled.

"It happens to the best of us," he admitted. Qu'Tee put down the quill and looked at what she had put on the scroll. She looked over at the robed Elf and then at the paper in her hands.

"Could you tell me what this means?" she asked as she showed him a recreation of the mark that was on Arrow's neck. His eyes widened. "My mind may be playing tricks on me and I am sure that you are more well versed in these matters," she asked curiously. Sugar, Evallion and Boo could sense something was amiss. Arrow was starting to pick up on it too.

"Very interesting. May I?" the Elf asked. She nodded and handed the piece of paper to him. They watched as he traced his finger over the symbol and then looked over at the king. "Sire, we have a bit of a problem," he stated seriously.

"Indeed?" the king asked.

"I fear that there may be some truth to what she speaks, and, to Arrow's suspicions. This mark, it is a crest used by the Order of the Hand. It is placed on an unsuspecting victim and through it, the witch," he began, the word sent a chill down Qu'Tee's spine. "Can manipulate him or her," he added.

"Then, my sister," Arrow began.

"Was most likely targeted by this witch, the one who used this very mark," the advisor answered. The king got up and walked over to where the Elf noble was.

"Are you saying that there was a witch in Lyte Wood all this time?" the king asked in modest disbelief.

"No. If there was, she would have been detected," he explained. It was then that both Sugar and Evallion began to follow the direction the Elf was taking this. Evallion began to reach for his weapon, but Sugar stopped him.

"Oddly enough, I find it quite the coincidence that a new Ken queen takes power, at the same time Arrow is lured away from home and found, her," the Elf pointed out.

"Are you telling me," the king began.

"What you must have suspected sire. She is a witch," he added, pointing at Qu'Tee.

Deception

For a few moments, everyone was stunned by the allegation.

"Has he been dipping into the sauce?" Evallion asked in disbelief. Sugar motioned for him to be silent. Evallion glared at the Elf that was accusing Qu'Tee.

"That is quite a bold accusation," Sugar admitted seriously.

"Would you chalk all of this up to coincidence? One who seems so young becoming queen so suddenly? Our prince is lured from the city to where she is waiting? The fact that goblins serve her and this?" he replied showing the mark she had drawn. "It would explain much as of late, the attacks, the unity among the goblin tribes," he added.

"Why would she tell us about the enchantment on the devices around us if that is the case?' Arrow asked. The robed Elf looked over at Qu'Tee and smiled.

"How better to avert attention from herself by telling you of her work? Very crafty," he rationalized. "You would be wise to detain them before she tries to bewitch your son, again," the Elf suggested. Qu'Tee wasn't scared. She just looked at him. It made him a little uneasy.

"You are versed in magic and you didn't notice the aura around those broken machines?" Qu'Tee challenged.

"I was busy maintaining the wards," he began but stopped. He looked as though he was feeling dizzy. "Do not try to use your puppet magic on me witch!" he hissed backing away from her. A few guards reached for their weapons, the king motioned for them to wait. Qu'Tee stared at her Elf accuser.

"There is something, odd about you. I thought it was that you knew magic at first, but, it is more than that, isn't it?" Qu'Tee asked. "When exactly did you get here?" she asked. He didn't answer.

"A little while before the goblins started attacking us," Arrow remarked getting their attention. Instantly he drew his bow and had an arrow ready aimed at the advisor. "Come to think about it, you spent a bit of time with my sister before she went missing. Where is she?" Arrow demanded. The advisor looked shocked. He looked over at the king.

"Highness? She has bewitched him! Do something before it is too late," he warned. He prepared to step away. An arrow shot over and pinned his robe to the floor. He looked over Arrow had another shot ready.

"Son, what are you doing?" the king asked. His son's eyes never left the eyes of the advisor. There was no fear looking back, only something dark and empty.

"There is no middle ground here father. You side with him, you condemn us all. Think about it! It makes sense! Ever since he got here! How our people were positioned when the goblins attacked? How his people could find no trace of my sister when she was lured away? He wants you to believe Qu'Tee is the witch? I think he has some hidden reason for wanting eyes to look away," Arrow stated seriously.

"This is outrageous highness!" the advisor protested. The king looked at his son and then at the advisor. He knew that one of them was telling the truth. The other was hiding behind a veil of magic and lies. "Highness? You can't believe this! I have served you," he began but he could see where the king was siding. He closed his eyes and smirked. "My lady spoke that she would come and that she would be crafty. I had no idea she would be so persuasive for one so young. Oh well, plan B," he began.

The next few seconds seemed to blur together. Arrow fired his shot. The guards reached for their weapons. The Elf advisor laughed maniacally as vines and roots exploded outward. Everyone in the room was bound by slimy roots and vines. The Elf advisor revealed his true form, a swamp beast. It looked down at the arrow that was imbedded where its chest would be. Effortlessly it plucked the arrow and snapped it in two.

"I am impressed prince Arrow," the beast mocked as it stalked its way towards him. "I thought the spell I put on you would have you in her waiting hands," the beast mocked as its putrid face inched forward. Arrow strained to get free, but no matter what he tried the vines and roots seemed to tighten. "Pity, you could have been with your sister," it mocked. It then looked over at the angry looking Elf king.

"Where is my advisor?" he demanded.

"He never existed. The irony, you will not see the final defeat of your ancient, arrogant people. I had hoped my ruse could go on further. I so wanted to see the look on your face when your people tried to fight back and her trap sprung," the beast of root, mud and vines then looked over at Qu'Tee.

"You won't get away with this," she stated. The beast laughed.

"Is there some ancient law that says you people have to say that? Look around you simple wench! Do you think that any of these pathetic Elves will be able to do anything? They don't even know what is going on. I sent them away as I came in," the beast remarked. Its arm elongated. A hand made of vines and roots coiled around her neck. "You my dear have become a thorn. One that shall be removed, slowly," the beast hissed as it began to choke her. She tried to fight it but there was nothing she could do. Sugar looked over and saw that Boo had been missed when the beast had attacked everyone.

"Boo, find the green potion in my pouch," she whispered. The goblin looked scared. "Be brave Boo," she reassured. The goblin climbed up the vines and roots that had Sugar trapped and reached into the pouch. He fished around for a few seconds and then pulled it out. "Good boy. Now, this will be hard. I need you to throw that in that things face," she instructed. She could see that Boo was still scared, but he could also see that Qu'Tee was in trouble. The fear faded.

"Boo do," it reassured as he scampered over the vines and roots that littered the room. The beast looked over and watched as the goblin threw something at him. Typical for a goblin that age. It was only when it was about to hit his face that he realized it wasn't a rock but a small vial. The glass shattered as a green liquid dripped all over his slimy face.

"If that was the best you could do you pathetic little beast," the swamp beast began, but was distracted when he heard one of his captives laughing. "You find this amusing?" it asked. Sugar stared at him in a way she shouldn't be. She was helpless and at his mercy. Why was she looking at him like that?

"Everyone has a specialty so it is said. Mine just happens to be making potions. Back at the temple, weeds were just terrible in the garden," she began.

"Is this going somewhere?" the beast demanded.

"I concocted a potion of sorts to kill weeds. Goes right to the roots and eats it away from the inside out. Nasty sort of business, if you are made up of roots and all," she explained. The beast was going to laugh, but he felt a sensation he had never felt before, pain. It was burning through him. His focus was slipping, enough for the Elves, and Evallion to get free. "Hurry up and die already!" she added impatiently.

"If I die, I will take her with me!" the beast threatened as it began to choke Qu'Tee with both hands. Evallion seemed to fly through the air. Light sparked in four arcs as he landed. The swamp beast stood stunned for a moment. Its arms fell limply to the floor. The rest fell into two uneven pieces. The vines and roots that were sprawled out all over the room began to wither and turn to ash. Qu'Tee then fell limply to the floor.

"Qu'Tee!" Evallion exclaimed as he caught her. He looked at her neck, it was badly bruised, but slowly the bruises began to heal. He sighed and allowed himself to relax. The Elf king walked over and looked at the pile of ash that had been his advisor.

"All this time," he began.

"You were right about that little goblin," Arrow admitted. His father smiled and nodded. Never had either of them seen a lone goblin act in such a fashion.

"Evallion? Could you take my daughter to a room until she is well?" she requested. The young fighter nodded and carried the sleeping cleric out of the room. "You want to go too Boo? Just to make sure nothing gets her?" she added with a wink.

"Boo do!" the goblin affirmed as it hurried to catch up with Evallion.

"How could I have not seen all of this?" the king asked in disgust.

"We tend to overlook things when distracted. When things happen fast, it is hard to notice the finer details," Sugar pointed out.

"Will she be safe? I mean twice she has been attacked here," the king said. Admitting it left a bad taste in his mouth.

"None here fault you or yours for any of this. Neither will Qu'Tee. By your leave, may I speak with your highness," she began as she looked over at the guards. "Privately," she added sincerely, without malice.

"I'm staying," Arrow added.

"I was hoping you would," Sugar reassured. The king motioned for the guards to leave the room. "There is much we need to speak of before my daughter returns," she added as the three began to talk.

A short way down the hall, Qu'Tee was resting on a bed in an empty room. Both Evallion and Boo were standing watch. As much as he was against the goblin being around, two times he came through when it counted. The Ken queen sighed as her eyes fluttered open.

"Welcome back," Evallion whispered with a wink. She was going to speak, but her throat hurt. "Take it easy. Do you remember what happened?" he asked. She nodded. "A lesser person wouldn't have pulled through," he added.

"Boo help!" the goblin piped in. Qu'Tee looked over at the goblin that was sitting on top of a big fluffy looking pillow. It looked like he was sitting on a cloud.

"He did. Stood up to that beast without a second thought," Evallion admitted.

"Eva went slash, slash, slash. Icky thing went ack!" the goblin rein act as it fell from the pillow. Qu'Tee giggled as she watched Boo climb back onto the pillow.

"You get some rest okay. We will be right here if you need us," Evallion offered. Qu'Tee rolled over onto her side and held his hand. She was fast asleep. It was then that he noticed Boo looking at him. "You okay?" he asked.

"Eva look sad," the goblin remarked. Evallion looked at Qu'Tee and sighed.

"I almost failed her again. I should have acted sooner," he remarked. It was then that he realized he was explaining himself to a goblin. "These must be odd times," he said shaking his head.

A couple hours later, back in the throne room, Sugar, the Elf king and Arrow were talking by the map of Elf territory. One of the guards got their attention. They looked over and saw the trio standing at the archway.

"Ah! They return at last! Come! Your mother has been telling us everything," the Elf king remarked. The three made their way over to where the others were. "Are you feeling better?" he asked sincerely. Qu'Tee nodded as she looked over at her mother, who was doing her worst to look innocent.

"I am almost hesitant to ask what she said," Qu'Tee remarked. Her mother giggled.

"You wound me daughter," Sugar mused.

"You have done much for my people Qu'Tee. I have spoken with your mother and my son on this matter. I understand the gravity and importance of what you are seeking to do, but as we are, there is little we can do to help you," the king said with a sigh. Evallion was going to say something but saw that the king wasn't finished. "You said, a magic was present. The magic that unifies the goblins, bewitched my daughter and son, you say it is not Bo'Glin?" he asked.

"It is a feeling I have," Qu'Tee replied. The king sighed as he looked over at Sugar.

"I trust your judgement. You saved many lives when you helped defend our wall. You saved many more noticing the magical traps that littered those devices surrounding us. You saved my life and my son by revealing that beast, that spy. But, I will say this. If the magic that empowers and unifies the goblins is dealt with, they will become as they were and we will be able to deal with them, and we will be able to help you in whatever way the Forest Nation, or what is left of it, can," the Elf king offered.

"How will we find this Hand witch? They tend to stay hidden," Evallion asked.

"I will go with you. After all she, she is after me for some reason," Arrow offered. Evallion looked over at the king. He could see that he didn't like his son's choice, but he didn't oppose it either.

"We will find her highness. And we will stop her," Qu'Tee reassured. The king smiled and bowed to her as she and the party slowly made their way out of the throne room. The Elf king then returned his attention to the map.

"I hope so queen of all Ken. If you fail, I fear we will all die," he said grimly as he continued to study the map.

The Web of the Witch

In a dark dank place, far from the Elf capital of Lyte Wood, a disturbingly beautiful, voluptuous, scantily clad woman sat within a glowing circle of runes. She was moving as though music was being played, but the only sounds present were from her humming.

Dark, twisted, horrific looking shadows danced on the walls of the cave around her. They looked like tortured souls. Spirits, trapped between worlds unable to find escape or freedom.

The woman slowly opened her eyes and looked at the glowing crystal that was floating before her. She sighed as she leaned against it.

"Master?" she asked as she looked over her shoulder. There was no answer. "He wasn't joking when he said that little girl was wretched. If she didn't show up, I would have had a matching set of Elf kids, and they would have charged eagerly into my trap. Pomph!" she pouted. She got up and began to dance to the music in her head. "But I can see why master fears her," she added. Just then a reptilian hand grabbed her by the throat and slammed her into the wall.

"I fear nothing and no one you insane bitch," the demonic frog reminded as he threw the woman aside. She giggled as she rolled over and looked up at him. "This is not a game," he reminded.

"But I like games," she replied. She floated up to her feet. "I thought you were here master. Can I get you something? A drink, a sacrifice, me?" she teased, as she resumed her dancing.

"I wouldn't drink or eat anything you offered," he began.

"That would be wise," she mused.

"I am well beyond needing sacrifices Samantha," he added as she continued to dance. He fumed as he slapped her down to the floor. "And if you keep testing my tolerance, you will find out just how much I need your likes," he added coldly. There was no fear in the woman's eyes, just one of depravity and cunning.

"You know you love me," she reminded. She rolled over and lounged against her crystal ball. "Is this, business or pleasure master?" she mused.

"With you, it is never a pleasure. Your plan with the Elves failed," he pointed out.

"Failure, success, it is all subjective," she replied. The demon's eyes glowed as he tried to suppress the rage he felt every time he had to talk to her.

"No, it isn't. it is black and white," he explained.

"I like it black, maybe off white, sometimes pink. I feel pretty when I wear pink," the woman pointed out. The demon groaned. "You are worried about her because you failed to kill her with that spell of yours?" she asked. A wave of force slammed her so hard into the rocky surface of the cave wall that it left an imprint. She gasped a bit. The effort didn't hurt her, it seemed to amuse her.

"Stay focused!" he snapped. She blinked and lowered her eyes. "I hadn't anticipated her friends interfering. It won't happen again," he added. The woman pulled herself out from the wall and leaned against the crystal again. "Explain how you let this happen?" he asked. She smirked, her expression was quite different.

"Please. Her arrival changes nothing with my plans. And so what if the stupid sharp ears know if they are surrounded by my traps? So what if my puppet was discovered. Does that change that I have another wave of over a hundred thousand goblins standing ready to make them extinct? No, it doesn't. The Elves still have the same choice now that they had before, that being, what I give them," she stated coldly. She slowly rose to her feet. The crystal ball floated up and seemed to balance on her finger.

"Her arrival changes everything. She is your priority. I don't want you playing your sick little games with this one. I want her dead," he explained his reptilian eyes narrowed and fixated on her.

"You really are scared of this one," she remarked. His hand shot over and gripped her throat. "Go ahead master. You don't put up with me because you like me, you do so because you need me. You know I can get the job done," she reminded. He growled as he released her.

"You, yes. The others that live in your messed up little mind are another story," the demon pointed out. The woman smirked. "I am warning you. Do not treat her like some child. Your puppet underestimated her. If you do, you will fare no better," he warned. Her eyes seemed to space out for a moment as her head lolled to the right. "Do you understand?" he demanded. She looked bored by the conversation now.

"Yes, yes. I heard you the first forty million times already. Why don't you go do that froggy demon thing that you do so well and let me do my job," she suggested. With a wave of her hand the demon was gone. "I love him dearly but some times he just won't shut up," she said to herself as she began to skip around. She clapped her hands. Hundreds of candles illuminated the cave. In one corner was a rusty looking cage. On the floor of the cage a barely moving woman laid. "Don't you just hate people like that?" the witch asked as she squatted down beside the cage. Slowly the Elf maiden looked up.

"What do you want of me mistress?" the Elf asked meekly.

"Many things come to mind. I know I promised you that your brother would be here to keep you company, but that rude wench stuck her nose where she shouldn't have," the witch sounded upset. "I hate not keeping my promises to you. Can you forgive me?" the witch asked passively.

"Please, leave him alone. Don't hurt him," she asked meekly.

"That would make you happy?" the witch asked curiously. The Elf nodded. The expression on the face of the witch began to change again. "Come on my precious. You should know by now, that all of this isn't about you. It is all about me. Arrow might have eluded my summon, but the result will be the same. He will come running to me, just like I wanted in the first place. Then I will have a matching set. One prince, one princess, then we can all play together," she said coldly.

She hopped up to her feet and began to dance around again. She stopped as she seemed to playfully ponder something. She looked around at her surroundings and smiled.

"I really do want to play with that young queen. Did you see how cute she was? I bet little precious is still a virgin even," she added. She shook her head and slapped the back of her hand. "No! that would be wrong," she argued. "Master said no," she reminded herself. But she didn't seem too convinced. "But, he wouldn't have to know. You wouldn't tell on me would you?" she asked as she ran over to the cage. The witch looked shaky at the thought. She whimpered as she rolled on the floor holding her head.

Slowly she began to regain her composure. All the candles in the room were snuffed out. Her eyes seemed to glow under the magical illumination from her conjuring circle and crystal ball.

"That little bitch. She ruined my beautiful plan. I spent so long getting all the pieces into place. Then she shows up and ruins everything! I hate her!" the witch screamed as her face contorted with rage. "I will make her suffer for ruining everything. Yes. That will make it better," she rationalized. The crystal ball floated up and hovered over to where she was. In it she could see Qu'Tee and Evallion. She could see they were talking, but she couldn't hear what they were talking about. "Cute boyfriend. A pity she corrupted him. He might have been cute in a couple of years. The image changed over to that of the Elf prince Arrow. The Elf maiden slowly pulled herself up from the floor of her cage. The witch looked over her shoulder at her captive.

"Please, I don't care what happens to me anymore. But please, don't hurt my brother," she pleaded passively. The witch fumed and returned her attention to the image in the crystal ball.

"Crown prince Arrow. Third born son to the fifteenth elf king. Big brother to a missing princess. Quite focused on one thing, finding and rescuing you," she mused. "That was how I managed to get my hooks as deep into him as I did. Known to be one of the most accurate shots in the Forest Nation," the witch said analytically as she walked around the image of the Elf prince. She waved her hand, the image changed and showed Sugar.

"Mommy of the new Ken queen, Sugar. A conjurer and alchemist," she fumed as she studied the image of Qu'Tee's adoptive mother. "There is something about you that just sets me off. I don't like you for some reason," she added. "maybe it is because you are one of those sneaky potion making potion makers. You have to hate people like that who aren't me," She snapped her fingers. The image changed to that of Evallion.

"Evallion, you have promise. Quite the little stud muffin if I do say so myself. I don't know what he sees in that wimpy Ken queen. But, there in lies his strength and weakness. He is in too deep with her. It clouds his judgement. He is too consumed with the past to see what is before him," she remarked as she thought for a moment. "I might be able to use him to hurt her. Will have to remember that," she added. She waved her hand. The image in the crystal changed and showed Boo.

"You are a freak. There is something just not right about you. You are a cute little animal, but there is something, I don't know, just too unpredictable about you. Maybe I could run some tests on you and find out what makes you tic-toc," she mused. Her head lolled from side to side like a pendulum. She tapped her finger on the crystal ball. The image of the goblin was replaced with Qu'Tee. Instantly she was dead serious.

"Qu'Tee of the Ken. Newest queen, a servant of the fallen angel, has a knack for healing, appears to be sensitive around magic," she began as she thought for a moment. "I just don't see it. What does Lord Bo'Glin see in her? What is in her that he fears? I have seen more powerful people who wielded magic. I have seen far better fighters. Physically she doesn't appear much stronger than a goblin. Emotionally she is just a child," she added. "Still has some sprouting to do too, but not too bad for one her age I guess," she pointed out. It was then that a wicked smile crossed her face. "I can't remember the last time I saw the boss so, froggy," she mused, allowing herself to laugh at her pun. "Bad, bad. He told us to kill the bitch, but, why is he so eager to have someone else do it? Is it because he can't?" she added as her mind began running in strange circles. "What if? Oh dark circles! What if she succeeded? What if, I helped her? Then master would be gone and I could have her all to myself," she pondered as she reached towards the crystal. Just then the image seemed to look up at her. The witch gasped as she felt as though she was being choked. The demonic frog stepped out from the shadows behind her.

"You stupid witch. Don't you ever imagine betraying me. I found you and saved you and I can just as easily destroy you," he reminded. He gripped her head in his mutated hand. Her eyes spaced out as memories stabbed at her mind like jagged knives. Samantha vividly remembered running through the forest with her mother when she was a child. They were being chased by religious zealots. She remembered as her mother and family were sadistically, brutally tortured and killed. She remembered it all too clearly. She got away some how. She happened upon an Elf party that was out hunting. She remembered begging them to help her, but they did nothing as she was caught again and dragged away. Her eyes watered as her body went limp and twitched.

"Can you still hear your mother crying for mercy?" the demon hissed. She couldn't answer, she was too far gone. He released her. She crumpled to the floor, still twitching. "They were supposed to kill you, but they didn't. they had their way with you, beat you, humiliated you and then left you alone in a swamp to die," he reminded.

"Forgive me master," she slurred, still shaking like a leaf.

"I am the one that found you, sick from eating things that were rotten or dead. Not to mention the state you were in physically. They really worked you over," he added. "I helped quiet the voices that were screaming in your messed up mind," he continued.

"I am nothing with you master," she whimpered, hesitant to look up at him. He reached down and ran his claw like fingers through her hair. "I'm weak and stupid. I am not well master," she pointed out.

"I know. Your unique perspective, your insanity makes you strong and impossible to predict. Why do you think I put up with you?" he reminded. She shrugged her shoulders. "You see things in a way that others can't. You perceive things others couldn't hope to comprehend," he pointed out. With a wave of his hand she floated back up to her feet. "But if you think, I will not know if you are trying anything against me, you are out of your mind. There is not one perverted, twisted thought that runs through your mind that I do not know about. Be wise, remember that if you can't remember anything else," he reminded coldly as he scratched her face with one of his claws. "Because, if you do forget, the horrors you endured physically at the hands of those sick, perverted zealots will seem mild compared to what I put you through," he concluded as he vanished into the shadows of the room.

Slowly Samantha, last of the witches of the Order of the Hand, wiped the trickle of blood from her cheek. She looked over at her crystal ball at the image of Qu'Tee and glared. Rage was welling inside her. She associated what she went through at the hands of her master with the image of the Ken queen.

"I will make you pay for this you little bitch," she said. She was laughing and crying as she pondered how she would deal with her master's enemy, her enemy.

Crown Prince Arrow's Quest

It took about a day and a half for the party to slip out from Lyte Wood. Many times they were almost discovered. It was almost as though they knew where they were going to be before they did. But soon they were out of the desecrated forest and found themselves in a part of the woods that seemed more alive. It still bore the taint of death, but it wasn't as bad as it was in other areas of Elf territory.

Arrow, Sugar, Evallion, Qu'Tee and Boo were once again camping. Sugar and Arrow were discussing possible ways to continue and course of action to take when they got there. Qu'Tee was more focused on her goblin friend.

"You okay Boo?" she asked, offering him another bowl of soup.

"Boo okay," the goblin answered. He took the bowl and sat down. Evallion looked over at Qu'Tee and could see the concern in her eyes.

"You seem worried. What's wrong?" he asked curiously.

"Whoever is doing all of this, she is controlling goblins. What if she tries something to Boo?" she replied. It was then that she noticed the soup faced goblin looking up at her. She giggled as she took out a cloth and wiped his face. "You can be so silly some times," she added. Boo, seemed to sense that she was still worried in spite of her smile.

"Boo be okay. Coo'Tee no be sad," he reassured.

"He sure is a perceptive little thing," Evallion remarked. He looked over at the elders in the group. "So where to from here?" he asked. Sugar sighed and shrugged her shoulders. "Tell me something. Don't tell me we are running blind through goblin infested forest," he began. He looked over at Boo and smirked. "No disrespect," he added.

"The problem is, this witch could be anywhere. She could be camped out somewhere near Lyte Wood, or on some island off the northern shore. It is one of the reasons that the witches from Order of the Hand were so dangerous," Sugar pointed out.

"How did they get taken down then?" Evallion asked.

"Years of scouting. Even then we weren't sure if all of them were taken down," Arrow began as he studied the map. "But, this witch seems fixated on the Forest nation for some reason. As such she most likely would be some where near to her handiwork," he added rationally. "But even still, that leaves a lot of ground to cover, and not a lot of time to cover it," he added grimly. Qu'Tee walked over and looked at the map.
"What is there?" Qu'Tee asked, pointing to a red dot on the map.

"A small village, Briar I think, why?" he asked. Qu'Tee traced her finger from that dot to the dot labelled Lyte Wood and then back.

"What direction were we going in before?" she asked curiously. Arrow blinked and returned his attention to the map. He remembered back and then pointed to a pathway that led away from where they were. "Then we encountered goblins, and ended up here?" she asked curiously.

"You think she is leading us to her?" Sugar asked.

"Why would she do that?" Arrow asked. Qu'Tee looked over at Arrow, her eyes looked older and deeper.

"She is after you. She has you marked. She went through a lot of trouble to lure you away from your home. She won't give up on you so soon," she pointed out.

"Makes a certain amount of sense, but where does that leave us then?" Evallion asked. Qu'Tee blinked and looked over at the others who were focused on her.

"What?" she hesitantly asked.

"You were just talking," Evallion reminded, she looked as though he had said the strangest thing. "Are you okay?" he asked seriously. Sugar sighed. She rolled up the map and put it away.
"My daughter tends to be, sensitive," she explained.

"I, don't understand," Evallion replied.

"The way that she is able to notice magic, see auras, spirits and such. Very few people are blessed with such a gift. Some of the people who have been blessed with such a gift have been known to see devils and speak with the voice of angels, as the saying goes," Arrow explained further.

"So, she gets possessed?" he asked.

"I wouldn't word it quite that way. But spirits and other such beings tend to be drawn towards her and can speak through her. She used to get in trouble in class because of it," Sugar pointed out. Qu'Tee blushed and looked down at the campfire.

"They thought I was making fun of the instructors," Qu'Tee pouted.

"We got it cleared up once we understood," Sugar reminded. Qu'Tee shook her head. There wasn't a moment that went by that she wasn't reminded in one form or another that she was different. "So please stop blaming yourself and beating yourself up over it. Having one martyr in the group is enough," she added with a smile.

"What is that supposed to mean?" Arrow and Evallion asked at the same time. The two looked at each other.

"I stand corrected. I swear some times you men make me question how it is that you survive so long. There are some things that you have no control over. Instead of seeing that and recognizing that you agonize as to why you should have done more," she added. She refilled Qu'Tee's bowl. Evallion lowered his eyes.

"Must be a guy thing," Qu'Tee added, thinking about the topic. Evallion sighed as he got up and began to walk away. "Where are you going? Aren't you still hungry?" she asked curiously. He said nothing, merely walked away into the shadows. Arrow sighed and got up. "You too?' she added.

"I will return shortly," Arrow reassured.

A short distance away, Evallion was sitting on a tree branch looking up at the sky. There weren't many clouds, but the odd one did drift slowly by, concealing the stars and moon as they passed.

"If it means anything, I'm sure she didn't mean anything by it," a voice remarked. Evallion looked down and saw the Elf prince looking over at him. "They, they don't understand. I don't think they can," he added.

"You know how me and Qu'Tee met?" he asked. The Elf prince shook his head. "I was just a kind. I saw her hiding in an alley by some garbage. I didn't know why she was hiding, but I found out that. There were some bullies after her, a group of them. I wasn't much bigger than her at the time. I tried to save her then, but, I was too weak, too small. I ended up almost dying. I wanted to save her, but, I ended up needing saving. I know, her mother doesn't mean it, but, she can't see it," he finished, shaking his head at the thought.

"I know what you are going through," Arrow admitted.

"You do?' Evallion asked.

"You blame yourself. You see the hardships she had to endure. You see the scars that have no physical form. You question yourself in the greater scheme of things. How could I have not seen it sooner? Why didn't I act? Why did I allow this to happen?" Arrow said, looking up at the sky. "My, sister, not a day goes by that I do not think about her and how I failed her," he admitted.

"You do know," Evallion remarked. He flopped forward and laid down on the branch. "So where does that leave us?" he asked curiously. Arrow looked at the point of an arrowhead and then over at the Pit Fighter.
"Where we were before. There is one difference between us though," he answered.

"The fact that you are an Elf and I am human?" Evallion pointed out.

"Besides that. Right now, the one that you are putting yourself though all this for, is here, now. She doesn't blame you for anything, as such, you have a chance," he answered grimly.

"You think your sister blames you for being lured away by a witch?" Evallion asked.

"At times. Some times there are quiet moments. I remember her smile, her face. Right now, I have no idea, if she is alive or dead. All I have, is hope," Arrow pointed out. He put the arrow with the others.

"Is that enough?" Evallion asked.

"It has to be," Arrow rebutted. "How about you?" he asked. Evallion sighed and closed his eyes.

"It isn't so simple. The bullies that tormented her so much, they did it on a regular basis. I don't know how many times I tried to stop them. I lost count. But, it didn't matter you know? I could take it. Besides, if they were focused on me, they were leaving her alone," he began. Arrow leaned against the tree.

"But, at some point they caught on?" Arrow asked.

"They weren't the brightest, but yeah. On that day that they did, they worked me over bad, then made me watch as they berated, humiliated and hurt her. There was nothing I could do. I wanted to kill them, I wanted to make them suffer a measure of what they had her through. After that day, I couldn't take it. I had to do something. That was when I left to study the ways of the Pit Fighters," he explained. "I worked hard to get strong, but it was for nothing. By the time I got back, the bullies and Qu'Tee were gone," he groaned at the frustration he was feeling.

"I was supposed to meet her," Arrow began. Evallion looked over at the Elf prince. He looked at though he was miles away.

"Nothing overly important, but I told her I would be there. I don't remember what happened, but, something distracted me. There wasn't a time in her life that she was in trouble, that she needed me, that I wasn't there," he continued. He looked over at the young fighter in the tree. "If the witch planned all this, she must have had a hand in that," he added.

"What happened?" Evallion asked.

"I got there late, not by much, but, she was gone," Arrow said, his hand clenching into a fist. I searched everywhere in Lyte Wood, the forest surrounding the capital, there was no sign of her anywhere. It was like she was there one day, and then, gone," he answered. "That day that we first met, I heard her voice calling to me, my sister's. A part of me knew that it was too good to be true, but the bond my sister and I had was so strong that I convinced myself that it was her," he added.

"Some times a soft lie is better than a hard truth?" Evallion remarked.

"Very profound. You surprise me," Arrow remarked.

"I heard a Ken elder at the village near to where Qu'Tee was say something like that. Never made any sense to me, not until now, oddly enough," Evallion admitted. "You do know that we will get her back?" he pointed out.

"If she is alive," Arrow rebutted.

"If all you have is hope, you definitely need more," he mused. The Elf shook his head.

"Don't spend the now, your today, looking to where you have been. Instead, save that for where you will go, your tomorrow," Arrow said eloquently.

"I liked my proverb better," Evallion remarked. Arrow quietly laughed. "I'm glad I met you. Until today I thought that all Pit Fighters were barbarians," Arrow concluded as he walked away.

"I won't say what I thought of Elves," Evallion affirmed as he rolled from the tree and landed gracefully on his feet. Arrow looked over his shoulder and smiled.

"That might be wise," Arrow admitted as he walked back towards the camp. It was then that Qu'Tee walked over and saw her friend staring up at the stars. She cleared her throat to get his attention.

"If, I made you feel bad earlier, I'm sorry. I was just teasing," she reassured.

"It's okay," he commented as he walked over to where she was standing. He looked at her for a few moments, then quickly looked away.
"The why can't you look at me?" she asked. You have been that way since we left the Citadel in Lyte Wood," she added. Hesitantly he backed away.

"You, don't remember? Let us best leave it at that," he remarked. Qu'Tee began to rapidly sift through the recent events to find what he might be talking about.

"Did you do something?' she asked suspiciously.

"Evallion? Do you want seconds?" Sugar called out.

"I'm on my way!" he replied as he hurried back towards the campsite. For a few seconds Qu'Tee stood there in a state between stunned and confused. Why was he being so evasive? Why couldn't he look her in the eye without…blushing?

"How did I get from the bathroom to the bed?" she then realized what must have happened. "Oh, my god," she whispered as she turned beet red. "He saw me," she began but stopped. She fumed as her hand clenched into a fist. "Evallion!" she yelled out as she charged back towards the campsite.

Goblin Raiders

Everything had quieted down after the, activity, that had happened the night before. Sugar was looking at a map. Qu'Tee was still pouting. Boo was doing his best to make Qu'Tee smile, but his best efforts weren't quite able to get the job done.

"You went a little overboard on your friend," Sugar remarked, not taking her attention from the map. "Is he back yet?" she asked. Her daughter was silent. "Daughter, it took almost four potions to heal him. Even by your standards that is a little extreme," she pointed out.

"You wouldn't understand," Qu'Tee rebutted. Sugar smiled as she looked over at her daughter.

"I know that you like him, if I had to guess, I would even say," Sugar began. Instantly Qu'Tee leaped over and put her hand over her mother's mouth. Sugar moved her daughter's hand. "Daughter, I know how you are. I know you are, how shall I say this, defensive? If you don't want him to leave, you better say something to him, if you don't, I will," she warned. Qu'Tee was going to protest. "Do you want him to go?" she asked seriously. Qu'Tee lowered her eyes.

"No, but," she began.

"No buts," Sugar interrupted. She motioned for her daughter to go.

A short distance away, Evallion was sitting in a tree looking around at the branches. Sugar had taken care of the injuries he had incurred when Qu'Tee had caught up with him. He wasn't mad though. He knew she didn't mean it.

"Looking for someone?" a familiar voice asked.

"What are you?" Evallion began. He looked over and saw Arrow standing under the tree looking up at him. On his shoulder was a rather familiar looking squirrel. "You little traitor," he scolded as he hopped down from the tree. The ears of the squirrel went down.

"Don't be too mad," Arrow began as he handed the familiar back to its owner. "I have a way with animals. Not many people opt for squirrel familiars," he pointed out.

"That was one of the reasons why I wanted one. Cats are for mages or wizards. Bats are too unpredictable," Evallion pointed out.

"Still, I never met a Pit Fighter with a familiar before," Arrow remarked.

"Their loss. Chi here helped me out on numerous occasions," Evallion said as he sat down at the base of the tree he had been in.

"He was the presence that I felt watching me when I was watching you, and threw that acorn at me too I would wager," the Elf added. Chi seemed to strike a pose at the Elf that recognized his handiwork.

"He tends to be a bit of a glory hound, and a bit of a pig that thinks with his stomach, but I wouldn't trade him away," Evallion remarked as he scratched the squirrel's ear. "You find anything?" he asked. The squirrel nodded.

"He can speak?" Arrow asked.

"Not exactly, but he has a, unique way of saying things," the fighter answered. Arrow watched as Chi grabbed a twig and began to draw on the ground before Arrow and Evallion. For a few moments Arrow had no idea what the familiar was drawing.

"He's pretty smart for a squirrel," Arrow remarked. He pointed to one symbol. "Is that our camp?" he asked. The squirrel seemed to smile and nod. "This is where we are?" he asked, again Chi smiled and nodded. "These five symbols, they are goblin encampments?" he asked, Chi clapped his paws together.

"How many goblins are we dealing with?" Evallion asked.

"Goblin raiding parties have five goblin warriors, ten that are cannon fodder, and one that is their leader," Arrow replied. Evallion looked over at the Elf and then at the drawing.

"That is a lot of goblins," Evallion began as he slowly got up. "And if they are organized by magic like they were at Lyte Wood, that is a lot of trouble," he added. It was then that they noticed Qu'Tee standing there. Arrow cleared his throat.

"I should tell Sugar about this turn of events," the Elf began as he motioned for Chi to tag along. The squirrel hopped up onto Arrow's shoulder. Qu'Tee watched as Arrow headed back to the camp. She then lowered her eyes.

"Are you mad?" she asked. It was a stupid question, but it was the only thing that came to mind. "I'm, sorry I overreacted like that," she added. Evallion smiled and shook his head.

"Don't worry about it. A couple of your mom's potions and I was good as new," he reassured casually. "Are, you still mad at me?" he hesitantly asked.

"No," she answered. There were a few long awkward moments of silence that followed.

"We should head back to camp," Evallion suggested. The two walked back.

At the campsite, Sugar was looking at the map. On it were markers indicating where they were and where the goblin encampments were.

"How many are following us?" Sugar asked.

"Enough to make us want to go forward," Arrow replied as Qu'Tee and Evallion returned. "Welcome back," he added with a bow. Chi scurried over and hopped up onto his master's shoulder.

"Seems we have a bit of a situation," Sugar began. "The witch seems to know where we are," she continued. Qu'Tee looked at the map. The goblin markers almost formed a semi-circle.

"What if we fight them?" she asked pointing to one marker.

"No good, they would signal the others. By the time we dealt with one batch, two more would be on top of us. Evallion closed his eyes and weighed the options in his head. He sighed as he walked over and looked at the map closely.

"I know this area pretty well. It is close to Pit Fighter territory," the fighter began. He pointed to one of the goblin markers. "We sneak by this group and then make a break to here," he said, tracing a path across the map towards a small lake. "Once we get here, it won't matter how many goblins come," he reassured.

"You sure? I've been there, it is pretty open," Arrow asked.

"I know of a place there. I'll explain more when we get there. Right now we should hurry. If we get there before nightfall we will be too dug in for them to touch," he reassured. Arrow and Sugar let it go. "Chi, scout around and meet at the teardrop," he added. The squirrel nodded and scurried away up a tree.

"How very intriguing. A mystery no less," Sugar mused.

"Sorry for the secrecy, but it has to be this way. We shouldn't be going there to begin with, but we don't have much choice," Evallion replied, packing his things quickly. "I'll get into trouble for doing this, but I will deal with it," he added. Within moments, they were all packed up and on route.

Hours later, the group was hidden in the bushes a short distance away from the goblin encampment that they needed to get by. For goblins they seemed disturbingly alert and organized. It was as though they were waiting for them.

"They look different from the goblins that attacked Lyte Wood," Evallion stated.

"They are. Raiders tend to live in swamps, bogs and mires. As such, their appearance looks," Arrow began as he fished for the right word.

"Creepy?" Qu'Tee suggested.

"That works. They are also more perceptive than a normal goblin. We may not be able to sneak around them," Arrow pointed out. Evallion looked around and then up at the canopy of leaves and branches above.

"You may be right, over them might be a better option," he suggested. "I doubt they would be expecting that," he added.

"True, but with the forest in the state it is in, the branches might not support us, and it is a long drop," Arrow pointed out.

"Why are they standing around a burnt out campfire?" Qu'Tee asked.

"Swamp water," Sugar replied.

"What?' her daughter asked.

"A black liquid. Pour it over something like sticks and leave even rocks become very flammable. Soon as we get spotted, they light that," she explained as she pointed way over to the east. There they could see another group of goblins waiting. "And they announce to their friends that the enemy is here," she explained.

"If we can get the drop on them before they light it, the other goblins might not realize we are here," Qu'Tee pointed out.

"That is a lot of ground to cover. And they are perched right beside it. Even if we did get there, there is no way that we could get them before they lit the signal," Evallion pointed out. Qu'Tee thought for a moment.

"Mom, do you have a potion that could make the swamp water stuff not work?" she asked. Sugar thought for a moment.

"I believe so," she answered. She fished around inside her robes and pulled out a small bluish potion. "But how?" she began as she then looked over at Arrow. She understood what Qu'Tee was suggesting. "You want Arrow to shoot the potion into their signal fire," she answered. Her daughter nodded.

Arrow took the potion and secured it to an arrow. He then held the projectile for a few moments. The weight was off, the object was top heavy. But he could compensate for it.

"Soon as I fire this, they will be all over us," Arrow pointed out as he readied himself for the shot. He took aim and focused on the signal fire.

"Evallion and I will take care of them," Qu'Tee reassured.

"You sure about that?" Arrow asked, still focused on his target.

"What do you mean?" she asked hesitantly.

"I mean no disrespect to your friend, but I have seen Pit Fighters. Their strength is their weakness. As they fight, a wave of crimson washes over them. It carries them to a place beyond reason and pain. Once in this state, some times, they lose focus and forget who is friend or foe. All they feel is the need to fight and survive," Arrow explained.

"He would never," Qu'Tee began.

"He's right," Evallion admitted.

"What?" she asked in disbelief.

"The longer a fight goes on, it grows harder to control the rage. Sort of like trying to pull a punch. If you are in control, you can stop it. If you aren't you will try, but the hit goes through," Evallion explained. "When I was training, the captain, he kept me in that state too long. It was like I was watching myself fight, like it wasn't me any longer," he added, remembering that fight vividly.

"Did he survive?" Sugar asked.

"Only because ten soldiers took me down, hard," he answered as he took his mask out.

"You didn't seem that way at Lyte Wood," Qu'Tee pointed out.

"I wasn't using my power there. When the fighting starts, stay out of my way, whatever you do, stay out of my Tantra," he insisted.

"What is Tantra?" she asked.

"The space that surrounds a Pit Fight. In other words, just stay out of his reach and do not try to get his attention until the fight is over," Arrow explained. "Just tell me when you want me to do this people," he added.

"Daughter, your healing gift will help him more that your fighting prowess. He may not be able to feel pain, but he will still get hurt," Sugar suggested. Qu'Tee nodded. "Okay, any time you are ready," she concluded. Arrow nodded. Everything save his target faded from sight.

"Lights out," he said as he let his arrow fly. It whistled past the waiting goblins and exploded a white foamy substance all over them. Instantly the goblins knew where they were hiding. They screamed out in rage and charged. Evallion knelt down. Qu'Tee could see a red aura pulsing around him.

"Blood, Blade, Bone," Evallion hissed. He leaped at the first wave of goblins. His glowing sword slashed and cut deep across the chests of the goblins, cleaving flesh and bone as though it was wet paper.

The second group of goblins leaped on him and began to pound on him. She was going to help him when a corkscrew punch sent one goblin soaring up and over. Evallion was back to his feet. He head butted a goblin with such force that the goblin's neck snapped like a withered twig.

Evallion slammed his sword to the hilt into the face of another goblin. He then grabbed the bloodied blade and ripped the head from the dead goblin. Three goblins pounced him. They managed to separate him from his weapon, but by no means was the barbarian done, he rolled with the impact and balanced himself on all fours like a feral beast. The goblins circled him. Looking for an opening. Qu'Tee moved as Evallion moved, staying out of her friend's line of vision.

The goblins made their move. The remnants of the goblin

cannon fodder rushed him. He blocked and dodged the bashing, slashing strikes of his enemies. A wicked smile crossed his face. They had their fun, now it was his turn!

Evallion's hand snapped out as he gripped one goblin by the face, his fingers pierced through the enraged goblin's eyes and nose. One goblin stabbed a knife into his shoulder. For a mere moment he winced, but the moment passed. He looked over at the goblin who was still holding the weapon. His free hand snapped over and gripped the goblin's face. He growled as he slammed the heads of the goblins together. The sickening sound of skulls cracking, made the cannon fodder goblins wary. They backed away. The warriors stepped forward.

Qu'Tee was surprised. She had heard that the Pit Fighters were strong, but she had no idea that they were like this. She extended a hand towards Evallion on concentrated. A dim aura began to glow around him. His wounds began to heal, slowly though. For her powers to be most effective she had to touch the person. For now she hoped what she was doing would be enough.

The five warriors circled Evallion. Part of the Pit Fighter was telling him that these ones were different. The rest didn't care. He seemed to move in slow motion. His steps seemed like that of an ancient dance. The goblins didn't know what to make of it. Their mistake!

Evallion seemed to slide from where he was to one startled warrior. Before they could do anything, the fighter was savagely relentlessly pummelling the goblin warrior. His bloody fists caving in flesh and bone with each strike. One of the other warriors stabbed his sword through Evallion's back. His head snapped over at the goblin. The goblin released the weapon. Another two stepped forward and stabbed their weapons into his stomach.

The goblins were smiling as they waited for him to fall, but he wasn't falling. He was still standing. He wasn't dying.

Evallion snapped as he drilled his elbow into the ribs of one goblin, sending the beast soaring into the cluster of remaining goblin cannon fodder. He then jerked two of the weapons from his body and watched as the wounds began to slowly heal. He looked at his blood on the weapons and then fixated on the goblins that were still standing. Thought and action were one frightening reality. Light flashed as he did four arching strikes. Blood exploded from the goblins.

"That was amazing!" Qu'Tee remarked. His eyes fixed on her. "Oops," she muttered. She could tell that the man before her was not her friend. This was a vassal fuelled only by rage and fury. A fury that was about to target her. Just then something was lobbed at him. Effortlessly he lashed out and shattered it. A mist exploded and engulfed the fighter. He coughed, staggered then fell over. Qu'Tee looked over and saw her mother. The Elf had an arrow ready in case Sugar missed.

"What did you do to him?" Qu'Tee asked. Evallion was sleeping. "He will wake up right?" she asked hesitantly.

"He'll be fine. Next time, don't try to get his attention," Sugar suggested. Within seconds Evallion stirred. His legs flung up over his head as he flipped himself back up to his feet. Qu'Tee could see that the red aura was still pulsing around him. "Damn," Sugar cursed. Arrow raised his weapon. Evallion raised his hand, motioning for them to stop. Slowly the aura began to fade. He dropped down to one knee and began gasping. "Have to use a stronger dose on you next time," she mused. Evallion gasped as he could vividly feel ever cut, stab and bruise.

"Was that all of them?" he asked between gasps. Qu'Tee nodded as she placed her hands on his chest. She concentrated on his wounds. Once again, the wounds began to heal, the cuts and bruises faded away along with the pain.

"The rest are out cold," Arrow answered. He looked over to the other goblin encampment. His eyes widened as a small fire could be seen. "They noticed us," he warned as he readied his bow. He fired a shot into the distance. One distant goblin seemed to be knocked off his feet.

"That place you mentioned before would be nice," Sugar pointed out. Evallion nodded.

"Take as many of them out as you can then follow us. Do yourself a favour and do not drag your feet. Follow me!" Evallion instructed as the others fled. Arrow focused on the distant goblins. They were still far away, but they were getting closer. He let another arrow sail. Another goblin fell. Without hesitation, he drew and fired, again and again. Each shot hit home. Every time a goblin was knocked down.

The Elf prince reached in his quiver, only three arrows remained. There were still goblins coming. He bit his lip and shook his head.

"I hope he knows what he is doing," he mumbled as he raced off in the direction the others had gone.

Teardrop

Night had come.

The party was holed up in a cave that looked like a barracks of some kind. Along the walls were shelves lined with weapons. The cave was at the end of a long winding tunnel. The mouth of the cave, concealed by a waterfall. Arrow was standing guard. Since they arrived, they had neither seen nor heard from any of the goblins that were pursuing them.

"How many times have I walked by this area?" Arrow asked himself. He looked over his shoulder and saw Evallion. "Why do I get the feeling that this is not a natural cave?" he asked curiously.

"This part was. The rest was dug out," Evallion stated as he sat down beside the Elf prince. Arrow looked over at the human and then over at the waterfall before them. "I'll stand watch," he offered. Arrow nodded and rose to his feet.

"Just to be clear, the treaty of Gaiwin, did forbid any nation from building in another nation's domain," he remarked. "This, is Elf domain last I checked," he added as he walked away. Sugar walked out from around the corner.

"Quite the place you have here," Sugar commented. Evallion shook his head. "This is clearly a staging ground. It makes me wonder how many others the Pit Fighters may have," she added seriously.

"Is Qu'Tee okay?" he asked.

"I need to know. Are the Pit Fighters planning on moving against the Elves," she asked seriously. Evallion was to his feet and reaching for his weapon, his restraint stopped him drawing. He scowled at her and returned his attention to the waterfall. "Touched a nerve it seems," she added as she stood beside him.

"I was at the temple. I heard the plight of the Ken. I know how much they lost. The difference between us, I can see that the other nations have lost a lot too. I know how the Ken see the Pit Fighters. I know how the Elves see us, I even know how the Defenders of the Crown and Pirate nations see us. But, there is one thing that seems to escape all of you. The enemy is here. Have the Ken been fighting it? No, the Ken are trying to save themselves. Have the Elves? No, they have been too busy debating the issue. Everyone has been busy protecting what little they have. Do you know what the Pit Fighters have been doing all this time? Keeping the goblins, orcs and other minions of the demon from overrunning the Veil," he stated defensively.

"Apparently you missed a spot," she commented.

"One nation can only do so much. We informed the Elves that our intelligence noticed increased activity along the border. Know what they said? They said that they could handle goblins. At first, we were content to let them deal with it, then we found out that they were more organized in their tactics," he explained.

"If the goblins took over Elf domain," Sugar began.

"They have a staging ground that touches just about every nation. We couldn't stand by and do nothing," he added grimly.

"Then this is a staging ground, that would be used in the event of the goblins taking over the remnants of the Forest nation," she completed. Evallion looked over at Sugar and sighed. "Sorry if I upset you," she added sincerely.

"Sorry for losing my temper. I respect what you and Qu'Tee are trying to do," he said.

"I would hope so. That is why you are here right?" she mused. He smiled and returned his attention to the waterfall. "I do not see you as a mindless barbarian. If you were, you wouldn't have found the temple to begin with," she said as she walked away. He looked over his shoulder, but she was gone.

Back in the barracks, Qu'Tee was looking up at the roof of the cave. The light from the wall torches made the oddest looking shadows dance across the crevices and support beams. It was then that the face of Boo seemed to just appear.

"Hi Coo'Tee," Boo said. Qu'Tee rolled over and smiled at her goblin friend.

"Hello. What do you think of this place?" she asked. The goblin stuck out its tongue. "I agree, these beds are horrid," she added as her mother walked back in. "Is everything okay?" she asked. Sugar smiled and sat down on the bed.

"More or less. Was talking to our friend about this place," Sugar answered.

"What is this place? Why do they have so many weapons here?" Qu'Tee asked. Sugar sighed and looked over at Arrow. The Elf prince was restocking his arrow supply from the surplus present.

"Evallion explained it to me," she answered.

"Do you trust them?" she asked.

"The Pit Fighter nation? Hard to say. My dealings with them have been, odd. To be perfectly honest, I am a little jaded about humans," she admitted. Qu'Tee lowered her eyes and sighed.

"Because of what happened to me?" she asked.

"That is part of it, not the whole," she reassured as she ran her fingers through her daughter's hair.

"Do you trust him?" Qu'Tee asked hesitantly.

"Do you think I would let him travel with us if I didn't? Besides, he seems just like the boy you described to me so long ago," she added with a wink. Just then Evallion walked in, cursing under his breath. "Problem at the gate?" she asked.

"Worse. I found out how the goblins knew where we were and where we were going," he answered as he threw a bat onto the floor. "We've been followed. This, thing has been spying on us. Probably since we left Lyte Wood," he added seriously.

"Bat familiars, that would explain a lot. Are you sure it belongs to the witch?" he asked. Evallion picked up the dead bat and showed him the underside of the flying cave rat. On its belly was a symbol, the same symbol that Qu'Tee had seen on Arrow's neck. "How did you catch it? They are annoying hard to hit," Arrow asked. Evallion smiled and shook his head.

"Only if they aren't trying to force their way through a wall of water. The witch knows where we are, meaning, we can expect a warm reception tomorrow, Arrow, I see you stocked up. Want to help me move the rest to the tunnel?" the Elf nodded. "Can either of you shoot straight?" Evallion asked.

"Odd question," Sugar teased.

"I think you know what I mean," Evallion rebutted.

"Not as well as the prince," Sugar answered.

"Not well at all. I always skipped class when they did range weapon stuff. What about you Boo? Can you use a bow and arrow?" Qu'Tee admitted. Evallion looked at the goblin and smirked as Boo picked an over sized bow. It was almost comedic seeing the goblin trying to figure out of the bow worked.

"I think Boo should sit this one out, and, no disrespect, but I think you should too," Evallion added. Qu'Tee glared at him. "Hear me out! This isn't going to be a fight. If the goblins try to take this cave they are getting slaughtered. I don't think Boo should be witness to it, and I don't think you want to leave Boo around so many weapons unattended? We wouldn't want him to get hurt right?" he pointed out.

"Nice save," Sugar commented.

"If you get hurt don't expect me to make you feel better," Qu'Tee pouted.

"Doesn't she look too cute when she does that?" Sugar teased. Qu'Tee blushed like a rose. "She is too precious. I'll help move the arrows. Do you want some spears there too?" she asked.

"Good idea," Evallion said, taking advantage of the opportunity to leave.

The rest of the night passed without incident
Early the next morning, they were awakened, by Evallion tripping over a small pile of swords. Almost instantly everyone woke up. It wasn't the desired way he wanted to get their attention, but it worked.

"They're coming," Evallion said from the floor. Boo looked worried as he watched Sugar and Arrow leave. "Don't worry,

Qu'Tee will protect you," Evallion reassured. He got up and hurried out.

"He did make quite the entrance," Qu'Tee said tiredly.

"Eva silly," Boo added.

At the mouth of the cave behind the waterfall, Evallion returned in time to see Arrow sneak back in.

"They have quite a reception out there," Arrow remarked. "Hope we have enough arrows for them," he added.

"They got organized last night. There must have been what? A couple thousand of them?" Evallion asked with a yawn.

"At least. They are building rafts," Arrow remarked with a smirk. "Won't do them much good. Soon as they get near the waterfall, the current will drag them under," he stated rationally.

"Everything the goblins do is aided by magic. I wouldn't count on it. If they are using rafts, they will probably make a bridge of them so that they can rush the cave like a mob. That will be where we come in. the ones that don't lose their footing, or thrust down into the murky depths, get to meet arrows and spears. Hopefully they will tire of this before we keel over from exhaustion," Evallion pointed out.

"I wouldn't put too much stock in that. They don't seem to care about such things. Their fear of their master compels them beyond where reason can reach. Plus there is the fact that they are bound by magic," Arrow pointed out. Evallion frowned.

"Any more optimism out of you and we will send you home," Evallion remarked. "That reminds me, set up the crates of arrows as a barricade. They might make it through, but some of them might be able to throw things," he pointed out. They moved the crates into rows then knelt down behind the first row. "Have I mentioned how much I hate waiting?" he asked curiously.

"Not today," Arrow replied.

"I hate waiting," the fighter complained.

The three waited. Bows ready. Through the roar of the waterfall, they could hear a distant chattering noise. The goblins were making their move. Just then a goblin tried to leap through the wall of water. He made it halfway through before the force of the water slammed him mercilessly into the unforgiving stone floor. It a panic it desperately clawed at the rock but was pushed down.

"It is going to be a long day," Sugar remarked.

Hours passed.
The goblins futile exercise to storm the cave was rewarded by death, either by arrow or drowning.
Night arrived as a crimson sun began to set. The three defenders were by the last row of crates. The tunnel before them was

littered with the bodies of hundreds of dead goblins. Each wave just climbed over the last.

"They must be running low in the ranks," Evallion remarked.

"Or are waiting for reinforcements," Arrow pointed out. Evallion scowled at the Elf.

"Go home if you are going to be that cheery," he rebutted. Wait here. I'll go see if they are still there," he offered. He drew his sword and made his way through the carnage and carefully slipped out around the waterfall.

"Did he tell you what this place was for?" Arrow asked. Sugar looked over at him.

"They aren't planning anything against the Elves," she reassured.

"You trust him?" he asked.

"I do, so does Qu'Tee albeit for different reasons," she answered. The answer didn't seem to sit too well with Arrow. She could tell that the Elf prince was suspicious and understood why. "What happens if the goblins win?" she asked.

"Here or at home?" he asked back.

"Lyte Wood," she clarified.

"The Forest nation would be splintered. The goblins would have our domain as a staging ground. One that touches almost every nation," he answered. "They made this because they thought we would lose?" he asked, almost feeling insulted.

"You know as well as I how humans think, and let us be honest, how well have the Elves been against these goblins?" she pointed out. Arrow groaned and shook his head.

"You have a point," he conceded as Evallion returned. "Anything?" he asked.

"Not a single one is left," he answered. "Look, you two go make sure Qu'Tee is okay," Evallion said with a sigh as he sat down amongst the dead goblins.

"What will you be doing?" Sugar asked.

"Well, I have to recover what arrows are still salvageable, then I have to dispose of this mess," he answered tiredly.

"How? There are a lot of them," Arrow asked.

"The waterfall, to the best of our knowledge is bottomless. It's one of the reasons we chose this spot," he answered.

"And you don't want any help?" Sugar asked, looking at all the goblins that were there.

"No, the responsibility for our being here is mine," he reassured.

Sugar and Arrow made their way from the carnage and vanished from sight. "I am going to be in so much trouble for this," he sighed as he began the tedious effort of retrieving the arrows.

After what felt like hours of work, he managed to save what arrows he could, which, unfortunately was less than half. He also managed to push all of the goblins into the waterfall, save one.

"Hey, you busy?" Qu'Tee asked. He looked over his shoulder and saw the young queen sitting on one of the empty crates.

"Not really," he answered. "What brings you this way?" he asked with a yawn.

"I wanted to see you. That was a silly question," she teased. She looked over her shoulder towards the barracks. "You know, Sugar and Arrow are sleeping," she pointed out.

"Sounds like a plan," he remarked. He began to walk towards the barracks. Her arm extended blocking his way. "Look if you want to train or something, can it wait until morning?" he asked. Qu'Tee smiled at him with a mischievous look in her eye.

"I didn't want to train silly," she said coyly as she slipped behind him and rested her chin on his shoulder. Evallion blushed and backed away from her. "Why are you acting like that?" she asked curiously.

"I could ask the same," he rebutted.

"What? Is it wrong for me to want to show the man I love how much I love him?" she asked. He could feel his heart in his throat. "Hey! You're blushing!" she said with a giggle. He sighed and waved a finger at her.

"You almost had me going there," he said.

"Oh. You think I'm joking?" she asked timidly. There was a look of hurt in her eyes. "You, you probably don't like me that way. You just see me like one of the guys," she said as she walked over and frowned at him. "But I'm not a guy in case you didn't notice," she added.

"I, noticed," he affirmed modestly.

"I never thanked you for saving me back in Lyte Wood," she pointed out. Evallion almost fell over, he was feeling dizzy and light headed. This was too much to take in all at once. He quickly looked away.

"I never expected anything," he replied.

"Come to me hero," a soft voice whispered. He looked around. Qu'Tee blinked as she watched Evallion searching the crates and by the cave entrance.

"Evallion? What are you doing?" she asked hesitantly.

"Did you hear something?" he asked seriously. Qu'Tee frowned and folded her arms across her chest.

"If you don't want to fool around you could just say so," she said coldly. He fell over. "I mean honestly. That is so lame," she added.

"But I swear," he began.

"I want you baby," the voice whispered to him again. He spun around looking for the source of the voice. That was when he noticed he had missed one goblin.

"Qu'Tee, wait here," he instructed. She looked bored as she leaned against one of the crates. She watched as Evallion drew his sword and stalked his way towards the dead goblin. He stalked closer, closer still. Slowly he reached towards the goblin. His hand was closer and closer.

"What are you doing?" Qu'Tee asked. Evallion jumped straight up. His head left a hole in the rocky surface above him. He fell down and was instantly was up to his feet.

"Are you trying to make my heart explode?" he exclaimed.

"But I wanted to kiss you," she pouted. He blushed, she leaned forward and saw the expression on his face. "Don't you want to kiss me?' she asked.

"Well, yes," he admitted.

"Then why?" she began but stopped. "Oh my, you never kissed a girl before have you?' she asked curiously. He looked seriously flustered.

"Of course, lots of times," he said defensively. She smiled at him and closed her eyes.

"Then kiss me silly," she offered. Hesitantly he reached towards her, unsure if he should hold her or not. He slowly leaned forward. He could hear her breathing. He could hear his heart jack hammering in his chest.

"Take me. I want you so bad," the soft voice whispered with a giggle. He spun around. His weapon flashed as he stabbed it into the dead goblin. He gasped as he turned the goblin over. Its eyes opened. He realized too late, it was no goblin!

The goblin's form exploded into a mass of roots, mud and vines. He desperately slashed at the vines and roots, but there were too many. Soon the beast had him pinned to the wall. He tried everything in his power to get free, but the beast had him. It was then that he realized something.

"Qu'Tee! Get out of here!" he exclaimed. It was the that Qu'Tee giggled as she danced over and stood before him. "Qu'Tee?" he asked passively. She giggled and shook her head. She began to seductively dance before her captive audience. The air around her began to sparkle. An aura began to glow around her. The aura flashed. The woman before him wasn't Qu'Tee, it was the witch Samantha.

"I have to say, you are something else," she said seductively. Every movement she made seemed to hypnotic, so sensual. "When I heard there was a barbarian in her ranks, I didn't think much of it. But you, you are different, special," she added. She stretched her arms out and arched her back, thrusting her chest forward. Instantly he looked away. Samantha giggled as she placed a finger on his chin and moved his head so that he was looking at her. "I think you like what you see. Do you see," she began as she traced a finger down his chest. "Do you see something in particular?" she teased. His eyes widened as her hand found something.

"I don't, uh, uhm," he stammered. But he could find the words. She smiled at him, amused by how easily she had him completely at her tender mercies.

"You have a girlfriend?" she asked curiously. He nodded. "You must like her a lot," she seemed to sniff his neck. "She, doesn't have to know. I won't tell. I know how to keep secrets. I know you want to," she pointed out making him blush.

"I'm not like that," he reassured. She pouted. She held her hands together and looked at him as though he was just too precious.

"It must be true love," she began as she undid the knot in the front of her top. Slowly she pulled the cord from her top exposing her ample breasts. He quickly closed his eyes as if sensing the beating he would get if he stared or peeked. "Don't you like girls?" she teased, touching the back of her hand to his cheek.

"I told you," he began.

"I told you, I won't tell. I'll never tell. I can take you places you never imagined. I can take your body to levels that no woman could ever imagine taking you," she whispered seductively. Her words danced in his mind like an whispering echo. Her scent was so powerful, so intoxicating that he could barely think. Hesitantly he opened his eyes. Her eyes seemed to paralyze him. It was that he realized the vines and roots that had bound him were gone. "Do you want me?" she whispered to him.

No. Evallion though. He tried to speak but no sound came out.. it was then that he felt his arms slowly rising up. His hands reaching for her. What am I doing? He thought as he tried to fight it. But it was no use. His arms slowly wrapped around her. She smiled at him playfully.

"I thought you might come around. Trust me honey, the world will seem so different when I am done with you," she reassured as she wrapped her arms around him and began to passionately kiss him. His mind felt as though it was on fire. His body began to shake. It was only then that he sensed how much trouble he was in. the world around him seemed to start spinning. His eyes seemed to space out as darkness totally engulfed him.

Under the Spell

Just then, a crate smashed into the back of Evallion's head. The witch hopped away from the young fighter. She looked down at the unconscious pit fighter then smiled at the young Ken queen.

"I see, you must be the jealous type," Samantha mocked.

"Who are you and why are you here?" Qu'Tee demanded as she stood between Evallion and the witch. Samantha looked hurt by the question. The witch removed her large, stereotypical witch's hat and bowed to the queen.

"How rude of me. I am known as Samantha, last survivor of the Order of the Hand. My friends call me Sam the Hand witch," she added playfully. Just then Arrow and Sugar hurried out. "Hey, y'all, the gangs all here," she added with a giggle. Arrow instantly had his bow armed and aimed.

"I must confess, you are by far the oddest gathering I have seen. Two Ken, a goblin, an Elf and a barbarian. Sounds like the cast for a play. Hey! Can I play the part of the witch?" she asked gleefully. Arrow fired. Her hand shot up and caught the projectile. He had another arrow ready.

"Where is my sister witch?" he demanded.

"Where she has been for quite some time, in deep, deep trouble. But, then again, so are you," she pointed out. He fired. Sam dodged to the side and caught that shot as well. "Do you ever get tired of wasting arrows like that?" she mocked, tossing the arrows aside.

"Why are you here?" Sugar asked.

"Maybe I was lonely? I mean, the goblins are good slaves, but they are poor company," she replied as she began to playfully dance around as though they weren't even there.

"I doubt that," Sugar replied. Sam continued to dance. "Excuse me?" she added. The witch stopped dancing and looked at them. "Why are you here?' she asked again. The witch sat down on the floor. Her crystal ball appeared in one hand, a wand in the other.

"I'm glad you asked," she began, tapping the wand to the crystal. Within the crystal a crudely printed sign was held up. It looked as though it was printed by a two year old. "Oh, the genie of the crystal is speaking to me," she added with a giggle. Let's see, a message! I love messages!" she added. The sign seemed to float out from the crystal and landed on the floor before the adventurers.

"Do as the witch says or the boy dies?" Sugar read out loud. Qu'Tee looked at Evallion. He wasn't moving, his breathing was shallow, his aura, slowly leaving his form. "What did you do to him?" she demanded. The witch smiled as she tapped the wand to the crystal ball again.

"I think the genie of the crystal knows the answer to that and many more," she mused. Another sign appeared. It slid out and landed before Arrow. "Oh my. It seems someone poisoned him. That's not good," the witch read aloud and remarked.

"No. I won't let you take him from me," Qu'Tee said. The witch laughed as the Ken queen knelt down beside her friend. The crystal ball and wand vanished.

"You are wasting your time dear. He is beyond your reach, but, I can save him," the witch pointed out. Qu'Tee ignored the witch. An aura began to glow around the two. "You are wasting your time," the witch pointed out.

"Come back to me," Qu'Tee whispered. She concentrated on her friend, trying to see the poison that was killing her friend. "It's not working," she strained. The witch shrugged her shoulders.

"I said that didn't I? Look, how about we make a trade of sort? For a limited time only, you too can have our patented witch's sure poison potion. Known to stimulate the sense and cure all the nasty side affects that poison induces. You know like throwing up and dying. What would such a miracle potion cost you ask? Why it costs nothing. If you act now, you get this potion and a picture painted by me!" she added gleefully as a painting of a crude looking smiley face appeared in her other hand. "I did it all by myself," she added proudly.

"You say that it costs nothing, why do I get the feeling there is more to this than that?" Sugar asked. Sam pouted as the painting and potion vanished.

"That was rude," the witch pointed out. "Just for that the price went up. If you want the potion now," the witch began as she moved her finger around and then pointed at Arrow. "You want the potion, I get the Elf prince. I have a princess, a prince would make my collection complete. "If you throw in the Ken queen I'll throw in the painting," the witch added as the painting reappeared before them. "I'm telling you, it will be a collector's item. One of a kind even," she remarked.

"I can feel him," Qu'Tee remarked. The witch looked down at the Ken queen and was befuddled at what she was witnessing. The eyes of the barbarian were beginning to slowly open. "He's fighting it," she added.

"That isn't possible," the witch said in disbelief.

"So you keep saying," Arrow remarked. "Apparently you were mistaken," he added. The witch fumed. She pointed at Evallion as if trying to ensnare him with a spell, but the aura prevented anything from working.

"That little bitch will be a problem. Seems master was right," the witch said as her fingers elongated into bony claws. With inhuman speed she leaped at the Ken queen. Qu'Tee was too focused on what she was doing to notice. Sugar threw a potion at the airborne attacker. The vial shattered as it hit her face. Arrow grabbed a spear and leaped at the witch, driving the point into her chest. His momentum carried them away from Qu'Tee and Evallion. He landed gracefully and slammed Samantha hard into the floor. He twisted the spear. The witch twitched and gasped, then stopped moving. Arrow slowly got up and began to walk away. The witch's eyes opened.

"Oh honey, you play so rough, I like that," she giggles as she sat up. She moaned as she pulled the spear free. "I can tell that you enjoyed, sticking it so deep inside me like that," she teased. Her body below the waist mutated into a ball of mud, vines and roots. The party watched as the witch became a beast that was half woman and half spider.

"She isn't the witch. She's just a puppet," Arrow cursed.

"I had a hunch she was," Sugar remarked. The mutated beast turned its attention to Qu'Tee's mother. "I mean, why would she risk her life?" she added. The beast wiped the dripping liquid from her face.

"I am no weed," the beast remarked.

"That wasn't the potion I used. It is a diluted acid. It gets soaked into the skin then spreads like a poison. By now you should be starting to feel it," Sugar pointed out. The beast looked confused. The witch/beast looked at the back of her hand, veins were starting to turn black and pulse. "Tell your master we are coming," she added coldly.

"No! I will not fail. Will kill," the beast slurred. It staggered towards Qu'Tee. It fell and began to twitch. Still it tried to drag itself towards the Ken queen. "Must, kill," it gasped, then slumped over. Its hand mere inches away from Qu'Tee. Arrow, Boo and Sugar watched as the beast rapidly decayed and then turned into a pile of ashes.

"How are you feeling?" Qu'Tee asked. Evallion groaned as Sugar and Arrow helped him up. He looked dizzy and still quiet sick, but he was alive.

"Terrible, but alive. Thanks," he answered.

"Do you have anything that might help?" Arrow asked Sugar. The Ken alchemist, looked at the sick looking Pit Fighter.

"Well, without knowing what the poison was from it would just be guess work," she pointed out.

"You have good instincts," Evallion slurred. "Take a guess," he added. Sugar sighed as she began to fish around inside her sleeve.

"No, not that, no, that might help later, no, ah! Here we go," she said as she pulled out a small blue vial. "As I said, this is just a guess. It might make you feel worse," she warned. Evallion coughed weakly.

"I sincerely doubt that is possible," he rebutted. He took the potion from her and downed it. He gasped and almost threw up. "My god! That tasted awful! What was that?" he groaned.

"Do you really want to know?" she challenged. He thought for a moment.

"On second thought no," he answered. He looked at his hands. His breathing began to slow down to normal. "Whatever that was, it seemed to do the trick," he added with a weak smile.

"Temporary fix unfortunately. Until we get that poison out of your system, you will still be at risk. Or, if we can find out what poison she used, I can make the antidote," Sugar warned. Evallion nodded and looked over at Qu'Tee who was scowling at him.

"Uh, did I do something?" he hesitantly asked. Qu'Tee got up and stood inches away from him.

"I should ask you that. When I came in you had your hands all over that witch," she replied. Arrow slipped away from Evallion as did Sugar.

"I don't remember a thing. Last thing I remember was cleaning the dead from the cave," Evallion reassured. Qu'Tee didn't look convinced. Arrow and Sugar smiled and backed away from the happy couple.

"I think we should clean up the barracks," Arrow suggested

"Good idea," she affirmed as they left the two to argue.

A short while later, in her lair, watching her crystal ball. She looked unamused as she watched the party of adventurers walking along the lake. It seemed as though Qu'Tee and Evallion were still enjoying their little tiff.

The witch sighed as she traced her finger over the surface of the crystal. She had grossly underestimated them. She made a mistake. It would not happen again.

"They are a crafty bunch of trouble makers," she said tiredly. She waved her hand over the crystal. The image went black. Slowly she floated over and sat down on a table near to a shelf full of oddities. She looked over at a severed head in a jar. "I mean, how was she able to save him? He should be dead. There should be no way her paltry gifts should have been able to help him. In fact, they should have done the opposite," she pondered. She quickly grabbed the jar and held it close to her ear, as though listening. "What? Use that to advance my own selfish needs? How?" she asked. She nodded as she listened to the silent jar. "I see. Well I guess with ideas like that, that would explain why you are a disembodied head and I am not," she rebutted as she threw the severed head into the fireplace. The glass shattered and a fireball wafted up engulfing the severed head. Within seconds the fire returned to normal.

The witch slumped forward and hit her wrists against her forehead. She needed to think. She needed a plan. She needed to do something, but the voices in her head were too chaotic. There was too much noise.

"Problem?" a familiar voice almost hissed. She looked over her shoulder and saw an unamused demonic frog glaring at her. "I told you to not take her lightly," he reminded. She shook her head and began rocking back and forth. "Get your act together!" his voice echoed in her mind. She fell off the table holding her head. Slowly the noise faded away.

"I, misjudged her. I sought to break her spirit by killing the love of her life. I had no idea, that her magic was at that stage," Sam said as she slowly limped over to where he was. "But, I always have a back up plan," she reassured.

"Do you?" he challenged.

"Of course. I dare not say it out loud just now though. They have spies everywhere. If they find out it will ruin everything," she replied suspiciously as she looked around frantically. Bo'Glin shook his head.

"I leave it in your, capable hands," he replied as he vanished into the shadows of the room. The witch mimicked the lording manner that she had been spoken to then sat back down on the table.

"I hate that pompous frog," with a wave of her hand, her large crystal ball floated over and hovered over her hand. She tapped the surface of the crystal with her finger. A magical glow once again filled the room. Within the crystal she saw Qu'Tee. She was still pouting. "I want to make her suffer. How best to do that?" she asked herself as the image seemed to pan over to Evallion. "He is the key," she began. She pondered the ways to use Evallion against her. She smiled a sick smile as she traced a finger over the image of Evallion. "Break her heart, break her spirit, break her body. If I seduce him, make him do such deliciously indecent things to me in front of her. That might do the trick. Even if he was enslaved, she would never be able to look at him without seeing my face," she remarked. She snapped her fingers. "I have an even better idea! What I said before, plus, having her tortured by those creative goblin inquisitors. They do so love their work," she corrected.

Sam hoped from the tabled and began to frantically knock things from the shelves until she found a scroll and a quill. A wild look consumed her as she stabbed the quill into her arm. A trickle of blood dripped from the self inflicted wound.

"I have to write this shit down. That one is definitely a keeper," she giggled insanely as she wrote down her idea. She looked up at the crystal ball and smiled at the unsuspecting travellers. "Take your time kids. The longer you take, the more fun we will have we you get here," she reassured as she continued to write, using her own poisonous blood as ink.

The Way of the Woods

About two days had passed since the unpleasant incident at the cave had occurred. What also was unpleasant was the fact that Sugar had yet to find the cure to the poison that was killing Evallion slowly. No matter what they tried, be it potion or magic, nothing seemed to keep the sickness at bay.

"It is getting worse," Qu'Tee said. Evallion leaned against a tree and did what he could to not think about it. "At this rate he won't make it," she began but stopped. "We have to do something," she protested.

"Dear, without knowing what poison is used, I can't cure it. And if your magic can't heal him, it means that a magic equal to or greater than yours is at work preventing it," Sugar pointed out.

"I'll be fine. It isn't as bad as it looks," Evallion reassured. "How can you say that?" Qu'Tee rebutted. "You are barely able to stand," she added. Evallion took a deep breath, concentrated on keeping himself ahead of the sickness and pain. Qu'Tee sighed. She was going to protest but, Sugar placed a hand on her shoulder.

"We aren't out of options yet. Do not lose hope," she reassured.

Back in her lair, the Hand witch Samantha was playfully rolling around on oversized pillows and cushions. She scampered from the small mountain of pillows and looked at the crystal ball upside down.

"Everything is upside down," she remarked. She turned the ball around so that it was the right way. "Much better," she added. She giggled insanely as she saw how everyone was fussing over Evallion. "So worried. So worried. The way they fuss and care for him, it just gets me right here," she said mockingly placing a hand on her chest. "Or some place like that," she added. She rolled over, holding the crystal at arms length. "I never anticipated the spell lasting this long. Odd that. Then again I had no idea that she could revive him. I guess I will have to try to make the best of a bad situation," she pointed out. "Elfy oh little pwetty Elfy?" the witch asked. She looked over at the Elf princess was. She was dressed like a harem girl and was manacled to the floor. Sam playfully bounced from the pillows and crawled over to where the passive prisoner was. "I want to play," she added with a friendly smile.

"Please just kill me," the Elf was shaking as the witch reached for her. The witch moved a rogue strand of hair from her face, then gently traced the back of her hand across the Elf's cheek.

"That wouldn't be fun," Sam said. He hand jolted and gripped the Elf princess by the throat. Effortlessly she lifted her prisoner up. The Elf struggled against the choking grip. The witch smiled. "Looks to me like someone still wants to live," she mocked. She dropped the Elf onto some pillows. "Don't worry. All of this, your time in this little drama, all of your suffering, all of it, will be over soon," Samantha reassured.

"Why are you doing this?" the Elf strained, coughing up a bit of blood.

"Because I can? Because I want to? I honestly don't know. It isn't for me to say. All you need to know is that, your brother is coming, just like I promised. So don't be a selfish little bitch. You behave, you be a good girl and you might live long enough to see him," the witch reassured. "Enough serious time!" she added. Before the Elf could react, the witch slammed a large pillow across her face, knocking her down. Pillow fight!" she said triumphantly, she readied to hit the Elf again, but she was out cold. "Pomph I say. Pomph and pomph again," she pouted. She sighed as she rolled along the cushion and pillow covered floor until she was by her crystal again. "I hope I didn't miss the best part," she added as she focused all of her attention on the party of adventurers that were on their way to see her.

Back in the forest, the party was taking another break because of the seriousness of Evallion's deteriorating condition. The proud Pit Fighter leaned against a near by tree. He was doing his best to not let his condition take him down, but it was a fight he was losing.

"Sorry about this," he said between gasps.

"Stop saying that or I will bop you," Qu'Tee retorted.

"So," he began. Her staff instantly went up into Evallion

bopping position. He raised his hands defensively and smiled meekly.

"I give up. You win," he relented. It was then that something. He motioned for the others to remain still. He concentrated, then leaped up into the braches of the tree above him. Seconds later he fell ungracefully back down to the ground.

"If you are trying to impress me, bad effort," Qu'Tee pointed out. It was then that the Pit Fighter showed a bat familiar he had crushed in his clenched fist. "Another familiar?" she asked hesitantly.

"We must be getting close," Sugar added.

Back in her lair…

The witch groaned as she began to hit the crystal that seemed to turn black.

"Damn it! I paid the bill last month. Why did they cut off my reception? How rude," the witch pouted. She looked up at the roof then slowly sat up. "Oh well. Some times, my perfectionism is my bane.
She rolled over and moved the cushions and pillows aside. On the floor was a detailed map of the Elf territory between her location and Lyte Wood.

"Eenie, meanie, miney, moe, which direction did they go?" she playfully sang as she moved her finger around on the map.

"They were at a cave thing here," she said placing her finger by the lake. "Then they walkied all the way to here," she said, tracing a path to where the bat familiar last saw them. "Quite a walk for the walking dead. They are making pretty good time. They might even get here within two days if they manage to keep this pace up," she pointed out.

In her mind she could see a dark cave.
"Go forth my batty bats. I am missing my new favourite show and will feed you to goblins if I miss something really good!" she threatened. The darkness of the cave was broken by hundreds of red eyes opening. Dozens upon dozens of bats swarmed their way out of the cave to find the witch's prey. Samantha sighed and opened her eyes. "And now, we wait, and wait and wait and wait," the witch sang as she seemed to play with the shadows that danced on the roof.

Back in the forest, the party took cover as the swarm of bats flew over them.

"We must be really close," Arrow pointed out.

"She definitely didn't like losing that familiar," Sugar added.

"Can they hear us?" Qu'Tee asked.

"No, bat familiars are used for their eyes. They can hear, but it is more distorted noise to them. They can't make out specific sounds. It is their only drawback," Arrow reassured. "If we don't want to be watched, we will have to be careful. Those bats will be everywhere," he added. Evallion motioned for him to be quiet.

"Can you hear that?" Evallion asked. Qu'Tee listened, but could hear nothing, neither could Sugar. Arrow listened for a few seconds. It was then that he could hear it too. "So I wasn't hearing things?" he asked.

"You put an Elf to shame," Arrow remarked.

"Must be something that witch did to me," Evallion replied.

"What are you boys talking about?" Sugar asked.

"Ceremony, big one, not far from here, that way," Evallion said, pointing in the direction of the noise.

"What kind of ceremony?" Qu'Tee asked.

"Goblin variety. They must have set up camp near by," Arrow answered. "There is a chance the witch may be there, but I doubt it," he added.

"If there are goblins celebrating though," Evallion pointed out. Arrow understood.

"There must be a reason," the Elf concluded. Cautiously they made their way through the forest. As they drew closer, Qu'Tee and Sugar could hear it too. Tribal drums, goblins cheering and chanting.

"There seems to be a clearing up ahead," Arrow said as they cautiously made their way to where the tree line seemed to stop.

"By the lady," Qu'Tee whispered.

Before them was a carved out canyon. Along the ridge was a winding path that led down to a primitive looking city by human standards, but disturbingly advanced by goblin standards. In the streets hordes of goblins were cheering as several banners were being carried and displayed.

"I found out why they are celebrating," Arrow said grimly. "They are celebrating their imminent victory over the Elves. They are planning their final assault," he added.

"I'm seeing mills, factories, mines, forges, armouries," Sugar added.

"How do you know that reason they are celebrating?" Qu'Tee asked.
"Those banners, that are in the streets now, those are tribal and are only present when the chief is near," Arrow began. "The leaders are here," he began as he looked over towards the rest of the party. "If they were gone," he continued.

"Might disrupt their plans for Lyte Wood. Might buy us more time," Sugar pointed out. The two elders looked over at Qu'Tee.

"Why are you looking at me like that?" the Ken queen asked

hesitantly.

"It is your call. This detour is risky and takes us in a direction away from where that bat swarm came from," Sugar pointed out. Qu'Tee looked at the goblin city below.

"If we can do something here, it will buy the Elves some time, and perhaps us as well," Qu'Tee reassured. The elders nodded as the group began to discuss possible courses of action. After what seemed like hours, they came to one choice.

"It is risky, but if we can make this happen, it will hinder their war efforts," Evallion admitted.

"Hugely," Arrow added.

"At least until they chose a new leader to step up," Sugar added.

"That could take weeks the way goblins are. If we haven't dealt with the witch by then, it won't matter," Arrow pointed out. Evallion nodded as he got up.

"I'll do it," he stated seriously.

"In your condition?" Sugar rebutted.

"Let us review, you are sick, poisoned and wounded. There is one way into that place in case you didn't notice. It is a fortified area with hundreds of goblins," she pointed out, clearly not happy with the idea of him going in.

"To get this job done, two of us are needed. If we fail, that leaves two to continue on to deal with the witch," he pointed out.

"Then I'm going with you," Qu'Tee replied without a second thought.

"You have bigger game targeted than this city. You have a bigger job on your plate. This is too risky for you," Evallion pointed out as he looked over at Sugar. "But I would wager you have done this sort of thing before. Shall we go?" he asked curiously.

Assassins

Down in the canyon city, Evallion and Sugar were concealed in the shadows of what appeared to be a factory of some kind. On several occasions the two were almost discovered but due to the activities they manage to remain unnoticed.

"You sure that you are up to this?" Sugar asked, seeing that Evallion was still a little shaky. The fighter nodded.

"You just keep your end and let me worry about mine," he reassured. "You make that potion we spoke of and just leave the rest to me," he stated confidently. Sugar nodded as they stalked their way through the alleys and shadows. They two stopped as a small band of goblins seemed to stop what they were doing and fixated on them. Evallion slowly stepped in front of Sugar as the goblins made their way towards them. Just then a chicken ran by and was promptly followed by what appeared to be a goblin butcher. The goblins that seemed to notice them lost interest and joined in the chicken chase.

"That was kind of close," Sugar pointed out.

"That guy looked like a cook. Would the ingredients we need be where he came from?" Evallion asked. Sugar thought for a moment then nodded.

"Most of them should be. The ones he doesn't have I should," she reassured. The two seemed to meld into the shadows. Silently they stalked behind the buildings until they happened onto a building that had a stink that could only be described as putrid.

"What is that smell?" Evallion asked, his eyes watering. Sugar wiped her eyes and covered her nose and mouth.

"You don't want to know. Wait here. What I need should be in here. Nothing else could stink like that," she replied as she checked in through one window. The structure seemed empty. She opened the window and slinked inside. "You wait here," she added. Evallion didn't argue. If the stench around the building was THAT bad, he could only imagine how bad it could be inside.

"Don't be too long," he instructed.

"You think I like it in here? Just be alert and tell me if company is coming," Sugar rebutted curtly. Evallion tried not to think about how the poison was affecting him. He tried not to think about how his injuries were killing him. But the unbearable stench was doing horrific things to his focus. He leaned against the nearest building, trying not to breath in too deeply. It was then that he saw the goblins from before, the ones that almost spotted them. They were going into the alley that they had just been hiding in,

"You might want to pick up your pace," Evallion suggested.

"A few minutes," her voice answered. He watched as the goblins seemed to leave the alley. They were looking for what they noticed before.

"I don't think we have that," he pointed out. She climbed out the window and gasped. He grabbed her by the wrist and quickly ran them in the opposite direction of the goblins that were looking for them.

After a few minutes they were in a spot where the air quality was notably better.

"My poor nose," Sugar complained. "It will take a week of bathing to wash this stink off," she added indignantly. "You owe me big time," she added.

"Whatever. Did you have time to make it?" he rebutted. She carefully took out a vial. In it was a bubbling black potion. It was corked.

"Whatever you do, be higher than the cloud this gives off. If you aren't, well, just make sure you are," she explained. He took the potion and put it into one of his pockets.

"If I'm not, I die, I'm dead, game over. I get it," he reassured. "You did your part, get out. I'll meet you up top," he replied seriously.

"What if you?" she began.

"Failure is not an option. And if you are worried about me doing something stupid, I wouldn't. Qu'Tee is counting on me. I won't let her down," he reassured. Sugar sighed and shook her head.

"If I can't talk some sense into you, I will wish you luck," she said politely. She bowed to him then vanished into the shadows behind them. Evallion sighed as he took a few deep breaths. He was still feeling dizzy. The fumes that came from that one building did not help his condition.

"This will not be pretty," he said to himself. He took a step but fell. His knees felt like noodles. "No. I will not die in a pit like this," he growled. He pushed himself into that place beyond reason and pain. Feel sick or hurt later. He had work to do now. He slowly got up. He looked forward and saw a goblin staring right art him. "great," he muttered. The goblin started screaming and motioning for others to notice. Evallion vanished into the shadows and hurried towards the tower like structure that had ten banners atop it.

After almost half an hour of stealthily running through the alleys, climbing cautious across ropes over the goblin roads, making his way up and down ladders, across rooftops, he finally made it to the building in question.

"If I didn't want these bastards dead before I sure as hell do now. I must have gone over every square inch of this miserable place," he complained. He scaled the wall and made his way into the top through one of the upper windows. He clung to the rafters and looked down below. It was at least a three story drop.

Below him was a large table. On it was a detailed map. He couldn't understand the writing on it, but he remembered where they were. He looked loosely and saw one dotted line that led from the lake to the spot where the goblin city was.

If that symbol is a city. He thought as he looked at how many of the symbols matched it. There were dozens of them. There are a lot of these cities. He thought. The doors slammed open. Two goblin foot soldiers went in and looked around, but not up. Once they were sure the room was safe they exited.

Then, Evallion silently watched as a goblin warlord stalked his way into the room. He had heard of goblin warlords, but this was the first time he saw one that closely. Hopefully he wouldn't have to again. Another then entered, we was painted differently. Then another and another until there were ten of them standing around the table. Once the doors closed they began to converse in a language he had never heard before.

Evallion coiled his legs around the rafter support beam and hung from it like a bat. He reached into his pocket and carefully removed the potion. He looked at it and noticed that the gas inside the vial had dissolved half of the cork.

"Potent stuff. Hope it works," he muttered as he dropped it. It was then, as though in slow motion that the goblins realized there was an intruder. Slowly they all looked up as the potion shattered. The liquid kissed the air and exploded into a thick, choking toxic cloud.

Evallion's eyes bulged as the cloud kept rising higher and higher. He pulled himself up onto the beam he was clinging too. The gas still rose up. He stood up. Stood on his toes and pressed his chin to the roof. The gas was already passed his hips and rising. Now it was up to his chest, his neck. It was only when then that the gas started to level off at eye level. From the corner of his eye he could see that the only reason it didn't go higher was because the rest had gone out the window.

"That was too close," he muttered as the cloud began to shrink. Once the last of the gas was gone, he dropped himself down to the table. Due to his condition his landing was less than graceful. Carefully he pulled himself up. He looked around at the ten dead goblin warlords. He sat up and shook off the panic, illness and other such maladies that were vexing him. "Part two of plan done time for part three," he began but stopped. He looked at the table and smiled at the map. He folded up the map and slipped it inside his armour. "Something tells me I might need that later," he said as he looked at the dead goblins around him. Time to make this look nasty," he remarked.

A short while later, the goblins standing guard entered the room to make sure everything was okay. When they saw the warlords dead in what appeared to be a chaotic fight between the warlords they screamed out.

In an alley a short distance away, Evallion watched the tower. He couldn't leave until he was sure the plan worked. He watched as goblins of each warlord began to argue, blaming each other for the deaths of the warlords. He smiled at his handiwork.

"Part three, success," he said to himself. He tensed up and looked over to his right. A startled goblin looked over at him. For a moment the two just stared at each other. Before the goblin could cry out. Evallion grabbed the goblin and effortlessly broke its neck. "Have to hurry or I will get caught in the chaos," he muttered as he raced away through the shadows that hugged the canyon wall.

A couple hours had passed.
Back where Qu'Tee and the others were waiting, the Ken queen was getting impatient and anxious. This was taking far too long.

"He's been down there too long," she stated.

"Do you think he succeeded?" Arrow asked. It was then that they noticed that there was a small riot in effect by the tower with all the banners. "Never mind," he added.

"He could be down there! We need to get him out of there," Qu'Tee pointed out. As she and the others debated the issue, they failed to notice that Evallion was leaning against a tree behind them.

"I wouldn't advise going down there," Evallion pointed out. They stopped talking and looked over at him. "It a nasty mess down there," he pointed out. Qu'Tee rushed over and hugged him tightly.

"You had me worried you creep!" she complained.

"That might have gotten the witch's attention. We should get going," Arrow pointed out. Qu'Tee then pushed Evallion away and covered her nose.

"You stink!" she complained. Evallion shrugged his shoulders. In his weakened condition he managed to infiltrate a fortified goblin infested canyon, assassinate ten goblin warlords and get out undetected. Did she acknowledge that? No, all she could recognize was that he stunk.

He let it go as they made their way towards where they believed the witch was hiding. Unbeknownst to them, one of the bats they had evaded earlier had found them and was following them closely.

Back in the lair of the witch, she was smiling at the her crystal ball. She then started jumping up and down like a giddy schoolgirl.

"Goody, goody! He's here at last," she sung happily as she watched as an unmoving man was tossed into an empty cell. Just then the crystal flashed. The image changed and showed the party on route to her domain. They were close. Less than a day away. "Oh the pieces are falling together marvellously," she added as she danced over to where the Elf princess was. She spun around on her toe and balanced herself before her captive and held the crystal between them. "Look precious, brother dearest is almost here," she added with a wicked smile. "The master, he said they had to die, but he never said how fast," she whispered naughtily.

"Brother," the Elf princess whispered timidly as she reached for the crystal. The witch scowled, spun around and kicked the Elf across the face. She would have hit the wall were she not manacled to the floor. The sound of a bone snapping filled the lair.

"Never touch my toys slave," Samantha hissed. She snapped her fingers. Two goblin warlords hurried in and bowed. "Torture the bitch until I send for her," she ordered coldly. She watched as the goblins unchained the trembling Elf and dragged her away. Samantha looked disgusted and pissed. "Don't worry precious, you won't be lonely anymore. You will have company until the day you, and every other miserable sharp eared Elf, is rotting in a shallow grave," she hissed. Her crystal ball violently exploded. She coughed as she waved the magical smoke away. "I go through more crystal balls that way. Manservant Albert, it happened again?" she called out. Another goblin with fake press on angel wings struggled to carry another crystal ball that was the same size as he was. The witch giggled as the goblin dropped it onto a large pillow. "Heavenly," she mused as the panting goblin bowed and scurried away before her mood changed.

The Village of Briar

Time seemed to stand still for the heroes as they stood on the outskirts of the Elf village once known as Briar. The taint of evil was thick in the air. The Elf prince knelt down and grabbed a handful of rancid soil. His hand began shake.

"She is here," Arrow said through gritted teeth. Sugar knelt down beside him and studied the ground. "You see something?" he asked, trying to stay focused, to not lose control.

"Evil has walked here," she stated seriously.

"Why do I get the feeling you aren't talking about the witch we are after?" Evallion remarked. Qu'Tee took a deep breath, having a small notion of what her mother was talking about.

"Is the demon here?" Qu'Tee asked.

"He was," Sugar answered as she placed her palm against the soil. "But I seriously doubt he is here now," she reassured. Qu'Tee sighed. She knew that the path she was on would place her before the demon Bo'Glin, but she was quite relieved to know that the day in question was not today. Evallion put his mask on and looked around at the surroundings.

The fields were in a state of decay and overrun with dying weeds. The buildings were desecrated and in a state of decay. Some of them looked vandalized by goblins or other such beasts. Somewhere in this long dead place, the witch they were hunting was hiding.

Qu'Tee looked around as well. She then stepped between the two time ravaged statues that marked the entrance to the village. A bright light blinded her for a moment, she staggered back and was caught by her mother.

"What happened?" Qu'Tee asked, wiping her eyes.

"I was going to ask you the same question," Sugar rebutted. Qu'Tee's eyes widened in modest disbelief as she stepped away from her mother. She felt light, almost as though she was floating, yet not.

All around her bright auras glowed around everything but her friends. She looked around at the structures. They looked new and untouched. The fields were being tended and maintained. All around her, Elves tended to their business as though nothing was wrong.

But something about this screamed at her. It was wrong. She walked over towards one Elf that was walking by. Her hand passed through him as though he was a ghost. Or was he. Two Elf children that were running through the streets headed straight for her. There was no time to move. Like phantoms, they passed through her as though she wasn't there.

Qu'Tee tried to speak, but no sound came out. It was then that an ill feeling came over her. Hesitantly she looked over her shoulder and looked over at her mother. It was then that she noticed her mother holding her body! In a panic she began to run towards her mother. But something stopped her. She looked to the forest behind her mother. On the path walking towards the village was a cloaked woman.

What is going on? Qu'Tee thought. What is happening to me? Her mind was racing as she tried to make sense of what was going on. The children that were running through the streets ran through her again. It was a most unnerving experience. The children rushed over and began to play around the cloaked woman. I wish they would stop doing that. She thought. One of the Elf farmers slowly approached the woman. He began talking in a language she had never heard. The woman giggled. A chill ran down her spine. She knew that voice. When the woman lowered her hood, all color drained from her face.

The hair color and style was different, the face was a little different, but the eyes, she could see the evil that welled within them. There was no doubt in her mind, the woman at the gateway to the village was the witch Samantha.

"Your hospitality is too generous. I come from a village far from here, my home, the paths of the forest," she began eloquently. She smiled at the children that were frolicking around her. It was not one of joy, but one a beast might show before it feasted upon its prey after a long chase and hunt.

Qu'Tee watched as the witch, disguised as an Elf lifted one child up and perched him on her shoulder. As the witched passed between the statues, all of the auras flickered. No one seemed to notice. The Elf walking with the witch started talking to her again.

"My name? I am but a humble bard. My story and my song are my name," she replied poetically. The Elf laughed. "I am called En'Vee. I thank you for inviting me," she began as she stopped. She blinked for a moment and then seemed to look over at Qu'Tee. For a moment she stared right at the Ken queen as though she could see her. The Elf spoke again. The witch looked at him and smiled. She looked back over at where Qu'Tee was standing but shook her head. "Forgive me. I must be weary from travelling. May I speak with your elder before I retire?" she asked curiously. The Elf nodded.

It was then that Qu'Tee began to grasp some of what was going on. She was seeing images of the past. The land and the spirits trapped there were speaking to her. A strong wind blew against her. She raised her arms to shield her eyes. When the wind stopped, something felt different. Day had turned to night.

Qu'Tee quickly looked around. The buildings looked okay, some of them looked a touch neglected. The fields, as much as she could see of them, looked as though they were still being tended to, but not as rigorously as before. She could see a party of sorts happening near to the center of the village. She didn't want to go, but something compelled her.

As she walked, she felt tired. It felt as though she was trying to wade through water. She looked forward to the gathering that was sitting around a large bonfire. Almost all of the Elf adults were present. A few of the children were there too, odd that, being the late hour that it seemed to be. All she could hear, was the sound of a large fire burning, faint clapping and the most beautiful music she had ever heard

Carefully, Qu'Tee walked through the crowd like a ghost. It was a sensation she did not enjoy, but something told her that she needed to move closer.

It was then that she saw her.

The witch Samantha was dancing, slowly, gracefully, hypnotically. Her every movement was precise, perfect, sensual. As she danced she played the most soothing song on an emerald hued violin.

Qu'Tee could feel herself blushing as she watched the witch dance. She shook her head and looked around at the other Elves that were around her. They looked tired, yet not. Their auras seemed different too.

It was then that she realized something about this was horrifically wrong.

Qu'Tee rubbed her eyes and looked at the Elves again. She could see thin threads of white mist flowing from all the Elves present, towards the dancing witch.

It wasn't a dance, it was a spell! A powerful one.

Qu'Tee looked down at the ground that the witch was dancing on. Around the fire was a conjuring circle with several runes and glyphs. The wind began to blow again. She didn't want to look away, but she had no choice.

Everything changed again.

It was day now.

How much time had passed? How long ago was it? Why did everything feel so different? She looked around at the village that surrounded her. How different it looked. The buildings looked run down and neglected. The fields looked as though they had not been properly tended to for several seasons and were now littered with thriving weeds. She could see the odd Elf lounging by the buildings, on the ground or other such places. But that wasn't what stood out the most.

Hesitantly she looked around. She looked for anything, something she needed to see, but knew she wouldn't. It was midday. It was sunny, yet, there was no sign of any children. Qu'Tee closed her eyes. She understood what it was that the land and the spirits wanted her to see. She felt herself floating again. She was falling backwards, then stopped. Slowly she opened her eyes to see Arrow, Evallion, Sugar and Boo looking down at her.

"You had us worried," Sugar admitted.
"She was here," Qu'Tee said passively.

"Who?" Arrow asked hesitantly.

"The witch Samantha," Qu'Tee answered as Evallion helped her sit up. "She came here, a long time ago," she added with a sniffle.

"What are you talking about?" Arrow asked, unsure where this was going.

"She looked different, sort of like an Elf, but it was her," Qu'Tee began. "I couldn't understand what the Elves were saying, but I could understand her. She told them she was a bard named En'Vee," she added. Arrow turned pale.

"You know that name?" Sugar asked.

"That long? All this time, we believed that she must have come a decade or two ago," Arrow began as he sat down.

"How much time are we talking about?" Evallion asked.

"There are books in the royal library that spoke of a bard named En'Vee. She was considered to be the best bard in all the Veil. The first time she was witnessed by the Elves was shortly after the fall of Bo'Glin," Arrow answered.

"That would mean," Evallion began.

"She has been here for a couple hundred years, at least," Arrow affirmed. "This monster needs to be stopped at all cost," he added grimly. Evallion knelt down beside Sugar and looked at Qu'Tee.

"Is she going to be okay?" he asked hesitantly.

"She will be fine. Do you remember a little while back? She is sensitive when it comes to magic. If something or someone is enchanted, blessed or cursed she can see it. It is both a blessing and a curse," Sugar stated.

"I don't understand," Evallion replied.

"I can't control it. I tried to learn how back at the temple, but nothing worked," Qu'Tee answered tiredly. "Every now and so often, they would bring in a cursed item, or something enchanted, or blessed. Some times it would be okay. Other times I lost control," Qu'Tee answered.

"If she is in a place that has been strongly enchanted, or cursed, as the present case may be, the magic will be drawn to her. Spirits, ghosts and other such entities can pull at her. Some will do so for good reasons, others, the opposite," Sugar explained further as she studied her daughter's face. "I am wagering this would be the first of the two?" she added curiously. Her daughter nodded.

"This place, it is in great pain. There are so many spirits trapped here," Qu'Tee affirmed.

"Is this going to be safe for her? I mean, she wasn't moving. She was barely breathing. If we go in, what if it happens again?" Evallion asked seriously.

"Her mind and body are connected even if apart, but, there is a risk," Sugar admitted.

"That being?" Evallion asked.

"If the spirits, or ghosts call to her, she will go. The ghosts and spirits cannot hurt her. All ghosts and spirits can do is remember, but, while she is with those spirits and ghosts, seeing what they are remembering," Sugar began. Evallion almost immediately understood.

"Her body is defenceless," he remarked grimly. Qu'Tee lowered her eyes.

"Sorry," she said passively.

"Don't be. No one is blaming you," Sugar reassured. Arrow walked over and knelt down before the Ken queen.

"I know this may be hard, but I need to know everything you can remember. Any little detail you can speak of may help us," Arrow pointed out. Qu'Tee nodded as she closed her eyes. In her mind she could see the images as clearly as if they were before her.

"There were three visions of sorts. The first I already told you about. Then, everything changed. I don't know how much time passed. There was a party, a big one. All of the Elves from the village, even some of the children," she added.

"Why is that odd?' Arrow asked.

"It was an unusually late hour," she answered. He nodded and motioned for her to continue. "En'Vee, or Samantha or whatever was dancing while playing a violin. But, it wasn't a dance. It was a spell, a big one," she explained.

"Go on," Arrow requested, knowing there was more to it than that.

"I don't know what the nature of the spell was, but, an energy was flowing from the people watching her dance and it seemed to swirl around her," she tried to explain. Sugar shook her head.

"It sounds as though she used the life essence of the Elves to poison the land," Sugar commented. Arrow almost spat at the idea.

"That is obscene beyond words," the Elf said in disgust. Qu'Tee reached up and tugged on her mother's sleeve. "I suppose I should be surprised with who we are dealing with," he added. His rage was clearly visible.

"There was more. I, I don't know what happened, or when, but something happened to the children," she added timidly.

"I don't even want to imagine what that witch would do with children," Arrow muttered to himself. The Elf prince slowly got up and stared at his clenched fist.

"It doesn't matter what she did, all that matters is what we do about it," Evallion reassured. The Elf looked over at the Pit Fighter. "Wherever the children and other victims of the witch are trapped, by the time we are done here, they will know peace. They will be free," he added confidently.

"Perhaps I should wait here," Qu'Tee began.

"What are you talking about?" Evallion rebutted.

"If I go in, the spirits might call to me again. Like mom said, I have no control over it. I don't want it to happen at the wrong moment and be used like a weapon against you," she pointed out.

"Do you think for an instant that I would let anything get that close to you?" Evallion reassured. Qu'Tee looked to the others and saw the same reaction. "Believe in yourself already. I mean we do," he pointed out. The Ken queen smiled and nodded.

"She knows we are here. There are too many bats all over the place for us to have gotten here unnoticed. So how do we play this?" Arrow asked. Sugar and the others pondered the issue. Behind his mask, Evallion smiled.

"I believe I have an idea," he reassured.

Battle of Briar

Within the town center of the village of Briar, nothing short of an all out war was under way. Around the heroes frenzied goblins were trying to swarm the out numbered heroes. In spite of the fact that the party got split up, each of them was holding his or her own against the goblin masses. At the spot where the Ken queen was, she was having a more testing task, as the beasts that were around her were undead.

"These skeletons and zombies are starting to piss me off! How do you make these damn things stay down?" Qu'Tee demanded as three more of the monsters she struck down either reformed or pulled themselves back up to a standing position.

"Watch your language," Sugar teased. She punched the skull from one of the slow moving skeletons. It crumbled to the ground then reformed almost instantly. "Although that can get annoying," she admitted.

"I think it is safe to say that the element of surprise is officially gone," Evallion said as he struck at the unending wave of goblins and undead. He tapped into the power of the Pit Fighters and savagely began to tear into anything that ventured near him.

Back in her lair, watching everything was a mildly amused Samantha. She traced her finger over the crystal and hummed a song to herself.

"They do make quite the team," the witch sighed. She looked at the image of the fighting and seemed to pout. "But where is my Arrow? Where is my Elf prince? It wouldn't be a party without the guest of honour," she asked herself. She looked over to her right and scowled. "Shut up! I didn't lose him!" she said to the emptiness beside her. She returned her attention to the crystal.

She tapped her finger on it. The image changed, showing a different picture of the area around the village. "No," she whispered. She tapped her finger on the crystal again, the image changed again showing a section of rotting fields. "Not there," she muttered. She tapped the crystal again. The image showed an area with numerous half buried bodied. "Nope," she sighed and tapped the crystal again the image showed the far side of the village. "Not there," she almost hissed. She tapped the crystal again, and again and again and again and again and again.

She screamed out in frustration as she threw the crystal at the neatest wall with such force that it exploded into a cloud of powder.

"Five hundred damnable channels and nothing on!" she screamed as she threw a temper tantrum. After a few long minutes she stopped. She took a few moments to regain her composure.

Slowly she got up and dusted herself off. She seemed more in control.

"Calm down. He wouldn't give up. Not now. He is so close that he can taste his sister's scent," the witch said to herself as she snapped her fingers. A goblin with strap on wings hurried in carrying yet another oversized crystal ball. He placed the ball down on a large pillow, bowed to her then hurried away.

"Thank you Albert!" she called out with a smile. Samantha sat down before the crystal ball and sighed. She looked over her shoulder at the barely moving Elf princess who was once again back in her rusty cage. "What are you looking at?' she almost hissed. The Elf was barely moving, but twitched at the sound of her voice. "Your brother is up to something but it won't work. You see, I know him. I know him well. I know how he thinks and he wants me! He wants me badly," the witch said with an insane giggle.

"He wants you dead," the weak Elf princess corrected. The witch sighed.

"Technicalities. He will get over it, just as you did sister," the witch said with a smile. "Master, he wants the Ken bitch dead, but your sexy little brother, he said nothing about him. I so want him. I want to see the look on his broken face as I bring his tortured ass back to the ruins of Lyte Wood," the witch said through gritted teeth. Her breathing was heavy, almost to the point of hyperventilating. She closed her eyes and placed her hands on the crystal ball. A dim aura seemed to pulse around the ball and the witch. Samantha seemed to calm down.

She slowly got up and walked over to where the cage was. She opened the door to the prison and slumped down to her knees.

"Why am I doing this? This is wrong," Sam said passively. "Mommy wouldn't approve of this," she added. She grabbed the Elf by her shoulders and shook her. "Mommy will be mad at me! What am I going to do?" she asked teary eyed. The Elf princess's head was lolled on her right shoulder, her eyes spaced out. She gasped and dropped the Elf as though her skin was toxic.

For a few moments she looked at the barely moving Elf with horror in her eyes.

"I have to stop this. I, I have to put an end to this," Samantha sobbed as she took out a dagger. She began cutting her arms. Just then, she threw the dagger aside. "You stupid bitch!" she hissed. She looked at the numerous cuts on her arms. Slowly they began to heal. "You did this! You confused that weak willed bitch!" the witch hissed as she reached down and began to choke the barely moving Elf. "I'll kill you!" she screamed. She twitched. Her face contorted as though her head was in pain. She released the Elf and exited her cage.

The witch staggered away from the cage. The voices, all of them were screaming. Slowly she began to hover. One by one, the voices began to quiet. The sea of chaos was once again calm. Her eyes slowly opened.

"He is near. He is waiting. He wants to see me so that he can imbed one of his precious witch warded arrows in my chest," Sam said calmly. She waved her hand at the cage, the door slowly closed and locked. "That will not happen. I will not meet my end at Elf hands," she stated calmly.

"What, what have Elves done to you?' the Elf princess weakly asked. The witch floated over to the cage then sat down before the weakened Elf.

"You don't know? I was a child at the time. But, I know how it happened. Many might think that I couldn't understand or appreciate what was happening, but I knew. My mother, she was on the council, of the Order of the Hand. We just wanted to be acknowledged as a nation, like the mages or wizards. But, they were afraid. They poisoned the minds of the other nations. They said we were dangerous. We just wanted to be acknowledged and left alone. But that was too much. We were too dangerous," Samantha said as her mind remembered those dark days of her youth.

"I remember, I stayed up late. I heard them. I heard the elders saying that the nations denied that we had the right to be a nation. I remember hearing them say that, if we continued to seek such status that we would be punished," she continued. "After that, we cut off all ties from all nations. All of the witches returned home. We had to move a lot, as the jealousy of the other nations hated our defiance," she added. She looked over at the barely moving Elf prisoner.

"On our holiest of days, while we were paying homage to the

elder gods, we were attacked. You see, Elves, they had tracked us to where we were camped," the witch stated coldly. "We never had a chance. The elders, they did what they could to buy the others time, time to escape, but, they were everywhere, like locusts. No matter where we tried to run, they were there. No matter where we tried to hide, they were there," Samantha continued, her hands clenching into fists. She glared at the Elf. "Did you know, that my mother and me, we were the last of our kind? We were hiding in the forest, like animals. All we wanted was to be left alone, but no! You and the other nations couldn't let go of your fear, your prejudice," she said through gritted teeth.

"I, I remember well that day, as clear as though it was yesterday. Those damned zealots came down on us. We had done nothing! Nothing! We hadn't seen anyone in years! But they came! My mother, she screamed at me to run. I froze. I was a child at the time. My place was with my mother. How could I leave her? But, the fear in my heart, with her words, they drove me to run. And I ran. As fast as my legs and feet could carry me. My legs, arms, face, I can still feel where the branches of the bushes and trees cut my flesh as I ran. It was then that I tripped. I was scared, alone, afraid. It was then that a small band of Elves happed by," she continued, a tear escaping her eye.

"I begged them. I was on my knees, gripping at their pant legs begging them to help me, to help my mother. It was then that those zealots arrived. They, spewed lies, about my mother and me. They ignored me. I was pushed aside. They walked away and let those, foul humans take me away," she said through gritted teeth.

"I know well now, I know how the Elves, how they made a pact with the humans who feared us the most, that they would not interfere. They, you and your kind just sat back while we were hunted like animals. You see, they didn't kill us right away. No, that would have been too merciful. No, they tortured the elders, my mother, my family, for years before they were giving the privilege of dying slowly within a large fire that burned them slowly, while they still had life in them," she said, a look of deep rooted hate in her eyes. "You know, to this day, I don't honestly know, if those elves I happened upon could have made a difference. I don't know if they could have stopped those humans. But, you see? They didn't even try. They didn't care," she explained.

"You blame all Elves?" the Elf princess strained to say.

"Oh no dear, not just Elves. There are precious few nations I can stomach. But you see, the Elves and humans, they hold a special place in my heart. You see, the other nations, they did nothing while we were hunted by the humans. As for the Elves, they helped the humans hunt us. We lived within the forests. There was no way humans could find us," she explained as she rubbed the arm that had been cut moments ago. "I will see all Elves all humans writhe in agony for countless years for the suffering that had been inflicted upon my people. You think what was brought against you was bad? What I have planned for the humans is far worse. Their memory is not long like the Elves. They may not remember, but I will always remember," she corrected. She frowned and folded her arms. "Get up," she ordered. The Elf was weak, but did everything within her power to obey. Her legs were wobbly, she had to support herself against the bars of the cage to stay up.

The witch walked over and stood before the imprisoned elf. She stared into the eyes of the elf princess until the elf lowered her eyes.

"Soon, all of your pain will end. You will have the blessing, of knowing some form of peace. You have no notion of the damage that was done to my people, my family, me, at the hands of humans. But the thing is, I never really cared about you. Once you were broken in a bit you were good for, some, things. But your father, he loved, cherished your brother. He is the one I wanted. The only reason that I chose you, did what I did to you, was for his benefit. Your pain, in a manner of speaking was his. He blames himself for your abduction, as well he should. Once I have him, as I have you, I will then go after your father. Both of you will get to watch as he is tortured and sacrificed. You will get to watch as he is carved up and served as a meal to my goblin slaves. Perhaps, I will let you both sit at the table. You know, one last chance to sit at the table with your daddy," she hissed. She smiled as she could see the horror in the Elf prisoner's eyes. In spite of everything she had been through, she still had some nerves left.

The witch reached into the cage and touched the back of her hand to the Elf princess's cheek. She could tell that the Elf wanted to recoil, but KNEW better than to try something that foolish.

"Be honest honey. You enjoyed some of those sessions we
shared. Me touching you, caressing you, kissing you? Even if,
by some miracle, those foolish heroes do save you, do you think
you will able to lay with another without seeing my face?" she
taunted. She smiled as she saw a tear escape the elf princess's
eye. "Hmm. You might be right. I doubt that any would be
willing to lay with you after everything that you have done with
me," she mocked. She shoved the Elf's face back, causing her to
crumple to the floor of the cage. "But you will stay alive long
enough to see your brother. I mean that is the only reason that I
kept you alive this long. I mean you have been gone so long, he
has come so far to see you, I figure it would be rude if he got
here and found you, well, dead," she explained. She waved her
hand. The large crystal ball floated over to her hand. "Time to
see how our fearless dedicated heroes are faring," she mocked as
she returned her attention to the crystal ball.

Back where the fighting was, little had changed. For every
goblin that they seemed to kill, strike down or knock out, three
more seemed to take its place.

"This is getting us no where," Evallion hissed as he leaped out
from a small mountain of dead goblins. "There is no end to this
wave of monsters," he added, not letting up his offensive.

Qu'Tee looked around as she fought. She could see that the
goblins and undead were starting to split. The goblins were
focusing on her mother and her. The undead were starting to

focus on Evallion.

"Mom, you and Evallion keep the goblins entertained. If you do, I can keep the zombies and skeletons amused," the Ken queen reassured.

"What do you think hero?" Sugar asked, throwing potions at any goblin or zombie, or skeleton that happened too close to her. "Sound like a plan?" she asked.

"I will be happy if the things I am killing stay dead," he hissed as he stabbed and slashed at three zombies and skeletons that were near him. His attacks seemed to have little staying power against such beasts. Just then, Qu'Tee leaped over to where he was and began attacking the zombies and skeletons with her staff. Evallion leaped over to where Qu'Tee had been.

For a few long seconds the goblins were stunned by the change up. Evallion took the initiative. He drove his fist into the face of one goblin causing a sickening, bone crunching sound. He then drilled his elbow into the back of the head of another goblin, spun around, kicked the side of his boot into the nose of another goblin, THEN slashed his sword across the chest of three other goblins before they snapped themselves out of their shock. Yet, for every one that he had hit and struck, three more seemed to willingly take their place.

"Persistent bunch," he hissed as he continued to attack the relentless mob.

Over where Sugar was, the scene was somewhat different. Around the mother of the Ken queen, was an odd sight to say the least. All around her, were dozens of goblins that were affected by her potions. Some were petrified, their skins, their flesh turned to stone. Some were encased in ice, some were encase within living crystal laces with throbbing vines, some laid on the ground twitching, some were unmoving, like living statues, some were pinned to the ground by choking vines, a few had become like feral beasts and were attacking other goblins. In spite of this, more goblins seemed to hesitantly inch their way through the carnage towards her.

"They want no part of me, yet their fear of the witch compels them to try," Sugar remarked as she hopped up onto the crystal prison that had one goblin trapped. She reached into her robes and revealed four more vials. "I don't suppose I could convince you critters to back off?" she mused. The goblins that slowly inched forward growled at her. Sugar sighed and shook her head. "Had a hunch you would say that," she muttered.

Where Qu'Tee was, the scene was far different. Around her, the undead seemed to refuse to stay down, but the Ken queen seemed unphased by it all. Her movements were methodical, precise, focused. It was as though she was a partner in a deadly dance. It didn't matter if her foes reassembled, rose up or were unphased by her deadly strikes. All that mattered was her movements, her strikes, her focus. It was as though the fight was taking no energy, no effort for her. The youthful queen of the Ken was displaying a skill and prowess with her weapon that would shame warriors twice her age. It was then that something strange happened. All of the undead around her seemed to back away.

Qu'Tee looked over, the goblins that were attacking Evallion and her mother had backed off as well.

"What are they doing?" Qu'Tee asked, watching as the skeletons and undead around her began to sway back and forth. The surrounding goblins were doing the same.

"Something is not right about this," Sugar remarked, four move vials ready. A light clapping sound got their attention.

"I must confess," an all too familiar voice began. "I didn't think you all could last this long against my minions," the voice continued. The three looked around for its source. It was then that they all saw an oversized hat bobbing up and down among the goblins. As it drew closer, they saw the smiling face of the Hand witch Samantha, sitting atop a stone chair carried by goblin slaves. "I dare say, you lot have merited my, personal interest,' she added. Slowly the goblins lowered the stone throne, careful as to not disturb their master. The witch smiled as she stepped from her perch and stretched her arms out. "Now, what say you show me just why it is that the master fears you lot?" she mused, her fingers growing into elongated talons.

Wiles of the Witch

The party watched as the witch removed her cloak.

"Is it really her?" Evallion asked.

"I think so," Qu'Tee answered, not totally sure. The witch smiled and removed her oversized witch's hat.

"I formally, and ever so humbly bid you welcome to my home. I apologize for the poor housekeeping, but good help these days is so hard to find," Samantha said with a giggle as she bowed to them. "Of course you know who I am," she began.

"En'Vee," Qu'Tee interrupted. The witch instantly looked up the Ken queen.

"Actually it's Samantha," she corrected. She stood upright and studied the face of Qu'Tee. "But I am curious as to why you thought that was my name," she stated as she stepped towards the ken queen. Qu'Tee stepped back and Evallion stepped in front of her. The witch sighed and shook her head.

"I saw what you did here," Qu'Tee stated calmly. A broad smile crossed the face of the witch as she tapped her claw like finger to her lip.

"I see. A sensitive one. I should be surprised. The master wouldn't fear just anyone. It figures. I suppose that is how you noticed my enchantment on the Elf prince, speaking of which where is he?" Samantha asked as she playfully looked around for any trace of Arrow. After a few seconds she stopped and sighed. "I never was very fond of hide and seek," she remarked.

"I do not know what you are planning, but we will stop you," Evallion remarked seriously. The witch smiled at him.

"I must confess. You, amaze me. I mean, here you are, slowly dying. You should have died back at that romantic cave hideaway of yours. Yet, not only do you survive, not only do you pull a stunt as ingenious as Assassinating my ten most decorated Goblin warlords and escaping that unscathed, you made it all the way here. Tell me, how do you feel right now?" she asked curiously.

"Once I kill you, I will feel great," he answered coldly. Qu'Tee stepped forward and stood in front of Evallion.

"Don't listen to her. She is just trying to get inside your head," she warned. The witch giggled and pretended to look impressed.

"You are just too precious," Samantha began as she put her hat back on and adjusted the brim to where she liked it. "Don't you get it yet? Where he is concerned, I am already in his head. How about, I make this even more interesting? I didn't use a spell to do what I did to your friend there, well, I did, but I didn't. The spell part is only half the problem. I used a poison. A rare one, from the old days. There is only one cure. Only one. It grows once every two hundred years, and the bloom only lives for two days. One dose, poisons the victim slowly. The second cures the victim completely," she explained as she looked over at Sugar. "Ask mommy. I know, that she knows what I am talking about," she goaded. Qu'Tee looked over at Sugar.

"Black Lotus Petal," Sugar stated calmly. Samantha clapped her hands proudly.

"I love smart ones. You know what the best part is? The plant bloomed, yesterday. Now, I had to choose carefully. You see, you and your mommy could live long enough to see the plant bloom again. With Ken, predicting life span is always tricky. All that Elf blood makes it difficult. But, Eva, the fearless hero, he is only human," she pointed out.

"Is this going somewhere?" Qu'Tee asked, not taking her eyes off the witch.

"Even if, you were able to kill me and stop the spell I placed on him, he would still die. You need me honey. Face the cold hard facts honey. You want to save the world but you are in way over your head. You can't save the world. You can't save yourself," she began as she pointed her claw like finger at Evallion. "But, you can save him," she pointed out. She could see the doubt in the eyes of the young queen. With her other hand she reached between her boobs and slowly pulled out a small pouch and held it up at eye level. "Be a dear and call out the Elf. I know he is here. I can smell his hatred," she mused.

"What is that?" Qu'Tee asked. Samantha smiled.

"The stuff that dreams are made of honey. Ground up Black Lotus Petal Powder. After I got what I needed to make my poison, I got enough to make the cure, just for this reason. I know you love him. To be honest I can see why. He is a cute little stud muffin. Call out the Elf, and I will give you this. What do you say?" the witch offered.

"How do we know it isn't a stronger poison?" Sugar asked. The witch sighed, looking deeply hurt by the accusation.

"Where is the love? Where is the trust?" she asked dramatically. The moment passed. "I suppose I could let mommy test it. She does like to do that sort of thing," she stated as she began to wave the bag back and forth. "So, what say you my delicious looking plaything? Is the life of an Elf you barely know worth more than that of your one true love?" she mused.

"What is to stop me from just taking it from you?' Evallion challenged. Samantha giggled. "You find that funny?" he asked through gritted teeth. Samantha cleared her throat and regained her composure.

"I do so love the ones that don't know just how deep they are in," the witch began. She arched her back a bit and struck a pose that accentuated every feminine curve of her body, so much so that even Qu'Tee was blushing. The witch smiled as she balanced the small pouch between her boobs. "If you want it

honey, come here, come to me and take it," she goaded. Before
Qu'Tee could stop him, Evallion leaped over at the witch and
lashed out with his swords. Samantha didn't move. She didn't
even try to block. Qu'Tee and Sugar stared as Evallion's attack
stopped inches away from the witch's neck. "I think what you
want is lower," the witch teased. Qu'Tee fumed and was about
to attack the witch herself, but was held back by her mother.
Evallion leaped back.

"I don't know how you stopped me," he almost spat.

"I told you dear. The poison was only half of what I did to you.
You couldn't hurt me if your life depended on it, which, in this
case it would," she pointed out. She walked over to where
Evallion was. The fighter growled as he leaped at her. The
witch's arm elongated and grabbed him by the throat and
slammed him into the ground. "Even if you weren't suffering
from the ill effects of that poison, such attacks are pointless
against me," she hissed. Her arm returned back to normal size.
Evallion gasped and slowly got up. "Concede to your fate boy,"
she said to the young barbarian.

"Never," he hissed. He sheathed his weapons and raced towards
the witch. He lashed out at her with focused punches and kicks,
yet no matter what he seemed to try, nothing got close enough. It
was as though she knew what he was doing before he did. A
strong backhand sent him rolling back to where Sugar and
Qu'Tee were.

"Tenacity will only carry you so far," the witch remarked. She was going to say more, but her train of thought was derailed when she heard the fighter laughing quietly. "What is so funny?" she asked hesitantly. Evallion held up his hand and showed her a familiar looking pouch. The witch looked down at her boobs. The pouch was gone.

"Lose something?" Evallion asked. The witch fumed and scowled as he handed the pouch to Sugar. She watched as Qu'Tee's mother opened the pouch and carefully sniffed it.

"This is Black Lotus Petal powder," she affirmed. The witch folded her arms across her chest as Evallion ingested a small handful of the powder. It was then that Qu'Tee noticed something odd. The witch, she was smiling.

"No," she whispered. Evallion reached for his throat. It was as though he was choking. "What did you do?" she demanded. The witch stepped back.

"Hey, I didn't give him that poison. I just like talking about it. You are the ones that gave that to him. Just so you know, there isn't enough Black Lotus Petal powder left in that pouch to undo the damage the fool boy did to himself. I do have more in my lair, but as you were so greedy, I must insist that Arrow come out of hiding," the witch called out to the hidden Elf. A whistle sounded. Her hand shot up and caught an arrow that was meant for her head. She looked over at the arrowhead that was inches from the side of her head. "Witch warded? Nasty business. A lesser person would be offended. I mean, I go through all this trouble to get you here and this is how you thank me?" she mocked. Another whistle sounded. Her other hand snapped up and caught another arrow that was meant for her chest. She sighed. "Now, I am offended. I mean, if someone violated someone I loved the way I violated your precious sister, I would at least want to see the face of the person responsible up close. I would want to see him writhing in agony as all life slowly leaked out of his rotting body," she pointed out. Three more arrows soared at her. Her arm arched and broke them into uneven pieces. The broken arrows then burst into flames. "Time is running out hero. You are playing with lives that are not yours. Her loving squeeze will pay, as will your sister. You had your shot, five to be exact," she commented. There was a long pause. Just then five goblins fell over. The witch looked over and saw Arrow with another arrow aimed at her.

"Where is my sister?" he demanded.

"Around. Somewhere here or there. I misplace so many of my playthings. I am quite the scatterbrain," she mused. Arrow was not amused.

"My sister is no one's plaything," he corrected.

"As you say. She would have come along to greet you properly, but, she hasn't been feeling too well as of late," she rebutted as Arrow rejoined with his allies, not taking his eyes off the witch.

"There must be something we can do? His aura, he is glowing," Qu'Tee asked, fear sinking in as her friend seemed to be dying before her. She looked up at her mother, the look she saw was one of sorrow and loss. "No! I will not give up on him!" she protested as she placed her hands on her dying friend and began to concentrate. The witch seemed to find the whole display quite amusing for some reason.

"You are wasting your time," Samantha began but stopped when she saw the human beginning to stir. "What? This is not possible," the witch protested as Evallion's eyes slowly opened.

"So you say," Arrow rebutted. The witch looked as though she was going to say something but changed her mind. She looked to her left and nodded.

"You have a point," she said to herself as she turned her attention to the party. "You fools. You think that touching little display changes anything? If you do, you are more delusional than she said you were," the witch remarked.

"What exactly is she talking about now?" Evallion asked weakly, still feeling the effects of the poison he had ingested.

"You stupid beast. You want me to spell it out for you? Fine. That, thing that you are clinging to so tenaciously, isn't your precious Evallion, it isn't even human," the witch explained.

"You lie," Qu'Tee began.

"Am I?" the witch interrupted. "Think back if you will. Why do you think your magic isn't working on him as it should? It was never like that before, was it?" she challenged. Qu'Tee wanted to answer but couldn't. "Face the reality of the situation. For the past odd number of days, your stud muffin in training has been laying, unmoving, in a cell hidden within the catacombs beneath us," she explained.

"I don't believe you," Qu'Tee rebutted.

"Were our roles reversed, I would probably say the same. Allow me to paint a picture for you. Knowing who is before you, tell me if this is possible. You and your band take refuge in a Pit Fighter staging ground in Elf territory. A small army of goblins try to storm the gates so to speak, but two of them aren't goblins. One is a puppet disguised as a goblin. The other a swamp beast, also disguised as a goblin. Valiantly you manage to stave off the goblin masses. Then, the danger passed, a tired Evallion begins the tedious effort of retrieving what arrows and weapons he can from the dead," the witch recounted with frightening accuracy. "Then, my puppet assumes a disguise. One that he wouldn't suspect. His guard is lowered due to fatigue and a spell woven around my puppet. The puppet in a daring move assumes my form and ensnares him with her whiles. I am kind of hard to resist. Plan A takes effect. The goblin/swamp beast splits into two. One takes on the form of Evallion. The other takes the unconscious hero away," the witch continued, deeply enthralled by the sound of her own voice.

"Why should I believe anything you say?' Qu'Tee asked seriously.

"I was getting to that. Be patient," the witch retorted. "Now where was I? Oh yes. My puppet then performed a little drama for your benefit. She was to cause you pain, by killing the Evallion or who you thought was Evallion. To be honest, I was mildly stunned when you were able to heal him," the witch admitted.

"You? You expect me to believe any of this? I am me!" he protested.

"No, you are a copy. My puppet probed your pathetic tiny human mind. Every secret, every emotion, every memory, is not yours. They belong to a small boy who is lying trapped in my dungeon. How true, how sad," she added poetically.

"That can't be," he began, uncertainty began to take root.

"Oh shut up you ungrateful plant! You didn't exist until about seven moons ago give or take. Everything you remember, feel is a lie. All you had to do was die back in that cave, to dishearten her, to turn her away from this fool's errand of a quest. But no! You couldn't even do that. You had to live. You had to miraculously survive that. You had to miraculously pull off the assassination to end all assassinations. You are nothing but a failure and a disgrace! How dare you show up here after failing me as you have!" the witch screamed. Evallion tensed up. Much to the horror of the rest of the party, Evallion mutated into a swamp beast.

For a few seconds the beast looked at its deformed hands. It then looked over at Qu'Tee. It stepped towards her, Qu'Tee stepped away. There was fear in her eyes. The swamp beast could see it. It then looked over at the witch.

"Get out of my site you miserable conjuring," she ordered. The beast seemed disheartened as it made its way into the nearby forest. The witch shook her head. "Some times I fear I am too good at what I do," she complained. "Goblins, undead, minions and other beasts. Kill all but the Elf!" she ordered.

Just then, Qu'Tee felt as though she was being pulled from her body. Her eyes spaced out as she fell to the ground. When she opened her eyes, she was in a dark tunnel. She knew that she had to be in the tunnels under Briar. The floor was stained with blood. Some looked fresh. The rest of the blood looked old, days, months or longer she couldn't say. A wind blew through the tunnel. On it were carried the whispered echoes of screams. She curled up on the floor, covering her ears. Slowly the screams subsided.

Hesitantly she got up and began to make her way down the tunnel. She had no idea where she was going, but it was as though a power greater than hers was guiding her. She rounded a corner and saw two barely living Elves standing guard beside a large set of bronze doors. On the doors were hand prints smeared with blood, as though something was desperately trying to get away from something.

Slowly the doors before her opened. She walked in. on the far side of the room, she saw Samantha, dressed as she remembered from mere moments ago. With her was a pale looking Elf maiden. She was dressed in white robes and was standing by a large blood stained alter. Much to the horror of the Ken queen, she watched as another Elf escorted an Elf child over to where the altar was. Mortified, Qu'Tee realized what was going to happen. She wanted to scream out. She wanted to grab the child and run. But it was as though something was sucking the energy out of her. She slumped down to the floor.

The Elf child was placed on the altar. He made no effort to run or cry. He just laid there on the bloody altar as though nothing odd was happening.

Qu'Tee watched as Samantha danced over to where the Elf maiden was. Her eyes were filled with pain and sorrow. The witch placed a dagger in the hands of the Elf. Although she whispered, Qu'Tee could hear the witch's words as clearly as if they were being screamed.

"Sacrifice your only son to our lord god Bo'Glin," the witch said. The dagger slowly raised, and then plummeted into the chest of the Elf child. Qu'Tee watched as a fountain of light, energy and life flowed from the sacrifice. It flowed and swirled around the ancient room until it finally flowed into the body of the witch. The ground began to shake. Ancient glyphs, runes and other magical symbols began to appear on the far wall behind the altar.

Qu'Tee wanted to run, scream, hide, anything! But nothing worked. All she could do was watch helplessly as a door forged from flesh and bone began to appear. A red light seeped through the cracks and holes in the door. The door slammed open and knocked the Elf maiden aside. A strong wind blew against Qu'Tee. She shielded her face from the foul wind. The ground was shaking again, but this time, it was because of something walking. Something big.

The Ken queen hesitantly looked over and saw the shadow of Bo'Glin standing within the archway of the doorway. With a wave of his hand the two elves that were present decayed and crumbled into piles of dust.

"You finished quicker than I expected," the demonic reptile croaked. The witch smiled and bowed to her master.

"Please forgive me master. I fear some times I fear I am too good at what I do," she said humbly. The two began to laugh as everything began to spin around Qu'Tee.

In the present, all fighting had stopped.

"I'm glad I got your attention. Lady Sugar, Crown Prince Arrow, do be dear guests and lower your weapons or I will carve another mouth in the young queen's pretty little neck!" the witch ordered, her claws gripping Qu'Tee's throat. Hesitantly Arrow and Sugar did as she said. As soon as they were unarmed, dozens of goblins jumped them and secured the captured prisoners. Samantha looked at the face of Qu'Tee. She was still gone, but she served her purpose. "By the way honey," she whispered to the Ken queen. "I win," she hissed triumphantly.

Worst Witch Way

A splash of cold water hit the face of a semi conscious Qu'Tee. For a few seconds she shivered before her eyes reluctantly began to open. Everything was foggy, but slowly she began to see. The witch Samantha was standing before her holding an empty pail.

"My, my dear. You are a heavy sleeper," the witch teased. Qu'Tee tried to get up but her arms and legs felt like leaded weights. Her clothes and armour were in a small pile of clutter across the room. She was dressed in tattered rags, as were the rest of the restrained prisoners. "Oh my. You don't seem to be doing too well?" she asked with a snicker.

"What did you do to me?' Qu'Tee slurred. She felt as though her mind was barely with her body. She could feel her limbs, but she couldn't move them. The witch walked over and effortlessly lifted the young queen up by her neck.

"That's the funny thing dear. I didn't do anything. There must be something about this place that is sucking the energy out of you. It is a common problem among those that are sensitive," the witch commented. She raked her claws across Qu'Tee's face, then watched with childlike glee as the wounds began to heal before her very eyes. "My dear, I do believe I could grow to love someone like you," she said with a giggle as she dropped her captive. She began to dance and playfully skip around. Qu'Tee forced herself up to her hands and knees.

"Evallion," Qu'Tee strained to say. The witch stopped dancing and looked over her shoulder at the young girl that was glaring at her.

"What about him?" the witch asked curiously.

"Where is he? What did you do to him?" she asked. Sam slinked over towards her on her tippy toes with a naughty look on her face, then squatted down before her prisoner.

"I don't know if I should tell you. You don't seem old enough to hear about," she began as she took a deep breath moved her hands over her chest. "These, kind of things," she teased. A look of hatred shot out from the Ken queen. The witch was going to taunt her further, but Qu'Tee leaped up and punched her across the face. The witch recoiled and staggered, staggered, staggered back and fell over. "Ow! That hurt!" the witch pouted.

"You go near him and I will make you suffer," Qu'Tee warned. The witch giggled as she rolled around on the floor. She then flopped over onto her back and looked over at the Ken queen.

"You and Arrow have a lot in common. You both care more about others than you do about yourselves. I find that so sexy, but, in life, often we must accept what is," the witch remarked as she floated up to her feet. "You, much like my new play toy Arrow over there, both of you should be far less concerned with his sister and your stud muffin boyfriend. Do you have the slightest inkling of just how much trouble you are in?" the witch asked seriously. She backhanded Qu'Tee across the face. She crumpled to the floor. The witch snapped her fingers. Vines and roots exploded from the floor and restrained Qu'Tee to the cold blood-stained rocky floor.

"What do you want?" Qu'Tee demanded as she tried to free herself, but the more she seemed to struggle, the tighter the vines and roots seemed to get. Samantha took out a knife and laid down beside her helpless victim. She moved the knife in a way that Qu'Tee's eyes would be drawn to it.

"I had a pet lizard once. He was named Fella. I would say, come here Fella. Fetch me this Fella. He was a good pet. I got bored one day. I cut off his tail and watched as his body began to slowly grow another," she whispered as she touched the flat of the blade to the young queen's cheek. The point dangerously close to her eye. "You heal kind of like Fella did. If I, plucked out your eye, do you think your funky healing thingy would grow you a new one?" she asked sadistically.

"Get away from my daughter you demented bitch!" Sugar hissed. Samantha giggled and looked over at the angry Ken alchemist.

"I don't think your mommy wants us to be friends. I don't think she likes me much," Samantha whispered as she licked Qu'Tee's cheek then flipped herself up to her feet. She licked her lips then skipped over to where Sugar was restrained. "You don't like me do you?" she asked, looking almost hurt by the question.

"Go near my daughter and I will make you wish you were never born," Sugar replied seriously. The witch shrugged her shoulders.

"Too late honey. I am already there. But, you are kind of cute. If you behave, I will go easy on you," she began as she traced her hand across Sugar's cheek. "I will even promise to make matters quick where your daughter is concerned. What do you say?" she asked curiously. Sugar looked over at her daughter and then lowered her eyes.

"If you promise," Sugar replied through gritted teeth. Samantha smiled. She grabbed Sugar by the cheeks and began to kiss her on the lips. Sugar growled and bit! For a few seconds Sugar refused to let up. Samantha punched Sugar hard in the stomach then slapped her across the face as she staggered back.

"Ow!" She whimpered. She backed away and moved a hand to her bleeding lip. "That was just plain rude, but then again, I do like things a little rough," she giggled. In the time it took to blink, the witch was before Sugar. She grabbed a handful of hair and slammed her head into the wall repeatedly then held her knife to the neck of the dazed Ken prisoner. "I want you to understand this you uppity little Ken bitch! You are my slave here. How long you live depends on my good mood and my sense of charity, and in case you haven't noticed, I am not revered as being a charitable woman," the witch hissed, a look of pure madness in her eyes.

"Is there a point to this?" Arrow asked. The head of the witch jerked over and glared at him. There was a hungry look in her eyes. A hunger mixed with hate, a hate that spanned hundreds of years. The witch smiled and took a deep breath.

"You are so much alike," she said softly. She walked away from the barely conscious Ken woman and made her way over to where Arrow was. "Your sister?" she added. The eyes of the Elf narrowed. "You have that same spark," she said as she pointed to a spot over one of his eyes. "Right there. It screams defiance, pride and all other proud Elf virtues. I will tell you this much, after about two months of my tender caress and touch, it all began to melt away," she whispered. Arrow spit in her face. Samantha wiped her hand over her face then licked the palm. "She did that too. She learned, and so will you," she said as she stepped away.

"She is no longer yours. She is mine. And she always will be. I broke her like a picturesque mirror. Even if all your artisans assembled the pieces and managed to fill in the cracks, the damage would still be there. I broke her in a way in which she will never, ever again be whole," she remarked, a look of disgust in her eyes. "You belong to me now. Body and soul, in life and death. Accepting it won't make the pain any less real, but it is better than clinging to some thin veil of hope," she remarked.

"Why are you doing this?" Qu'Tee asked. The witch blinked and looked over at her master's most feared enemy. "This, this isn't about your master. This is personal for you," she added. The witch blinked as she walked over to where Qu'Tee was. She snapped her fingers. The vines and roots lifted the Ken queen up.

"You are very perceptive. Maybe I just don't like people that get in the way of my master?" she suggested.

"But, that isn't it," Qu'Tee replied quietly.

"You are right. It is personal. Do you know what it is like? To see everyone you love hunted like animals? Do you know what it is like to hear your family screaming, screaming, screaming," she began as she shook her head. "Shut up!" she screamed. The voices in her head were all screaming and shouting and yelling incoherently. "Make them stop," she whimpered. Samantha cringed on the floor for a few moments before she managed to regain her composure. Tears stained her cheeks as she looked over at Qu'Tee. "Humans, they did this to me, my friends, my family," she said repressing her emotions. "Elves, they could have done something. They could have tried something, said something, but they did nothing. They let all of it happen," she said as she wiped her nose with the back of her hand. "Then there is you my dear. You and your mother. Ken, the best of both worlds. The embodiment of everything I hate," she hissed. Her hand snapped over and gripped Qu'Tee by the throat.

"You won't get away with this," she strained as the witch slowly tightened her grip. A cruel smile crossed the witch's face.

"Is that like some unsaid hero rule or something? I mean do you have to say that? Who is going to stop me? Boo? Even if he was more than your garden variety waif goblin, how could he hope to succeed where a master Ken Alchemist, an Elf prince, a human barbarian, and a high and mighty cleric from the holy Order of the Butterfly all failed?" the witch asked. There was a look unlike anything Qu'Tee had ever witnessed in the eyes of the witch. "And if you are clinging to the thread of hope in that the Elves might charge in to save the day, well, I wouldn't hold my breath. As we speak, an army of goblins, unlike anything the Elves have ever witnessed is marching on Lyte Wood. Your little gambit with the warlords was pointless. Amusing for me, but pointless," the witch added sweetly. She didn't have to look. She could sense that Arrow had turned pale.

"You won't win," Qu'Tee replied calmly. Sam was notably stunned by the remark. "You are the key. Your magic is what binds them together and makes them strong. Once you are gone, they will be as they were before your magic aided them. They will not be a match for the Elves," she added passively. Samantha growled as she slapped the young queen across the face. A look of madness gripping the witch.

"You don't listen much do you? You want me use small words?" she asked intolerantly. She was going to hit Qu'Tee again, but some measure of restraint kicked in. a cold look replaced the madness that had been there moments before. "You are good. I think that we are alike you and I," she began as she tapped a finger to her temple. "I think you know about voices too," she remarked.

"I am nothing like you," Qu'Tee rejected any similarity. The witch snapped her fingers. The vines and chains restraining the

Ken queen vanished.

"Hear me out, please," the witch requested with a frightening amount of sincerity. "You, you lived among them, the humans," she began. Hesitantly, Qu'Tee rose to her feet.

"How do you know?" she began.

"My dear, where you are concerned, my master knows everything," Sam stated as a matter of fact. The witch walked over to a table and motioned for Qu'Tee to follow. The young queen looked over at her mother. She still wasn't moving. "Look, I could get in a lot of trouble over this. Please," the witch added. The Ken queen hesitantly walked over and sat across from the witch.

"What, what do you want?" she asked hesitantly. She had seen first hand how quickly the mood of the witch could change.

"You, you know," Samantha began as she grabbed a dusty bottle and two glasses. "You are different, even by Ken standards. You were among the humans. You, know what it is like to be picked on, tortured. I wager there was more than one occasion when you were back there, that you just wished, prayed, that they would just end it all. That death would just take you," she continued as she poured a clear liquid into each glass.

"Once or twice," Qu'Tee admitted.

"It never came though. No matter what, it just wouldn't stop.

The pain, the humiliation. Even if it happened so long ago, it is always there, like a stain that you can never really get out. You hope that others might be able to accept you, but you fear, you dread that they can see it," she continued. Qu'Tee could barely breathe as the witch spoke. Her words seemed to carve a path straight to the core of her being. "You push yourself hard?" she asked with a half smile. Qu'Tee nodded and accepted the glass that was offered to her but didn't drink.

"What is this?" she asked timidly. The witch smiled and took a sip from her glass.

"Elf spring water. I bottled a lot of the stuff shortly after I arrived. The water here is toxic now, but, every now and so often, I indulge. You were humiliated at the hands of the humans. I know what that is like. But, you are wrong," she pointed out.

"What do you mean?" Qu'Tee asked.

"You are drawn to the Elves because the humans treated you so badly. Elves are little different from the humans that bullied you. The only reason the Elves are being nice to you is because they are out of other options. If they thought for an instant that they could pull themselves out from the trouble they are in, do you honestly think that they would rally behind you? They do not care about my master's grand design. All Elves care about are trees and Elves. They have little use for half-breeds, an Elf word," she pointed out. Qu'Tee looked over at the prisoners that were bound to the wall.

"I, I don't understand. Where is this going?" the Ken queen remarked. The witch sighed and seemed to take a moment to choose her words carefully.

"A lot of stuff is going on. It is all part of a tapestry far greater than you could hope to understand, at this moment," she added, she looked up at the roof. Hesitantly Qu'Tee looked up and saw a detailed map of the Veil carved into the rocky surface. "Things are not always easy to understand. Things are not always black and white," she began. It was then that Qu'Tee began to sense the pattern. She began to see the direction that all this was going in.

"You want me to join you?" she asked.

"Would that be so bad?" she asked sincerely.

"I thought you hated me," Qu'Tee reminded. The witch giggled.

"You might have noticed that I am somewhat fickle at times. Some times, I chose the wrong words. It gets me in trouble a lot," she admitted. "Before you answer, hear me out," she began as she took another sip from her glass. "May I continue?" she asked. Qu'Tee looked down at the glass then found herself nodding. "Thank you. Master, he may be cross, but I am sure I could make him understand. Side with me. Stand with me as the walls of Lyte Wood crumble. Stand with me as we crush every single cold hearted human that infests the Veil. There is a place for all who stand in the shadow of our master. He is quite generous with those who are loyal. Your family, your friends, your boyfriend?" she added. That part perked the Ken queen's interest. "You would be able to save them all. And those bullies? Those humans that subjected you to those humiliations, they would be found and brought to justice," she added. Although she was reluctant to admit, there was more than one part of Qu'Tee that liked the sound of that.

"Don't listen to her," a weak voice stated. The two looked over and saw that Sugar had regained consciousness. "She will just trying to confuse you," she added. Sam sighed and shook her head.

"As I said before, I don't think your mommy likes me much. Do not let her values confuse the issue. Think about what you are trying to accomplish? You are trying to unite the splintered nations under one banner? Four of those nations are human. They carry a lot of sway among the other nations even under these trying times. They poison the rest against any that are different because of their narrow minded views," she pointed out.

"Who was it exactly that decimated the Ken capital?" Sugar asked. The witch fumed as she placed her hands on the table.

"You and the rest were meddling in matters that you should have let go. You continued to defy the will of the master. He was going to just leave you to your devices?" the witch rebutted. She closed her eyes. The voices were starting to get louder again. "Not now!" she hissed. She shook her head and took a few deep breaths. Her eyes snapped open and fixated back on Qu'Tee. "I was there. I was the one that unified the goblins that day. I gain nothing by lying. Ask yourself this though. Where were the other nations that day? Where were the humans? Where were the Elves, Wizards, Mages and whatever? They knew that an army was moving against the Ken, yet, they did, nothing," she pointed out. "You seek to ally yourself with the very people that watched as your capital, crumbled," she pointed out.

"You were there?" Qu'Tee asked. The witch sighed.

"Look honey, you can live in the past. Not for long mind you, but, if you look to the future, you will see that what I am saying is true. Opposing the master may seem noble and good and all that other good stuff that epics are written of. But, at what cost?" she asked. From the corner of her eye she could see the disgust in the eyes of Qu'Tee's mother. It was a look that was mixed with worry.

"All you have to do is turn your back on everything you believe in and love. How many years has the demon hounded you and tormented you?" Sugar reminded. Sam sighed and shrugged her shoulders.

"The master is not used to, rogue, elements. He is a creature of chaos true, but only chaos that is within his control," the witch pointed out.

"She would use you, as she uses everyone near her," Arrow remarked.

"They say such mean things. I am wounded," the witch sarcastically remarked. "They are using you too you know, but you are too young and trusting to see it," she continued as she got up and walked over to a shelf. "I should be surprised I guess," she added as she looked over her shoulder at the confused looking Qu'Tee. "One person cannot stand against a wave," she stated.

"Many can though," Qu'Tee pointed out. The witch looked at her for a few long seconds. There was deep disappointment there. She snapped her fingers. A vine shot up from the floor and coiled around Qu'Tee's neck and jerked her away from the table.

"Pride go-ith before the fall," the witch remarked as Qu'Tee slammed into the floor. "That had to hurt," she mused as she picked up Qu'Tee's glass and slowly poured it out. "I had hoped that you would have sampled the water. It has a sweet taste to it. Mildly toxic, but sweet," she mused. She walked over to where Arrow was. "You know, I am pretty sure that I could have had her. She was this close to toasting a new tomorrow with me, but I do believe that you were the voice that swayed her," she remarked.

"Am I supposed to feel bad?" Arrow asked. The witch smiled at him.

"Not yet, but you will. I can be very creative when I get angry," she began. She gripped his chin and glared at him. "You got me angry, but she will be the one that suffers. Ironic that. Her fate was once cursed by humans, and now by an Elf that she sought to help," she mused as she pushed his head against the wall. "But wait! There's more! Honey? Come on in! We have company," the witch mocked as she danced away from the restrained prisoners. Arrow and Sugar looked over and watched as a pale looking Elf maiden hesitantly made her way into the room.

"Geia," Arrow whispered as his sister timidly walked over to where Samantha was. The witch smiled at the hurt look on Arrow's face.
"Down girl," the witch said as though talking to a dog. The Elf princess passively slumped down to her knees before the witch. "But wait, there is more! On our wall of shame is room for one more guest. That is right dear! You wanted him? You got him! Bring him in!" the witch energetically beaconed. Arrow and Sugar watched as an unmoving Evallion was brought in and secured to the wall beside Sugar. "And now that we are all here," the witch mused as an insane look consumed her. "What fun games shall we play?" she asked as her head jerked over and once again fixated on Qu'Tee.

Meanwhile, unaware of the peril, or all too aware, the goblin boo found himself alone by the spot where the last battle had been fought. In his mind, the goblin could remember how they fought against the waves of goblins and undead. He wanted to help Qu'Tee and the others, but he was scared. He wasn't like the other goblins. He wasn't a fighter like Evallion. He wasn't accurate like Arrow. He wanted to help, to do something, to make a difference, but when he saw the witch, he got scared. He hid while the goblins and undead swarmed over his friends like a foul tide.

He slumped down to the ground that was littered with dead goblins and other undead things. Everyday that he was with Qu'Tee he learned something new. This day, he was feeling deeply ashamed.

"Mean girl has Coo'Tee," he said passively. He looked the ring that was around his neck. In his mind he could see her smiling at him as she gave it to him. "Boo should have saved Coo'Tee" he pouted as he sighed. He wanted to make a difference, but he remembered how scared he was when he saw the witch, how she moved, acted and spoke. "But what Boo do alone?" he asked himself. It was then that a familiar looking squirrel pounced from the trees, across the goblin laden area.

For a few long, silent seconds, the goblin and the squirrel seemed to study each other.

"Boo know you," the goblin stated. "You Eva squirrel," he stated. The squirrel perched on its hind legs and see bow at the recognition. "Boo was no there for Coo'Tee. Coo'Tee got taken by mean lady," he said sadly. The squirrel familiar Chi sat down before him. "Coo'Tee was in trouble. BIG trouble. But Boo was too scared," he tried to explain. The squirrel snorted, clearly unsympathetic. At first Boo was upset, but it passed.

Boo got up and began to pace among the dead goblins. For a few seconds, Chi just seemed to watch, then the squirrel scurried over and began to follow the goblin, mimicking him. Boo looked over his shoulder and saw the seemingly smiling squirrel.

"But what Boo can do?" he asked timidly. The squirrel seemed to ponder the issue, then ran off. Boo watched as Chi scurried around and then hurried back to the goblin, dropping four of the Elf prince's arrows at the feet of the tiny goblin.

Boo knelt down and looked at the arrows that as big as spears to him. In his head he could remember Arrow say the tips were made special, to hurt witches.

"Arrows is magic. They hurt bad lady," he understood, but he was still scared. But as much as he was scared, he was still thinking about Qu'Tee and what the witch was doing to her or might do her. "Boo scared, but Coo'Tee need Boo!" he stated, a confidence that was mildly stronger than his fear taking control.

The goblin picked up one arrow and held it like a spear. He knew that what he was holding could hurt the witch. He knew that it could hurt the mean lady that was a danger to Qu'Tee, but even still, would he be enough?

"This help Boo, but is enough?" he asked hesitantly. The squirrel familiar began to scurry around him. "Chi help Boo?" he asked. The squirrel familiar seemed to salute him. The goblin sat down and tried to think how a goblin waif and a squirrel familiar could hope to stop a witch as strong and as scary as Samantha.

An idea came to him.

He looked at the spear-like weapon he had. He knew that Chi couldn't use the arrows like he could, but maybe, if they were shorter, he might! Chi watched as Boo struggled to break the arrowheads free from two of the arrows Chi had recovered.

"If Chi has on feets, Chi can hurt bad lady," the goblin pointed out. The squirrel seemed hesitant, but decided to relent to his reluctant ally's judgement.

Over the course of minutes, Boo managed to secure two severed arrowheads to the front paws of his familiar ally.

It was quite clear that Chi did not like the items being bound to his paws.

"Now if Chi scratch mean lady, mean lady hurt bad," Boo pointed out. The squirrel seemed strike a martial arts pose, displaying his newly acquired arsenal. The unity of the new alliance was interrupted as a swamp beast swaggered out from the forest. The two hesitantly backed away at first, but then Chi seemed to twitch.

The squirrel seemed to study the creation of the swamp witch. Boo looked at the squirrel and then at the swamp beast. For some reason, it seemed familiar. In his mind, the goblin remembered how he saw Chi and Evallion. The way that Chi and this swamp beast were looking at each other was the same.

"You," the hesitant goblin stated, getting the swamp beast's attention. "You is a friend to Coo'Tee?" he asked seriously. There were a few, long seconds, that passed before the swamp beast seemed to nod and then drop to one knee before the tiny goblin. "You like Eva?" he asked. The swamp beast nodded. Boo was afraid of the swamp beast, almost as much as he was of the swamp witch, but something inside the tiny goblin reasoned, it screamed at him that the beast before him, the creation of the swamp witch, was sincere.

Boo began to circle the swamp beast, seemingly evaluating if the beast was sincere, worthy of being an ally in what they were seeking to do.

The tiny goblin stood before the swamp beast.

"Is you a friend of Coo'Tee?" he asked bluntly. The swamp beast nodded. "You want help Coo'Tee?" he asked seriously. The swamp beast again nodded. "Even though scary lady is there?" he asked. Without hesitation, the swamp beast nodded. "You help free Coo'Tee?" he asked. Again the swamp beast seemed to nod. Boo looked over at Chi, to see what his ally thought of this.

The squirrel looked at the swamp beast for a few moments.

Chi scurried around the kneeling swamp beast, the creation of the swamp witch Samantha. Then after a few more seconds hopped up onto its shoulders and sat there as though the beast present was Evallion.

"Chi trust you," Boo began. "You want help Coo'Tee?" the goblin asked. Once again the swamp beast seemed to nod. Boo held up another of the arrows Chi had gathered. "Then you need this," he stated seriously. The swamp beast nodded. Vines and roots shot out from its arm and seemed to absorb the projectile into its arm.

Back in the lair of the witch…

Samantha was watching, deeply amused as one of her goblin minions savagely whipped at the back of the helpless Qu'Tee. The witch seemed seriously amused as Arrow and Sugar watched, but was equally perturbed that Evallion was still unconscious.

"Stop. Stop, stop," she began as she sat up amongst the pillows she was sitting. "This doesn't feel right The hero is still out cold. He must hear her cries and whimpers, yet he still isn't moved? That is so not right," the witch pointed out. She looked and watched as the lash marks on the back of Qu'Tee miraculously began to heal before her eyes.

The witch flopped from her pillow perch and crawled over to where Qu'Tee was.

"I could do anything to you," the witch whispered. Qu'Tee knew better than to respond. "No matter what I do, your gift, your power, will make you as good as new," she pointed out. Qu'Tee could feel the presence of the witch as she perched over her, while balanced on her hand and toes. "You know, my master wants you dead, but, I honestly don't know if he said, how quick," the witch pointed out.

"I would sooner die than," Qu'Tee began, but before she could finish, the witch flashed out her serrated dagger and held it before the face of her helpless prisoner. Qu'Tee could see her reflection on the smooth surface of the blade.

"You remember, do you not? About my old pet Fella?" the witch asked. Qu'Tee didn't answer. "I wonder," the witch seemed to muse. The blade was moved away from Qu'Tee's face. "Does, every part of your body heal as quickly as your pretty little face?" the witch taunted. Qu'Tee gasped as she felt the tip of the witch's dagger touch her inner thigh. "I heard you stifle your cries as my goblin whipped you. Tell me honey, are you that strong? I wonder," the witch whispered to Qu'Tee as she traced the dagger up Qu'Tee's inner thigh.

The courage of the Ken queen began to melt the further the dagger moved.

"Please, no," Qu'Tee stammered. Just then, the entrance to the lair exploded. Samantha hopped away from her bound captive, weapon ready to repel whatever dared to enter her domain.

The debris from the explosion began to settle.

The witch's eyes could see someone standing amidst the smoke and debris. It was then that the witch seemed to go cross-eyed. She stood up and shook her head in modest disbelief.

"You have to be joking. You of all things, dares, to oppose me?" the witch demanded in a state between disbelief and disgust. The smoke began to settle. By the entrance to the lair of the witch stood her creation, the swamp beast she herself had created. On its shoulder was a squirrel familiar. By its feet was the goblin familiar named Boo.

"Mean lady no hurt Coo'Tee while Boo here," Boo stated defiantly.

Rescue Party

For a few long moments the witch jovially rolled around on the floor, laughing near hysterically at the would be rescue party.

Samantha stopped laughing and slowly stood up. She paused as if thinking to say something to the intruders, but instead began laughing again.

"Oh my, I can't remember the last time I laughed so hard," she gasped. "But seriously, joke is over. Leave now and I will forget your rude intrusion," she offered. She turned her back and began to walk over to where Qu'Tee was.

Again she stopped. She looked over her shoulder. The swamp beast, her creation, a squirrel familiar and the goblin were still there.

"You are testing my patience you mindless beast," she warned. It was then that the swamp beast began to glow. "What?" the witch began as the beast once again took on the form of Evallion. "What manner of trickery is this?" the witch demanded.

"It seems as though my daughter's magic is more potent than yours," Sugar stated. Samantha glared at the Ken alchemist. A look of madness consumed the witch as she returned her attention to her defiant creation.

"I do not know how it is that you changed. I do not know how it is that you still exist. I, do not care," the witch began. "I created you, seems only fitting and fair that I kill you proper," she stated. Her hands became a blur of motion. The fake Evallion dodged to the right. His hand snapped over and caught the blade the witch had tossed.

"Boo, Chi, find a way to free the others," the fake Evallion instructed. The witch didn't blink as the tiny rescuers hurried towards the chained prisoners. She didn't remotely care about them. All she could see, think of was the defiant beast she had created that was undoing what she was so close to completing.

"You stupid, ignorant beast. You don't seem to get it. You aren't Evallion," she pointed out as the two began to circle each other.

"It doesn't matter," he rebutted. "Just because I am not real to her, that does not mean she is not real to me," he pointed out. The witch watched as the fake Evallion snapped the blade between his fingers.

"I see," the witch mused. "You say it doesn't matter, but you are wrong. What you feel for her is so strong that I can feel it from here. But you are a monster to her. She could never love you," she mocked. The fake Evallion closed his eyes. In his mind, he remembered the look of fear in Qu'Tee's eyes when the witch revealed his true form. The witch was right. For all he felt, he knew that Qu'Tee never would or could feel that way for him.

He was just a copy, a spell gone awry. But, that didn't change the situation or what he felt he had to do. His arm elongated and grabbed one of Evallion's swords from the assorted pile of belongings.

"There is a monster here, perhaps two. What I feel for her may be someone else's, but," he began as his arm reformed and took on human shape. "I will make you suffer for what you have done to Qu'Tee," he hissed as he leaped at her.

Over by the wall, Sugar and Arrow watched as the fake Evallion fought the witch. Boo looked over and smiled.

"Eva help," Boo pointed out. The two conscious prisoners looked down at the goblin and squirrel that were before them. "Now Boo help Coo'Tee mom," the goblin added as he looked at the restraints.

"You sure he is up to this?" Arrow asked curiously. Boo walked over and kicked Arrow in the shin. "Ow!"

"Boo can do!" the goblin protested. Sugar couldn't stifle her giggle.

"I guess he told you," she mused as she watched as Boo carefully began to scale the wall until he reached the chains. "Careful Boo. It is a long drop for a tiny goblin," she pointed out. Boo looked down and nodded.

"Boo be careful," he reassured. Arrow watched as the goblin

hung himself upside down from the wall restraints. For a few long seconds he seemed to study the way they were put together.

"Can you do it Boo?" Sugar asked. Boo didn't reply. He was too fixated on what he was doing to hear her. It was then that Boo seemed to smile. He reached over and pushed on one spot. A latch moved. He then moved another part of the metal restraint. It was loosened enough for Sugar to slide her hand free. "You are quite the hero Boo. Go help Arrow, I'll help Qu'Tee," she suggested. Boo nodded and made his way along the wall restraints until he was over Arrow.

"Elf need Boo help?" the goblin teased.

"Very funny," he remarked. He looked down at the squirrel who was watching the furious exchange that was happening between the witch and the fake Evallion. It was then that he noticed something about the squirrel. "What is?" he began but stopped. He recognized what he saw. The goblin had secured two of his witch warded arrow heads to the squirrel familiar's paws. "He is a crafty little thing," he admitted to himself

Over where Qu'Tee was, Sugar was doing her best to free her daughter from the magical restraints.

"I'll have you free in a moment," Sugar reassured.

"After the last time," Qu'Tee began. "After that last time that those bullies beat me up and humiliated me, I swore that I would never let anything shake me," she added. Sugar managed to free her arms from the chains and vines.

"No one is judging you except you," Sugar rebutted. She could see that Qu'Tee was in a state between disgust and rage. "Look, if you dwell on this, she wins," she pointed out. "Let us talk about this later. Right now we need to get out of here and regroup, okay?" she reassured. Qu'Tee nodded. She looked over at the fake Evallion. He was just a copy made by the witch. He was fighting for her – to protect her, just like Evallion would do. Sugar placed her hand on Qu'Tee's shoulder. "He is doing what he can to buy us time to get out," she pointed out.

"Right," Qu'Tee said. She was about to head towards the exit when she noticed the Elf princess Geia. "Geia," she said quietly. The Elf maiden looked over and cringed from her hiding place amongst the pillows. Qu'Tee walked over and knelt down beside the terrified Elf. "We have to get out of here," she added.

"No. I have to stay. She will be mad if I run," the Elf stammered passively.

"She will kill you if you stay. You must know that," Qu'Tee pointed out.

"She will punish me," she answered.

"No, she won't," Qu'Tee reassured. For a few moments everything seemed to vanish around the two of them. "She will never hurt you, ever again," she added confidently.

"But, where would I go?" Geia hesitantly asked.

"Home," Qu'Tee answered.

"But she, I," Geia began.

"They won't care," Qu'Tee reassured. Slowly, she extended her hand to the Elf princess. For a few seconds, she just looked at the hand. "I am asking a lot, but trust me, believe in me. I promise you, after today, the witch will never hurt you or anyone ever again," she requested. Almost as if by magic, the Elf princess watched as her hand slowly, timidly began to reach for Qu'Tee's hand. For the first time since she had been captured by the Hand witch, she felt something, hope.

"Okay," she said passively. It was then that she noticed that the two of them were glowing. "What is happening?" she asked hesitantly. Slowly, every ache and hurt in her body began to heal.

"Healing magic," Sugar answered. Geia looked over and saw the rest of the gathering. "My daughter really is quite talented," she added proudly.

"We should have this talk elsewhere," Arrow pointed out. The entire room began to shake as the fight between the fake Evallion and the witch escalated. Qu'Tee nodded as they quickly made their way out of the cavern lair of the witch. Samantha growled as she saw her prisoners escaping!

"I do not have time for this!" she hissed. A force bolt sent her attacker soaring through the air to the far side of the room. She watched as his feet touched the wall. For what seemed like a few seconds he was balanced on the wall. Then he launched himself back at her.

"Make the time!" he growled. She dodged to the side. Her hand snapped over and gripped the wrist wielding the weapon. She then spun around and slammed him hard into the floor. A dagger flew into her free hand.

"Game over you fake," she hissed as she stabbed the knife into the chest of the fake Evallion. "If the real thing was helpless against me, what made you think a copy could fare any better?" she taunted. The fake Evallion smiled at her. Something was wrong. It was then that she remembered. What she faced wasn't human! The beast mutated into its true form. Vines and roots propelled an arrow at her. "No," she gasped. She tried to dodge but there wasn't enough time. She could hear the sound of the magical arrow as it pierced her flesh.

She staggered back and fell to the floor. She glared at the beast that had hurt her.

Her eyes fixated on the arrow embedded in her shoulder. With a shaking hand she jerked the arrow from her body and gasped. She looked at the arrow that was stained with her blood. Her eyes then fixated on the swamp beast that had hurt her.

"You know, I never stopped to wonder if, you filthy beast could feel pain," she began as her fingers elongated into feral claws. "But I will take exquisite pleasure in finding out," she hissed as she leaped at the swamp beast.

A short while later, the group regrouped topside. They were free of the witch's lair, but they were far from being safe. Goblins and undead creatures were everywhere and were going crazy. Some were attacking each other, some were ravaging the remnants of the still standing structures of Briar

But luckily for those that escaped the lair, the goblins and undead didn't notice the escaped prisoners that were hiding in the remnants of a barely standing house.

"What is with the locals?" Sugar asked.

"The witch needs to be focused to control minions. The fight must be taking more effort than she anticipated," Arrow replied as he looked over at his sister. She cringed and looked away.

"Don't look at me," Geia stammered.

"Why?" Arrow asked.

"Because, she made me," she began but couldn't say the rest.

"I don't care about that, well, I do, but, all that matters is that you are here. That we are together and will be going home," he reassured.

Sugar looked over at the two elves and then over at her daughter who was still doing everything she could to revive Evallion, but no matter what she seemed to do, he just wouldn't wake up.

"Nothing is working," Qu'Tee said, a sense of hopelessness beginning to set in. it was then that she felt his hand touch hers. She looked down and saw his eyes slowly opening. "You dummy. Do you know how scared I was?" she asked.

"I wasn't scared," he answered quietly.

"Why?" she asked.

"I knew you would save me. You always do," he replied. Just then a powerful explosion rocked the area. The party looked over to the secret entrance to the lair of the witch. The confusion that seemed to grip the goblins and undead, had passed. A familiar laugh echoed from the smoke filled entrance to the cavern lair.

"Where, or where did everybody go?" the voice of the witch taunted.

"Not good," Arrow muttered. He and the others watched as the witch emerged from the smoke. She was a little bruised, but other than that she looked less than phased from her fight with the fake Evallion.

"If you naughty slaves are good and come crawling back to me I will grant you, all of you a quick, relatively painless death," she offered. She extended her hand towards the dilapidated house that they were hiding in. the wall nearest to her exploded sending them soaring. "Do not think that you can hide from me," she warned. Her eyes fixated on Geia. "You, have been bad. You should have stayed like a good puppy," she taunted. "If you thought what I did to you before was painful, just wait until you are back underground," she threatened. Qu'Tee stepped over and stood in front of the cringing Elf.

"If you want her, you will have to go through me first," she warned. The witch smiled a wicked smile.

"My dear, that can be arranged," the witch pointed out as she stared at her claws.

Unlikely Hero

It was a grim situation.

Before the questing band was their enemy, the very powerful and very insane Hand Witch Samantha. That in itself would be bad, but add to that they had no armour or weapons handy made things feel somewhat apocalyptic.

"The master told me as sure as I am standing here he did. He told me not to take any of you lightly. How was I supposed to know that included a spell gone awry, a waif goblin and a squirrel?" she asked as she slowly raked her claws over her chest. "Who knew?" she added with a deeply insane look in her eyes.

"Why did she do that?" Qu'Tee asked.

"Witch's blood is poisonous," Arrow answered.

"The older the witch, the more potent," Sugar added.

"Any more good news?" Evallion slurred.

"She is mine," Qu'Tee stated seriously. Her tone shocked everyone present. "The rest of you stay out of this," she ordered as she stepped ahead of her allies, friends and family.

"Daughter?" Sugar began.

"You heard me mother. And that goes double for you Evallion. This is my fight," she added, sensing her weakened friends attempt to argue the issue.

Having said her piece, she walked over to where an old Elf spear was. The blade was rusted and the shaft was in a mild state of decay. It wasn't her first choice for a weapon, but currently, it was better than nothing. She looked over at the witch, who found this bravado sincerely amusing.

"Honey, I would ask if you have been dipping into the wine, but I know for a fact that you haven't. what makes you think that you, some fresh faced Ken wench could best me? I have crumbled cities, humbled kings, and princesses," she added, smirking at Geia. Arrow was going to interject himself into the equation, but a weakened Evallion managed to sway him. "I know what you are thinking honey. You are thinking that I can heal. He poisonous claws won't kill me, but, what if I'm wrong?" she taunted as she began to dance around. Qu'Tee could see glowing strands flowing from the land into the witch.

"I do not know if your poisonous blood could harm me or not, but I do know that you have to get close enough to scratch me to find out," Qu'Tee rebutted confidently. The witch laughed hysterically and then stopped. She stopped dancing. Her head lolled onto her shoulder. For a few moments she stood, motionless, like a statue. The witch blinked. Slowly she looked over at the young Ken queen. There was something deeply disturbed and evil in the eyes of the witch.

"The others had their chance to play. Now it is my turn," Sam remarked. Although the sound of her voice sent a shiver down her spine, Qu'Tee stayed focused.

"You say your master wants me dead? If that is the case, he will have to send someone better than you to do the job," Qu'Tee goaded. A look of unrestrained madness consumed the witch. She screamed out as she seemed to fly at her enemy. The witch raked her claws in an arching motion at the young queen. Effortlessly she evaded the strike and the numerous attacks that followed. Nothing the witch seemed to do could breach the defences of her enemy.

Much to the surprise of those watching, Qu'Tee dodged one of the witch's strikes and in one fluid motion stabbed the rusty spear into the wound that was still raw and exposed in her shoulder.

The witch seemed frozen as the sensations of the pain of being stabbed with a rusty spear, having a previous wound being aggravated further and being shown up by some uppity young Ken began to set in.

"I have spent the past five years of my life training and preparing to face evil creatures like you," Qu'Tee stated. She spun around, drilling the shaft of the spear across the back of the witch's head. Everyone watched as the witch staggered and crumpled to the ground. Qu'Tee stood ready, in the event that she might mount a counter attack.

The witch shivered and twitched as she forced herself back up to her feet. She began to quietly laugh as she nursed her bleeding shoulder wound. Everything around Qu'Tee seemed to warp and twist.

The only thing that was steady was the glowing eyes of the witch.

"What is the matter dear? Feeling under the weather? Remembering something you wished would stay forgotten?" the voice of the witch taunted.

Qu'Tee staggered and blacked out. A jolt of pain shocked her back to reality, only everything was different.

"Get up you stupid witch!" a familiar voice taunted. A strong kick to her ribs caused her eyes to open. A feeling of dread overpowered her. She looked at her hands, they were so tiny. She hesitantly looked up and saw the bullies that tormented her. A feeling of panic began to grip her. She tried to get up to run, but one of the bullies grabbed her by the hair and threw her down to the ground. "I don't remember telling you to move," she goaded, her friends laughed. Qu'Tee cringed as she looked over. She saw that the bullies had Evallion too!

"Please. Let him go. I promise I'll be good," a young Qu'Tee pleaded passively. The leader of the bullies smirked at her.

"You really like him don't you?" the bully taunted. Qu'Tee could feel tears welling in her eyes. She didn't have to answer. The bully knew. "Rough him up a bit!" she ordered. Qu'Tee watched helplessly as the older girls began to beat on her best and only friend.

"Please stop!" Qu'Tee pleaded. She tried to rush over to help him, but the leader of the bullies grabbed her by the hair and threw her down to the ground.

"I tried being nice. I tried giving you the benefit of a doubt," the leader of the bullies remarked. "But, what has that gotten me? You still are acting up. You are still being a stupid little bitch," the bully stated coldly. Qu'Tee could hear the others still beating and kicking Evallion.

"I'm, sorry," she stammered passively. The leader of the bullies motioned for the others to stop. "I'll be good. I promise," she added timidly.

"I recall you saying that before. Yet here we are," the bully taunted.
"I am the one you hate. I am the one you despise. He has nothing to do with this," Qu'Tee pleaded. The leader of the bullies laughed.

"Girls! I think the witch has a crush on junior! Do you like him witch? Do you love him?" the bully taunted. Qu'Tee could hear the others laughing.

"Yes, I do. Please, I don't care what you do to me, but please leave him alone," Qu'Tee admitted passively. The leader of the bullies grabbed her by the hair and jerked her head back. Qu'Tee kept her eyes closed. She didn't want to see Evallion to see her like this.

"Hey girls, maybe we should leave the witch alone and just pick on her boyfriend," the bully suggested. Qu'Tee opened her eyes in a state of panic.

"No! Please! I promise I won't be late or complain or anything," Qu'Tee pleaded. The bully smirked as she knelt down by the trembling Qu'Tee.

"You make me sick," she almost hissed. She spit in Qu'Tee's face. "You think you are so special. You think you are better than everyone," she stated, a look of hatred in her eyes. "If you do not do everything I say you little slut, I swear we will kill him in a way that even your witchy magic can't fix," the bully whispered to her. A feeling of helplessness overpowered Qu'Tee. All she could do was passively nod. The bully stepped away from her and motioned for the others to pay attention. "You filthy little witch! You are nothing but a dog in heat! On all fours bitch!" the bully ordered. Qu'Tee looked over at Evallion. She could see the hurt in his eyes. Passively she did as she was told. The other bullies laughed as their leader motioned for her to move around and make noises like a dog.

How many times had she replayed this very day in her mind?

How many times had she lived this humiliation? Hearing the taunts and laughter of the bullies, feeling the shame of acting like that, doing as they told her in front of Evallion no less. It was then that she noticed something, different.

Qu'Tee looked over at the leader of the bullies. She looked different.

"What are you doing dog? Did I tell you to stop?" the leader of the bullies demanded. Qu'Tee blinked. The face of the bully was wrong. She looked like the witch Samantha. She wiped the tears from her eyes and slowly got up. "What do you think you are doing?" the bully demanded. Qu'Tee kicked the old spear up to her hand.

"I'm not playing your game anymore," Qu'Tee stated calmly. Everything around her shattered like brittle glass. Once again she was in the ruined, tainted village. "Making me relive my past won't make me forget the future. Several paces away glaring at her was the Hand witch   .

"How dare you!" the witch screamed as she lunged at Qu'Tee. Her attacks were like those of a rabid, savage beast. Qu'Tee was able to stay ahead of her attacker, was able to stay one step out of reach of the witch's poisonous claws, but for reason her focus slipped, just for one second. That was all the time the witch needed. A strong rock hard fist slammed into Qu'Tee's stomach. A starburst blinded her as the witch drove her knee into Qu'Tee's face, knocking the Ken queen off the ground. "Time to die bitch!" she hissed. She spun around and raked her claws across Qu'Tee's belly.

"Qu'Tee!" Evallion screamed out as he watched her fall to the ground. Sugar and Arrow had to hold him back. The witch smiled as she looked down at the one person her master feared more than anything.

"Hard to believe that the master was afraid of you," Samantha remarked. Her eyes widened as Qu'Tee began to stir. "What?" she muttered in modest disbelief. The Ken queen was gasping. "Why aren't you dead?" she demanded as she looked at her blood stained claws. Qu'Tee slowly sat up.

"You won't win," Qu'Tee began as she used the spear to support her as she got up. "Whether it is one or one hundred that stand against your master, he will never win," Qu'Tee stated calmly as a dim aura began to glow around her.

"What? What are you?" the witch demanded as she hesitantly backed away from Qu'Tee. Just then a blur of motion landed on the Ken queen's shoulder then leaped at the witch. "What is?" she began as the squirrel Chi slashed his paws across the face of the witch. She screamed out! Her skin blistered and burned where the arrowheads cut her. One of her eyes swelled shut. "Damn you all! I'll kill you all!" the witch screamed as wisps of unholy power began to lash out at anything around her. Goblins, bat familiars, undead, structures, vegetation, all withered and crumbled. Any thing that her magic touched, anything except Qu'Tee. The aura that was pulsing around her protected her.

"Your time is done," Qu'Tee stated coldly. Her voice was older, her eyes were glowing with holy power. The witch glared at her.

"I refuse to let you stand in the way of my vengeance!" Samantha screamed. She extended her arms out. The wisps of power and unholy energy took on the shape of hands and slowly arched towards the Ken queen. The others watched as the tendrils of unholy power tried to overpower the aura that surrounded Qu'Tee.

"You don't," Qu'Tee began, but the strain of the witch's power was starting to catch up with her. She could feel the pressure beyond the aura. "You don't have a say in the matter," she rebutted.

"You are running on fumes dear. I can see it in your pretty little face. You can't hold out much longer," the witch goaded. Just then Boo leaped at the witch. Wielding an arrow like a tiny spear, he stabbed his weapon into the back of the witch's knee. The witch lost her focus and screamed out. The witch screamed out and reached for the goblin. But he rolled out of the way then stabbed the spear through the back of her hand, pinning her bleeding hand to her thigh.

Qu'Tee watched as the witch began to shake and twitch. The wisps of unholy power around her began to slowly evaporate. In a frantic state, she began to look around.

"Master? Master?" the witch stammered. "I need help master. They," she began. A loud thud cut her off. For a few seconds, a calm fell over the witch. She slumped down to her knees then fell over, an arrow embedded in her back.

Qu'Tee looked over and saw the swamp beast, the fake Evallion standing there. He bowed to her, resumed his true form, and then crumbled into dust. The spell that made him, was broken.

The Ken queen looked over at the body of the witch. Her power seeped from her wounds and flowed into the land. She then watched as spirits, hundreds of them slowly rose up from the land and fly up into the sky. The spirits of the Elves the witch had sacrificed and murdered, were free.

"Her spell," Qu'Tee began, as the accumulated effect of her injuries caught up with her. "Is broken," she slurred as she collapsed. Darkness, all to familiar engulfed her.

There sounds all around her. They were distant. She couldn't make them out. Slowly her eyes opened. Her vision slowly came back into focus. She was looking up at the star filled sky. She groaned as she tried to sit up.

"Hey! She's awake!" Evallion alerted the others. Qu'Tee looked over and saw Evallion and the others. "How are you feeling?" he asked.

"Terrible. I ache and hurt all over," Qu'Tee began. "How long was I out?" she asked.

"A couple days. You had us worried for a bit, but when your

bruises and cuts started to heal, we knew you would pull through," Geia stated with a smile.

"Is the witch?" Qu'Tee began.

"Dead," Sugar answered as she helped her daughter sit up.

"Lyte Wood?" Qu'Tee asked.

"Stop worrying about everything already. Lyte Wood is fine. Just like you said, as soon as the witch fell, the spell that unified the goblin factions faded. The war machines exploded, as did the traps outside the city walls. Most of the goblins fled, many turned on each other, some just refused to retreat and were cut down by Elf arrows," Arrow stated with a smile as he handed her the note he had received from the Elf capital.

"We did it," Qu'Tee said to herself.

"I'm glad I happened onto you people, especially Boo," Arrow said as he got up. "Had I not seen it with my own eyes, I don't think I would have believed it," he mused as Boo struck a hero pose.

"You, you're leaving?" Qu'Tee asked.

"I have to take my sister home, plus it will take a great deal of time and effort to heal the damage that has been done to the forest," he explained as he walked over, knelt before her and bowed his head. "On behalf of the king, and all Elves, I thank you for what you have done this day," he stated diplomatically. He reached forward and placed a pin with the crest of the Forest Nation on it. "Know that where you travel, you speak with the voice of all Elves. When you need the aid of the Elves, we will be there," he concluded.

"Two nations out of ten. Off to a good start I'd say," Sugar pointed out.

"Arrow? Could I have a word with you? In private?" Evallion requested. Geia continued to talk with Sugar and Qu'Tee as Arrow and Evallion walked out of ear shot of the others. "I need to ask a favour of you," he began.

"I'm listening," Arrow replied seriously.

"I need you to forget about that cave," Evallion stated flatly.

"That could be a problem. A staging ground in Elf territory," he began.

"It is not a weapon meant for the Elves," Evallion interrupted.

"Are there other such, locations in Elf territory?" the Elf asked. Evallion sighed and looked away for a moment.

"There are. I need you to understand, I know that witch was insane, but she was right about one thing, the Elves tend not to involve themselves in matters that do not directly concern them. We tried to reason with you that there was a threat marching against the Forest Nation," Evallion began but stopped.

"It is hard to dispute that," Arrow admitted. "But, what you are asking of me is to remain quiet about a weapon that could be used against my people. It is true that we tend to stay out of the affairs of the Veil. This is so we can be unbiased, so that we can see without hate or prejudice," he explained.

"I understand that," Evallion agreed.

"We, know that the human heart, it is easily swayed. It is what makes humans so weak, and so strong. Who is to say that your people, unhappy with how Elves are tending to the affairs of our territory, would step in and try to impose marshal law?" he asked.

"Pit Fighters have no quarrel with the Forest Nation," Evallion began as he reached into his leather armour and pulled out a scroll. "Secrecy, well intentioned or no, comes with a price. I ask you to respect this secret, tell no one of what you have seen and what we have spoken of, if you swear this, I'll give you this," he offered.

"What is that?" Arrow asked.

"A map. I have no idea how it happened into my armour, but on it are the locations of what I would guess are goblin strongholds," Evallion answered. Arrow looked at the rolled up scroll.

"Your replacement must have picked it up when he went into that goblin city," the Elf remarked. "May I see it?" he asked. Evallion nodded and handed it to him. Arrow studied the scroll and the foreign markings on it. "I, will presume, that you are sincere. I will presume that you are telling the truth, as I am sure your people would want this map as badly as the Elves do," he began, Evallion nodded. Arrow sighed shook his head. "What cave?" he asked with a smile, extending his hand.

"War with the Elves serves no one, no one save the demon," Evallion replied as he shook the Elf prince's hand.

"Well said. So where are you and your merry band heading from here?" Arrow asked.

"My people aren't far from here. That will probably be the next obstacle," he answered.

"You expect trouble?" the Elf asked as he put the map into one of his pouches.

"I didn't leave there on the best of terms. That could complicate things. Time will tell," he answered grimly.

"Would that I could join you," Arrow began.

"No disrespect, but, where we are going, you wouldn't be much help. You know how we barbarians feel about Elves," Evallion remarked. Arrow quietly laughed.
"I suppose you are right. Regardless, I wish you the best of luck

on your journey. I fear you will need it. The road ahead, it will only get harder to travel down the further you go," the Elf admitted. The two walked back over to where the others were. "Geia, we should be heading back now. We don't want to keep father waiting," he stated.

"Now?" she asked.

"It is best that we go now. We will be able to move undetected," he explained. His sister hurried over and hugged him.

"Good luck!" Geia called out as she and her brother vanished into the shadows of the surrounding trees. Qu'Tee looked over and scowled at Evallion.

"What is that look for?" Evallion asked.

"Did you say something to him?" she asked defensively.

"What? He wants to get his sister home," he rebutted.

"You aren't telling me something," she pointed out.

"Come on," he protested.

"You are the one keeping secrets. See if I care," she stated as she focused her attention on Boo. Sugar quietly laughed as she handed Evallion a bowl of the stew she made. They had done much in a short period of time. They had stopped one of the demon's minions, but there were more. It was to early to celebrate, but they were off to a good start.

At that moment, back in the ruined lair of the Hand witch, a demonic figure waddle through the mess. The fight between the fake Evallion and the witch had trashed the place beyond repair.

"I should have known better than to leave this to that insane witch," he croaked. "No matter, her purpose was severed here. Her usefulness was almost expired anyway," he rationalized. "Now where is the piece of talisman that I entrusted to her care?" he asked. An aura of green light glowed around his reptilian hand. His eyes panned the room until he saw a small statuette glowing the same colour.

The demon frog made his way over to where the statue was. He crushed the small statue into dust within his fist. When he opened his hand, a golden puzzle piece was there.

"You will fail my dear. You will understand soon enough that nothing can stop me. No mortal being can," he said as he vanished into the shadows of the ruined lair.

The story continues in
Bo'Glin book II:
The Present and the Past

www.ingramcontent.com/pod-product-compliance
Lightning Source LLC
Chambersburg PA
CBHW060936030726
47503CB00003B/619

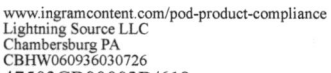

* 9 7 8 0 9 7 8 3 2 3 7 0 7 *